THE
HANGING
WOMEN

THE HANGING WOMEN

John Mead

The Book Guild Ltd

First published in Great Britain in 2018 by
The Book Guild Ltd
9 Priory Business Park
Wistow Road, Kibworth
Leicestershire, LE8 0RX
Freephone: 0800 999 2982
www.bookguild.co.uk
Email: info@bookguild.co.uk
Twitter: @bookguild

Typeset in Adobe Garamond Pro

Printed and bound in Great Britain by CPI Group (UK) Ltd, Croydon, CR0 4YY

ISBN 978 1912362 059

British Library Cataloguing in Publication Data.
A catalogue record for this book is available from the British Library.

*Dedicated to my family, for ensuring
I know what to value in this life.*

1

DERELICT

Day One – Tuesday April 15th 1886

He was finding the twisting of the two bodies, in the cold April wind coming off the river and flowing through the broken walls and empty windows, mesmerising. The pair, a black woman and a white woman both in their twenties, were tied together facing each other and were suspended by their right and left leg respectively. The wind seemed to catch them, like a sail, twisting them gently until the rope from which they were suspended was tightened to the point where it twirled them back to their starting point, the breeze then once again prevailing; the motion repeating over and over. It wasn't so much the movement that held his attention, it was waiting for the turning pair to reach the zenith of their journey, just at the point where the rope tightened enough to twist them back. At this point the black woman's thigh, buttocks and small of her back was silhouetted against the weak midday light of an overcast day, the flowing curve of the woman's outline reminding him of Kitty as she had stretched naked, front down on the bed but half-turned, her smiling face towards him.

What troubled him, as he sat on the pile of debris in the derelict warehouse on the north side of the Chicago River, was where he had been for the past day and two nights. *He had been crawling across a meadow, looking for his rifle, and he was aware of the men and women, in formal wear, dancing just at the edge of his vision as he searched the ground. He was in formal dress himself and, though he always felt slightly ridiculous when putting it on, he knew it suited him so it wasn't this that concerned him; it was what tugged at his right leg. Something black and shapeless clutched at his right foot and ankle, he dared not look back and went on with his search knowing if he could find his rifle the thing behind him would evaporate. Just as he put his hand on his rifle icy fingers distinctly gripped his foot and he involuntarily kicked out, fear gripping his chest.* As he awoke the hand still held his foot in its death-like clasp and he continued to kick, tipping himself off the couch with a startled shout and onto his parlour floor.

Martha, his wife, sat impassive and barely startled watching him; her knitting, her constant hobby now she had grandchildren, not that the pair required any supplementary knitwear as all their needs were provided by their wealthy parents, lay unheeded in her lap. "Are you alright?" she asked with genuine concern, "I was beginning to think you would sleep the morning away."

"What?" Jack asked testily, still disorientated and uncertain how he had ended up sprawled on the parlour floor, his voice horse and his mouth and tongue dry as dust.

"You returned in the early hours, your attempts to enter the house woke Hettie and myself," she placidly informed him, knowing it best to leave him to find his own way off the floor, his erratic ill-temper having grown worse over recent years as he drank more, "but we could not manage to help you up the stairs so thought you would fare better on the couch in here. We had been quite worried about you, Jack."

"Why's that?" he asked, having managed to leaver himself back onto the couch, it was a three-seater but even so his long frame made it uncomfortable to sleep on and he ached in every muscle and joint. His vision, however, had stopped dancing and he was able to focus on the room and his wife; for a woman in her late forties she was still handsome, her auburn hair framed her strong face, whilst her brown eyes were warm and passionate. She was tall and curvaceous, her dress and jewellery were modest but clearly showed her to be of a class whose wealth gives them a comfortable if not an extravagant lifestyle. Had Jack felt in better humour he would have smiled at her sitting there concerned over his well-being.

"You have been gone all of yesterday, the night and much of the afternoon before, it is unlike you not to send word," Martha's tone was neutral, she did not rebuke her husband as many wives would have, "I understand the work you do keeps you out but you have never been away so long." It was the slightest emphasis on the word 'work' that grated with Jack as he knew that in practice she considered his work a euphemism for drinking, that plus the fact he could not find his hip-flask. His colt was still in his shoulder holster and his five-shot revolver was in the right pocket of his jacket but his flask was missing and, more than anything, he wanted a mouthful of whiskey to clear his head.

"Do you want something to eat?' Martha continued not getting any response from her husband who seemed preoccupied looking for something. "If it is your wallet you look for it is on the table in front of you, it fell out as we got you on the couch." If it had been Lillian there to cook for him he might have given in to his hunger but Martha's elderly maid and cook had died in January, a simple cold she had refused to give in to had laid her low, then put her in the ground. She had recently been replaced by Hettie, who had a Boston accent and cooked in the 'french style' that she inherited from her mother which Jack found not to his taste. Whilst Hortense and Gideon, a colored couple who between them looked after the house and garden, had been hired by Martha five years ago and were more used to Jack's ways and

3

tastes. As all three servants lived-in and, as Martha was often out visiting family and friends, it made Jack feel as if he stayed in a hotel with so many at hand to wait on him, yet never giving him the privacy or peace he wanted in his own home.

"Do you not feel well, Jack?" the the merest hint of annoyance crept into Maratha's voice at her husband's silence.

"Damn your eyes!" Jack's temper erupted, he'd been only too aware of Martha's searching gaze during her 'interrogation' of him. He lurched forward as he stood up, half-kicking, half-knocking over the small table and vase in front of him, spilling water and flowers across the carpet. "What business is it of yours where I've been, you may think little of the work I do but some consider it of value." He made certain to kick the overturned table across the room as he stormed out, leaving his stunned and confused spouse in his wake.

He didn't get far down Rush Street before his temper cooled and he realised he was hungry, thirsty and disheveled but he had no intention of going back. He caught a cab and had it wait whilst he went to his customary barber. He had the shop boy fetch him a clean suit and shirt from his home, whilst the barber trimmed his sparse, greying hair and thick, downturned pepper and salt moustache and side-whiskers. The barber knew his customer's moods well enough to know when to talk and when to be silent, and also when to provide him with plentiful cups of hot, black Arbuckle; Jack's favourite brand of coffee. Jack might have fallen asleep, with the hot towels around his face, had not the boy returned with his clothes and set the shop bell tinkling. Even so, changed and shaved he felt a new man and, having dispensed large tips, left the barber shop smiling; at least, what he thought of as a smile though others considered it something closer to a scowl.

His dirty suit, returned home for cleaning, had given him little information about what he had done the previous day. It was grimy and looked as if he had, at least once, rolled about the street in it and it smelt of beer, smoke and cheap scent, which was hardly surprising given his tendency to frequent bars, though

Kitty's distinctive perfume was not evident. He remembered leaving home in the mid-afternoon and going to the River Bar, which was in an alley north of the river. It was here he had his usual fortnightly meeting with Hank Tipwell, to swap gossip and information about Chicago's more criminally inclined and less salubrious citizens and events. However, after Hank left things started to get hazy, he was certain at one point he had been walking the streets and thought he remembered an argument and tussle with a youngish man but beyond that nothing; the previous day held no memories for him.

As he crossed Rush Bridge in the cab he caught a glimpse of the Home Insurance building, on Adams and LaSalle, towering over all its neighbours. It had been on that corner he had first met Kitty. The ten storey building was newly finished but yet to open. Its height remained a novelty, even to the locals, and pedestrians tended to walk the crowded crossroads constantly looking up, so Jack and Kitty walking into each other was not without precedent. After the usual embarrassed apologises she had continued to engage him about the wondrous height of the building and Jack was happy to participate, supplying what little knowledge he had of the steel construction, not being adverse to conversing with a pretty woman.

It was only later, as they ate an early dinner at Jack's invitation, did she reveal they had already met and she had been waiting for him to recall her: Kathleen, Kitty to her family and friends, McGuire, née Tipwell, Hank's elder sister. Jack could not recall her at Hank's wedding, which he had attended with his wife, where Kitty had first seen him. Her younger brother, Hank, was Brandon Edward O'Shea's godson and right hand man. The Tipwells, along with the McGuire's and Murphy's, were all cousins, aunts and uncles to the O'Shea's and, as such, formed one large clan that were involved in all the political, financial and criminal deals across Chicago. Hank was, therefore, 'a man to be reckoned with' and as Kitty was a widow he took his guardianship of his sister seriously, which though she appreciated, she found irksome, restrictive and put off potential suitors. She had been rather taken by Jack, one of the few men Hank seemingly respected, and had deliberately walked into him at the crossroads.

Kitty, a widow with a grown son of twenty, looked younger than her years and, despite the loss of a husband and daughter some ten years previously, went through life with a smile and lightness of heart. It was a surprise to her that she should find anything attractive in a morse, married man, fifteen years her senior but she quickly decided he would take her to bed. So, on their second meeting and against all properties and his own expectations, Jack found himself steering them both to a small, discreet hotel in order to spend the afternoon in love making. Jack, not being a passionate man, except about imbibing whiskey, was not the best of lovers but she seemed content and, at the end of the afternoon, she had stretched herself, half-turned towards him with her lower-back, buttocks and thigh making the same flowing, bow-like, line that he was to see reproduced a year later in the the silhouette of a naked, dead, black woman.

Jack was disturbed from his reverie, still none the wiser as to how he had spent the previous day, by the sound of a heavy step on the warehouse's rotten stairs.

"Stevens, I got your message that you have found a body," Inspector Uriah Micajah O'Leary, 'Cage' when off-duty, was a small, dark, muscular man, with sideburns and a moustache, of Irish and polish descent; he'd been in the force for sixteen years and a detective for ten. Although his sack suit and derby might not have marked him out as anything different from a prosperous business man, his voice or stare was enough to send a shiver down any wrong-doer's spine.

"As you see, Inspector, I did not play you false for I have two," Jack informed him, his tone solemn despite the light hearted nature of his response.

The inspector took in the scene before saying anything else.

In the dusty grime of the floor he saw two sets of boot prints mingling with each other around where the bodies hung, though the larger sized prints were less frequent and had not approached so close. The larger set he traced back to Jack, sitting on a pile of debris off to the side where the smaller sized boots had not trod. The naked women, one black and the other white, had been hung upside down, using a double-block and tackle, suspended from a roof rafter. Their hands had been tied behind each others back as if embracing each other, the colored woman's right ankle tied to the other woman's left; their free legs had been bent and tied so as to cross behind their respective knee. Had the pair been the right way up it would look as if they were pirouetting on tip-toe, clasping each other in some macabre dance.

The blood in both bodies had drained towards the head, discolouring and distending the skin and features, though as both had been garrotted their faces resembled no living person. The hair of the white female, who appeared the slightly elder of the two, had been loosened and hung down, in a golden stream, to brush the grime of the the floor; the black woman's naturally curling hair still framed her face. In life the pair, both in their twenty's, would have been considered attractive, both of medium height, the colored woman a hand's breadth taller, both slim with figures that were likely to have attracted glances. In death, their contorted faces and starting eyes were far from appealing.

"It was you that found them like this? You've touched nothing?" Inspector O'Leary asked, his tone professional, he'd know Jack Stevens for five years, having met him not too long after Stevens and his wife moved to Chicago and taken possession of their house near Oak and Rush. Despite everything he heard about Jack he rather liked the man and, along with the Pinkertons with whom he seemed to work, considered him a useful person to know; if for no other reason than he moved freely amongst both the highest and lowest of Chicago's citizens yet was not aligned with nor gave favour to any fraction.

"Yes," Jack lied, "I happened to be strolling along the river, watching the boats and the like when I saw two boys of about eight or so run pell-mell from this building, therefore, I entered to take a look and found these dancing pair." In actuality Jack had been in the Gripmans Bar and Diner, just starting on his steak and eggs and his second beer, when he was approached by a lanky youth in rather showy clothing.

"Mr Jack Stevens?" the young man asked, his tone respectful enough though his accent was decidedly from the waterfront tenements, which combined with his excessively stylish clothing, marked him as a member of the Dead Hands, the largest of Chicago's Irish gangs and currently run by the Tipwell contingent of the O'Shea clan.

"None other," Jack smiled back, his hand from habit slipping onto the revolver he carried in his right coat pocket. "Would you care to take a seat?"

"Under normal circumstances that would be an honour, sir," the young man responded, feeling in his element at this exchange of 'gentlemanly niceties', "but I have an urgent message for you, from Mr Henry Tipwell." The youngster paused as if expecting a trumpet blast to sound at the mention of such an exalted name, but getting no reaction from Jack other than his swallowing another mouthful of steak, continued, "He asks that you go, as a matter of urgency, to the north side of the river and speak with his cousin, Mr Jaunty Tipwell, on a matter most urgent and delicate."

"Very well," Jack happily agreed, wondering if this had to do with his missing day. "Why don't you sit whilst I finish my food and you can explain how I find Mr Jaunty Tipwell."

"Mr Henry Tipwell," the youth, bending closer to Jack's right ear and lowering his tone, so as to sound more discrete, "asked me to say that it was his personal wish you treat this matter with urgency, even if you are already otherwise engaged." Jack was torn, he hated to waste food especially when he was hungry, but there were few men that Hank would ask a personal favour from and fewer men still who would not have jumped up and rushed to Jaunty's side at the first asking.

It turned out that the youth took him not to Mr Jaunty Tipwell, who ran the north side river front and was intending to stay as far away as he could from any dead bodies, but to a disused warehouse in a decaying and generally deserted part of the riverbank. On the cab ride there the youth had explained how two young sailors, either lost or looking for a place of considerable privacy, had found the bodies and told a local bar owner who, not wanting to unnecessarily trouble the police, had passed the message on to the nearest Dead Hand. And so it went up through the ranks until it reached Hank who, not wanting to bother either the police or Mr O'Shea on such a matter, had thought of Jack.

"You say you sent for the police straight away?" the inspector wanted to know.

"I did," Jack lied a second time as he had spent a good half hour carefully examining the scene before sending for Cage, "though I did take a quick look around after I had done so. The pair were obviously dead but I thought I should look more closely."

"They appear to have been dead for some hours," Inspector O'Leary informed him, the smell of their decay despite the chill weather being stronger as he approached to examine the pair, "so they probably died late last night. As you found them, could you tell me where you were yesterday?"

"I wish I could," Jack explained. "Apparently I arrived home, somewhat disorientated and my suit begrimed, in the early hours of this morning, though unfortunately I have no memory of yesterday at all. Given my state I believe I had fallen into some type of stupor, unnoticed in an alleyway, and only made my way home by habit and luck."

"Really? That is your alibi?" Cage shook his head in disbelief. "Anyone else, even the mayor himself, and I would have them run in this instant."

"I'm sorry, Cage, but I see no reason to lie, at my age such things happen. As far as I can tell I have never met either of these two unfortunate souls before," Jack understood the difficult spot he put the inspector in. "Nor have I ever killed anyone without a reason and, if I did, I would not go to such elaborate lengths as those undertaken here as I much prefer the simplicity of a gunshot or silence of the knife. All this," Jack waved distractedly at the hanging women, a degree of disdain in his voice, "is excessive and unnecessarily provocative."

"Provocative? An odd word to use?" Cage wondered.

"You agree it has been planned?" Cage nodded in response to Jack's question. "Someone has thought this through and brought a double-pulley to use, knowing they could not otherwise hoist the dead weight of even two such slender bodies. The single set of foot prints and the pulleys suggests one man did this, he would also have needed to plan how to take and hold both women. How he did so I can't say but he must have gotten them here without attracting attention somehow, carried them in singularly, stripped and tied them together. They would both need to be subdued for him to do so, otherwise one might have struggled or escaped whilst he dealt with the other. He cut the clothing from them, it is over there in a heap behind the debris in the corner, bound them together in this somewhat obscene way that you see before you and hoisted them up. He has posed them, otherwise why tie them in the odd shape they are in, and if he has posed them then it must be to send a sign to provoke others.

"Having hoisted them up he then proceeds to use the carriage whip, the one lying by the wall there, to beat them about the buttocks and thighs. Given the welts and blood this has produced they would have been alive and screamed mightily, so he would have known it was safe to do this here, having picked the one part of the riverfront which is derelict and hardly used; it was sheer luck they were found so quickly. His message delivered he finishes them off by garrotting." Jack paused thoughtfully before adding, "I pity the one who had to listen to the other's dying breath."

"Amen to that, Jack," Cage crossed himself, he had followed Stevens' reasoning and agreed with it in full. "Anything to add before I call my men up? My sergeant will be saying we should take you in, though my superiors might ask why I thought it necessary to arrest the father-in-law of our state attorney and prospective future governor."

"Politics is a difficult tightrope to traverse, Cage," Jack sympathised. "Personally I try to steer clear of it myself."

"Very wise," Cage agreed, moving to the stairs and calling his men, setting them tasks and sending his sergeant over to officially take Jack's statement.

Martha had no shame and she knew it because her 'beautiful' Belarusian told her so, and did so over and over again as they sweated together in their love making. His apartment was small, being one of four created from what had originally been one large house. The walls were thin whilst Martha's vocalisations of the passion, that her lover sweated to produce in her, were loud. Fortunately Minsky did not mind, the apartment opposite being empty and if the widow below or the old couple who lived opposite her found it objectionable then, to his mind, they had not lived. Martha's exhortations to her maker, usually in the form of, "God, yes!" or "God, please more! More!" or at the zenith of her passion, "Dear God, harder!" were he thought not blasphemous but divinely poetic; words that stirred him to greater effort, to toss his beloved and shameless Martha all the more strenuously.

They lay for sometime after they were spent side by side, breathing loudly, naked and sweaty, whilst their bodies and minds regained some composure.

"That, my darling Ibrahim, was like old times," Martha, once she got her breath back, smilingly informed him. "You are like a stallion."

"You have no shame, Martha," Ibrahim, Karl to anyone who asked his first name, Mikhailovich Minsky was a Belarusian Jew from Minsk. He was a head shorter than Martha and of a stocky build, clean shaven with long, black, curly hair and dark brown eyes that were rarely angry and never still.

"I have only been shameless since meeting you, it is you who made me a happy adulterous, you corrupted me, you vile seducer," she laughed, turning to him. Her body was twelve years older since they first met in early '74 and, though she felt much the same now as then, she considered herself less attractive with the passing of time. However, Minsky did not seem to notice and still looked at her with eyes that only saw the same captivating and passionate woman of more than a decade ago. They had originally met at a time when Jack had deserted her and was thought dead, they had been neighbours and were both down on their luck and, though the difference in their height made them a comical looking couple, they found an ease and contentment in each others company that quickly led to them becoming lovers.

"You needed little encouragement," Minsky laughed back, "and as for seduction you have many more conquests amour than I."

She rolled over onto him, pinning his arms, her legs straddling his sex and her breasts hanging in his face, "I shall crush you for the worm you are for saying such things," she laughed down at him. There was a playfulness in their relationship, a freedom that allowed for honesty, even when hurtful that she treasured but somehow did not seem to give the solid foundation she required; certainly she could never see herself running away with Minsky. Despite his diminutive stature, Minsky was more than strong enough to overthrow her and took possession of his prize by straddling her in his turn, pinning her by her shoulders as his loins pressed against hers.

"No," she squirmed beneath him, only adding to his pleasure, "don't start again, there isn't time as I must go soon."

"Ahhh…" he sighed falling back, "can't you stay a little longer?"

"I am due at Abby's and my grandchildren expect me," she

explained, though feeling embarrassed at admitting to having grandchildren, although he already knew this, somehow their current post-coital nakedness hardly seemed appropriate for a grandmother.

"Your granddaughter is a little beauty and tall like you," Minsky commented, hoping to distract her and keep her at his side for a little longer.

"She has a temper like her grandfather," Martha huffed, "when she does not get her way. She is but two and yet she stamps her foot and screams if she does not get to wear the dress she wants. Whilst her brother is five and quite solemn and uncommunicative and only wants to shoot everything with his toy guns, which is also rather like Jack." Despite themselves they both laughed at Jack's expense. "We shouldn't laugh," Martha eventually managed, "it isn't respectful."

"Tell me," Minsky observed, still smiling though his tone was suddenly serious, "if your husband came into the room now do you think he would be more annoyed at your saying he is ill tempered and uncommunicative or at the fact that we are still both bathed in sweat from our love making?"

"I doubt if we would have time to ask," Martha languidly replied, "as he would shoot us both without thought or hesitation." then adding after a moments reflection and with much more emotion, "At least I hope he would, I hope he still loves me enough to do so."

"Personally, I would prefer him to hate me if he shows his love by shooting us," Minsky grinned, causing Martha to hug and kiss him.

"Time is short," Martha pulled away, realising that their passions were rising once again, "and we have yet to resolve the predicament you are currently in."

"I have made it clear I will not involve you," Minsky sat up his tone sincere and insistent, his ability to lie to himself meant that he could lie with complete sincerity even to the woman he truly loved and admired.

13

"I can tell by the degree that your accent returns that you do not really believe what you say," Martha laughed at him, her own affection for her 'beautiful' Russian enabled her to speak as she saw fit. "When you first met me all those years ago, you plotted to seduce me and use me to gain the favours of various gentlemen so we could both profit. Now, out of the blue, you return to me expressing once again your undying love for me whilst all the time hinting at the debts you have outstanding."

"Did I not confess this to you all those years ago?" Minsky stated, somewhat hurt at the accusation, taking her smile as agreement. "And, didn't you readily fall in with my plans, shameless as you are?" Again she smiled and nodded. "And, did I not graciously leave the field when it seemed you had found happiness? I went without making any further demands on you or your purse as a lesser man would have."

"That is true, my dearest," Martha agreed, trying to remain serious, despite her growing smile, "you disappeared without a goodbye as soon as I told you that Jacob DeWert had serious intentions towards me. Though at the time I did wonder if it was because Brandon O'Shea suspected you regularly bedded me whilst I was his mistress?"

"That is not true, if he suspected I would not have gotten away so cleanly," Minsky stated ruefully. "I went the moment I heard the rumours that your long dead husband had been *resurrected*. I thought your life complicated enough."

Martha turned to face him, placing her hands either side of his head, "Let us play a little game, each time you answer a question with the truth I will kiss you and allow you a liberty with your hands, if you lie I will twist your ears until you cry out. Is it a agreed?" He nodded and she twisted his ears causing him to cry out, "Just testing, so you know what to expect," she smiled at his scowling face.

Minsky gained a kiss and various liberties with her breasts for confirming he had gone to New York City from Chicago all those years ago and had initially done rather well for himself.

Then another kiss and further freedom to caress her buttocks for explaining that he had returned when a particular deal had gone badly wrong and he thought it best to vacate the great metropolis.

"When you first came back you kept away from me?" Martha asked, imparting another kiss as he nodded, "Because I had grown old and ugly?"

"No!" Minsky was quick to respond and was prepared to pinch her back if she thought it a lie, but she allowed him to continue, giving permission with another kiss, "I did not intend to stay and I thought you so well established and happy, I did not want to intrude or rekindle something that was only short term. Quite frankly, with your daughter married to Chester DeWert and your son being the senior manager of DeWert Holdings, with its railroad, mining and shipping interests, and you with your large house, grand dresses and jewellery and a husband with a formidable reputation; I did not think you would look kindly on my reappearance in your life."

"You did not think I would sweep you up in my arms and give you a big kiss in the middle of Adams and LaSalle?" Martha recollected her immodest behaviour on recognising Minsky as he stood looking at the Home Insurance building.

"I certainly did not, you truly showed yourself shameless for the whole of Chicago to see," Minsky laughed, remembering his own blushes at her enthusiastic greeting.

"And, you had not arranged for me to accidentally see you on that corner?" she asked the laughter gone from her whilst her eyes fixed his.

"I swear by my God, and my love for you, that I, Ibrahim Mikhailovich Minsky, did not plan or intend our reunion," he stated with sincerity and received a kiss in return. "Though I must say I am glad it happened all the same as I missed the enthusiasm and shamelessness of your lovemaking," for which he nearly had both ears pulled off.

"As you have pointed out I am now the wife, mother and

mother-in-law of wealthy men so you will allow me to pay your debts," she said watching him as he rubbed his ill-treated auricles, after their brief but satisfying tussle.

"And, as I explained previously," he said, a little testily as he thought she had rather over done the twisting, although he could deny her nothing that gave her pleasure, "even if it were possible I would not allow it, I do not want you mixed up in this."

"I do not understand," Martha was overdue at her daughter's and wanted the matter done with, it was nothing but money and what was that between friends such as they? "At least tell me the amount that you owe."

"It is not the sum," Minsky explained, trying unsuccessfully not to sound dismayed. "They have bought up all my debts, including those from New York. It is a large sum, though not to the likes of a DeWert, but they do not want money in exchange for my scrip but a service, they want me to gain for them a particular item."

"Surely they cannot refuse cash?" Martha was perplexed but seeing how despondent Minsky was went on, "Perhaps, with the correct story, Jack could be persuaded to intervene… "

"I'm sure he would be in his element," Minsky ruefully grinned, "these men are of the most violent and ill-tempered disposition, what is more they grow impatient, but I will not take the risk and will certainly not involve you."

"What exactly is it they want you to obtain for them?" Martha asked, her expression clearly showing she would not be put off from knowing all about her lover's predicament.

"It is the O'Shea diamonds," Minsky told her, his head in his hands.

"You are quite certain you do not know who the colored woman is?" the sergeant asked Jack for the fourth or fifth time in their brief interview.

"No, Sergeant," Jack reaffirmed, wishing he had not lost his hip-flask as he was sorely in need of a drink, "as I have already said, I do not associate with many coloreds, of those I do few are female and even fewer young women. Now, I grow cold and stiff sitting here on this pile of old wood and bricks and, at my age, a chill is something to be avoided as are pains in the arse, so would you mind asking Inspector O'Leary if I may go about my business?" The sergeant, who still bent over Jack taking notes, hesitated for a while, but unable to think of anymore questions nor a response to the jibe about 'pains in the arse', relented and walked over to the inspector.

Cage was watching his men, the bodies had been lowered onto a sheet and the ropes cut from them, their torn clothing had been collected and, with the carriage whip, tackle, ropes and other items, were all being taken to the police station. The doctor, who had confirmed the time of death as being between nine and midnight of the previous night, was finishing his cursory examination. The sergeant waited patiently, a good five minutes knowing Jack's eyes were on him the whole time, until O'Leary finished speaking with the doctor and turned to him. The inspector and sergeant muttered together for a few moments then Cage with the sergeant, now smiling, in tow walked back to Jack.

"Now, Mr Stevens," Inspector O'Leary stated in his best policeman's voice, which was both neutral and suspicious at the same time, "you persist in telling us you do not know the young black woman."

"You know, I served in the war before either of you had kissed your first girl," Jack responded truculently, annoyed they should doubt his word; the word of a veteran after all.

"I was born the year after the war ended," the young sergeant informed them both. "My father was a corporal in the union infantry and it was the year he was mustered out, I expect mother was glad to see him back. Which side were you on Mr Stevens?" the question causing O'Leary to cough, covering his laugh at the sergeant's jest at Jack's expense.

"I served with the 1st Battalion New York Sharpshooters from '62 to '65 and was mustered out in Washington, a sergeant major,"

Jack looked the young man up and down, thinking him a measure of the time since the war had ended: his life as a babe and child, then as a youth between hay and grass until he'd grown a man and was now a sergeant in the Chicago police. Whilst over the same time span Jack had fought the rage inside him, brought on by the death of his best friend who was blown to bits by a mortar shell that left Jack unscathed and happy to live but guilt-ridden. The years that followed of waking nightmares that left Stevens unmanned and branded him, in his mind only, a coward. How he had taken Martha and his young family west to start a new life but had failed. Eventually he had put his family on a train to Chicago with a promise to follow, but had deserted them and disappeared into the wilds of the Black Hills. His years of hunting, of living with and fighting the Indians, his time as a bounty hunter, then a more peaceful existence as a drifter and cattle drive cook before becoming a sheriff of a small town in the middle of nowhere. His accidental reunion with his family, who had thought him dead, his reconciliation and rekindled love. Followed by what? Not the peace he had sort, it was as if all feeling had drained from him since his coming to Chicago. He had become an observer of his own life, distant from Martha, his children and grandchildren; even his relationship with Kitty seemed to occur at arms length from himself, a passive actor in his own life.

The silence which followed Jack's statement, and the passivity of his stare as he looked back over time, grew to such a length that the inspector relented in his questioning and instead took a small, slightly under-exposed photograph from his jacket pocket and showed it to Jack, "Does this help jog your memory?" he asked.

The photo was of a prosperous colored family, a middle aged man and woman seated, with their son and daughter standing behind them. The family resemblance was clear and the young woman, of about twenty, was attractive and intelligent looking. Her older brother in his early thirties, was tall, broad and muscular with somewhat angry eyes dominating his stern and clean shaven features. The father, though seated, leaned upon a walking cane, his bewhiskered visage almost glowed with benevolence, tinged with the self-righteousness of one who knew he did God's work and did so with all his heart and energy. Whilst the wife reminded Jack of a colored woman he had once known, a woman from a very different station in life as the one in the picture, but whose only concern was seeing her family through the storms of their lives.

"I'm sorry, but I don't recognise any of them," Jack handed the photograph back with a shake of his head.

"If I said she was well known as a pianist and her father is Reverend Blackstaff?"

"The name does ring a bell, but the only colored I know who plays the piano is a male and he currently abides nigh on 600 miles west of here." Jack shrugged, unapologetically.

"Inspector, sir," a police constable, clomped up the stairs, holding something silvery in his hand, "this has been found on the floor below, behind the broken door."

"What is it, Davies?" the inspector asked, though Jack had already recognised it and clamped his mouth shut.

"A silver hip flask, sir."

2

THE REVEREND

How the flask had ended up behind the broken door of the derelict warehouse Jack had no idea nor did he enlighten the police as to his ownership. Despite this, Inspector O'Leary was determined to take Stevens with him to the Blackstaff residence, partly to help break the news of their daughter's death and partly to see if they recognised him. However, Jack made a bad companion for the cab ride as he spent most of the journey deep in his own thoughts trying to piece together the few memories he had of the previous day. His problem was the scarcity of the pieces he had to complete the puzzle: a vague memory of the River Bar, a night-time walk along Clarke, a young man in a brown check suit with whom he recollected having had an argument. As they turned into North Astor Street Jack gave up, he was too hungry and thirsty to concentrate and the conversation that the inspector was having with his sergeant intruded too much.

He let the inspector and sergeant lead the way, not being overly keen on what was to come, Cage telling him to hold his tongue and for the sergeant to keep notes of all that was said. The house was large: a spacious hall and imposing staircase, library cum music room, drawing room, dining room, a parlour at the rear for the family to use, a half dozen bedrooms and a bathroom, servant quarters in the attic more than ample enough for the two white maids, colored butler and cook. The place even boasted an indoor privy, though the outdoor ones were still used by the servants. Whilst the the kitchen and laundry room were built onto the side and obscured by bushes and trees, which filled the large, path strewn gardens surrounding the house.

The family looked much as they did in the photograph Cage had shown to Stevens at the warehouse. However, the reverend was smaller and older than Jack expected and, although he appeared sprightly for a man in his late sixties, he had a slight limp, which explained his use of the walking stick, and his hair and whiskers were grey. The reverend's son was much more imposing being tall and muscular; the restrained anger showing in his eyes, movements and voice was only too evident for all to recognise. Whilst his wife, also in her sixties, appeared outwardly calm she had the look of someone on the brink of shattering, all too aware that her world was at the point of disintegrating.

Cage reintroduced the sergeant and simply referred to Jack as "… and Mr Stevens accompanies us," then broke the news of their daughter's death as quickly and as simply as he could with no reference to the actual circumstances. Jack had grown used to dealing with the dead, his spending time with the two deceased women in the early afternoon was no great matter to him, but he could not stomach the out pouring to grief from those who remained behind. Even the son, a six foot sculpture of inward rage had melted at the news, falling to his knees and with a hand on each of his parents shoulders joined them in prayer. Or at least the father and son prayed, the mother simply intoned some ancestral wail, that came as part of a long drawn out breath from deep within her soul. Jack could not abide it and left the room, passing the butler who stood in the doorway: immobile, face pale and drawn, with his mouth half-open, frozen in shock.

Jack waited in the library, which also housed the dead woman's piano and music collection as well as a many shelves of books which where mainly text of a religious nature. One entire shelf was dedicated to the writings, published books, pamphlets and hand written sermons and lectures, of Reverend Blackstaff. Stevens had plenty of time to look around the room, half an ear on what was occurring in the drawing room, waiting for the moment he thought he should return. In all fairness he had to admit that Cage and the sergeant had remained at their post waiting in silence then answering the family's uncomprehending questions.

"Mr Stevens," Jack hadn't noted the butler's presence as he was engrossed reading a small notebook he had found, "if I may ask you something?" The mother was holding onto the butler's arm, her head bowed and seemingly on the point of collapse, the butler's attention was more on her rather than Jack, "Mrs Blackstaff has been given to understand that you were the person who found..." the butler was an elderly man, in his late fifties, portly and dignified of bearing, but his eyes pleaded with Jack for him to speak before he had to complete his sentence.

"Yes, my condolences, ma'am," Jack affirmed, his voice even and clear, his eyes on the mother. "I waited with your daughter until the police arrived. She appeared composed and at peace, quite serene I would say; I would think she passed quickly and without pain."

There was a brief pause whilst the mother whispered something and the butler relayed, "We thank you, Mr Stevens, it eases the pain we feel to know someone was with her to watch over her." Jack watched as the pair shuffled out, wondering how many mothers had grieved over a son or daughter that he had put in the ground. Once they were gone Jack slipped the notebook into his inside jacket pocket and returned to the drawing room. Coffee and small cakes had been served, the habit of hospitality prevailing despite the circumstances, though none had touched them. However, Jack's hunger got the better of him and he filled a cup and plate before seating himself.

"As I explained last night," the reverend was saying, his voice calm though tremulous, "I thought my daughter had gone to teach, she gives… gave, private lessons but also taught music and gave recitals at various clubs that my foundation organises for the improvement of the labourers of this city."

"These are located around the city but it was to the one near the docks that she was expected?" O'Leary checked the information he had been given the night before when the woman had been reported missing.

"Yes," it was the son, John Wesley Blackstaff, who answered, "I also teach, as do many of father's supporters, though my subject is mathematics and far less popular than Philomena's recitals. There is a published rota of who gives the classes and when."

"When we went from here it was the first place we searched last night," the inspector explained, "but it would seem that she was not expected, she had swapped the class with a friend. We also checked the other venues you informed us of and she did not attend any of those either."

"There is some mistake, Inspector," the reverend stated firmly, "my daughter would not lie."

"Is there any possibility she was going elsewhere, to meet with someone or… "

"None whatsoever, Inspector," the reverend insisted, "my daughter was a quite girl, shy when not performing. Her music was her world and when not teaching or reciting she would be here practising. As I have told you she would not aim to deceive or dissemble it is… was not in her nature."

"We have also spoken to her friends, from the list you gave us," the inspector led the father and brother as gently as he could with his questions trying to unearth as much as they knew or, more difficultly, suspected about the recently deceased young woman, whose reputation her loved ones would not willing besmirch, "they could not shed any light on where she may have been. We will, of course, try to retrace her steps once more but she must have left here last night with the intention of going somewhere; though it does not appear to have been to where you thought. If there are any other possibilities, other friends or family, anyone else she may have gone to?" Cage glanced at his sergeant as the two he questioned shook their heads and seemed genuinely perplexed.

"Is there anything you can help us with, that would give us some direction as to where we should start?" the sergeant asked, taking the inspector's hint to further push the grieving pair for information. "Miss Blackstaff may have muddled her appointments so anything, no matter how unlikely, you can add then now is the time to tell us."

"Your foundation is a popular movement, across all strata of society, I believe?" Jack asked in the deepening silence that followed the sergeant's question and though the inspector scowled at Jack he had nothing else to ask so waited to see where Jack's line of enquiry took them.

"A better description would be a 'broad church'," the reverend stated, answering with more certainty on a topic he knew well and found a comfort to discuss. "It has a wide membership of all races and stations in life, with many advocates amongst the powerful and wealthy of this city."

"You are also an ardent supporter of the Knights of Labour?" Jack asked, showing a greater knowledge of the reverend than he had led Cage to believe he possessed.

"What of it?" the son, John Wesley, almost barked, then looked down at his father's reproving glance.

"My foundation is a charitable one, it has no political nor really any religious affiliation," the reverend amicably explained. "Its aims are to help the poor and the working men and women of this city; through education, to support the growth of the mind, and to supply medical treatments, for bodily welfare. We teach a doctrine of 'all men are equal' and propagate a belief based on the attitude of 'turning the other cheek' along with the values expounded in the parable of the 'good samaritan'. In these doctrines there exists an affinity to the views of the Knights of Labour, but no direct connection to their political aims. It is true, however, that I occasionally speak at their rallies and meetings and write in support of their collective ideals, that all are equal and should be treated fairly regardless of sex, race or wealth. Though I do not expound their political goals nor their agenda on improving working conditions."

"Unfortunately not everyone is as nuanced in distinguishing between your ideological and religious beliefs and the politics of the Knights," Jack stated quietly, ignoring the agitated fidgeting of the son. "I was wondering if you or your family have received any threats?"

"We receive them simply for the color of our skin," the son broke in, this time ignoring his father's expression. "We have grown used to them and the lack of action in dealing with them by the authorities."

"You think my daughter has been the victim of an attack that ultimately is directed at myself and my work?" the reverend's face had again fallen at the thought that he had some part to play in his daughter's murder.

"It is possible that someone has thought to get at you through your daughter," Jack gently elaborated, "given the quietness of her life it must be considered a possibility. Have you had any threats of late that have been aimed at your family or may suggest they hold you collectively responsible?"

"Apart from those shouted at us in the street or at public events, those that are written are often no more than a rambling of obscenities. I have them burned and take no notice, as my son says, these are the sort of tribulations to which we 'turn to him the other also'; as is our way."

"Mr Stevens has a point," the inspector persisted, seeing Jack had resumed drinking his coffee whilst reflecting on the reverend's words, "your daughter may have been attacked because of the family's link with the Knights or, as your son states, simply for being what she was; an educated and successful black woman. If there have been any threats made recently, no matter how vague or unlikely sounding, it might be of help."

"Matthew, our butler, may be more able to help, he vets our post and burns the more obviously unfit communications. Anything he considers I should look at he passes directly to me but over the last few weeks there has been nothing out of the ordinary and he has dealt with everything that has come to us."

Cage sent the sergeant to find and question the butler before asking, "The woman who was found with your daughter, you said her description is unfamiliar to you and as generalised as it is you can put no specific name to it?"

"You have described a woman who could be anyone of a dozen or so," the reverend despaired. "If that poor young woman has not herself been reported missing then it suggests she has no family and few acquaintances, I cannot think of anyone my daughter has mentioned that is in such a situation."

"There is of course an obvious explanation as to why your daughter may not have mentioned to you a meeting that she considered private," Jack stated, replacing his empty cup on a small table at his side, unconcernedly brushing crumbs from his lap. "If she was going with her friend to meet with her friend's gentleman… "

"My sister would not go behind her parents back nor take part in a secret meeting with a man," John Wesley spluttered in indignation and anger, though Jack ignored him watching instead the father's face which creased in thought and concern at the suggestion. "I find these questions unacceptable and unnecessarily intrusive, nor do I understand your role and position here to put such inflammatory questions to us at this hour of our grief."

"Mr Stevens, regularly helps with our enquiries and he is also associated with the Pinkertons," Cage explained, his voice even but authoritative, an edge of warning in his tone that John should hold his temper.

"A Pinkerton!" John's voice had grown loud and he was near out of his seat, but directing his words to his father. "There you have your answer, they come here not to help nor find Philomena's murderer but to cast vile lies upon her character and do all they can to undermine your teachings."

"I am not a Pinkerton," Jack explained calmly still ignoring the irate brother. "It is true that many years ago, in the Black Hills, I worked alongside a couple of Pinkertons but the association has long ended." Jack lied but the father's gaze softened from the sudden animosity he had portrayed at his son's insinuation.

"John, please, regain your composure," the reverend was doing his best to remain calm and keep at bay the overwhelming wave of despair he felt about his daughter's death that was dammed up somewhere inside his heart. "The Pinkertons have been troublesome in dealing with the Knights and a thorn in the side of all their supporters, including ourselves, but I do not believe we are singled out by them especially not in this. As for my daughter being involved with a young man, either on her own account or in support of a friend, I believe my wife would be aware of this and she has made no mention of it. My daughter was naturally shy and though she had attracted attention from one or two young men she had shied away from them."

John Wesley could stand to hear no more and with a grunted, "I will see how mother is," pushed back his chair, nearly tipping it over, and went through the door banging it behind him.

"You must forgive… " the reverend began but Cage was already assuring him of his understanding. Then after a pause, whilst the reverend fiddled with his cup of cold coffee first taking then replacing it on the table besides Jack's empty one, asked, "Do either of you have any notion as to why she was… attacked?"

"None," Cage admitted, then drawing breadth, knowing what

the father's next question must be, explained. "The circumstances suggest her death was premeditated but, until we are able to identify the young woman who died with her, we cannot say which, if either, was the primary victim. I should tell you, whilst we are alone, that your daughter died quickly," Cage readily lied on this point. "Over the next few days much scurrilous and unfounded detail will be printed in the papers about this, you should ignore what they say. Perhaps your butler could ensure they are kept from your wife, he should also shield you both from any unwanted callers, unfortunately curiosity knows no bounds of propriety. If you have any questions then send for me and I will come."

As the sergeant reappeared during O'Leary's final words, he might have made his farewells and left at this point had Jack not asked, "Your son, what is his occupation? I understand your daughter was fully occupied with her music and teaching, and you, I assume, with your charitable work and writings, but your son?"

"In my life I hope I have contributed to the public good but from a financial standpoint I make very little from my writing nor my sermons and lectures. My son runs the family business founded by my father, which is the basis of our wealth and good fortune."

"What is this business?" Jack asked, though realising that Cage must already know as he was waiting to leave.

"My father and his brother escaped here from the south as very young men, and worked on the docks and boats," the reverend explained, once again happy to reflect on matters that did not take account of his daughter's death and the emotions this raised in him. "When he married my mother he wanted an occupation that was more secure and obtained a position in a chandlery. As a black man he was lucky to secure such a position but quickly proved his worth. The owner was an elderly man, a widower without any heir, and he eventually agreed to my father buying the shop from him. After my father died, my uncle ran the place briefly until my son finished his studies and took over as manager. John has further built on his grandfather's labours and now employs a large number of men, as well as his two cousins, and in addition to the chandlery the company has a number of properties on the north bank of the river."

"This would be 'Blackstaff Chandlery and Warehousing'?" Jack connected the name, as the reverend spoke, with the dilapidated sign over the door of the derelict warehouse.

Jack had asked to be dropped at the Gripmans near Washington and Wabash, despite their passing his home he preferred to eat out. As the road became crowded and they approached Rush Bridge the cabman became involved in an altercation with another driver, even the horse seemed to join in with loud whinny's and clattering of hooves, in the end the sergeant dismounted and got them moving again. Jack took the opportunity to show Cage the notebook he had found.

"You have taken this without permission?" the inspector stated, though Jack could not tell if he joked or not.

"I believe it is Philomena's diary," Jack explained, "it was hidden in the piano stool under a pile of old music sheets, so I doubt it will be missed. The pages are dated and contain musical notations but also written observations."

"Yet you thought to steal it from the grieving parents," Cage admonished, then scowled as Jack plucked it from his hands and replaced it in his jacket pocket as the sergeant regained his seat in the cramped carriage.

"Take the cab, Sergeant," O'Leary told his assistant as the cab pulled over. "It was a late night yesterday and you should not further neglect that young family of yours. I will dine with Mr Stevens, but we shall meet at the station early tomorrow to plan our day." The sergeant readily agreed and the cab was off the moment Jack had closed the door behind him. "I'll meet you inside, order me a steak and trimmings with pie to follow and a beer, I'm going to report back to the precinct station that I am here if I need be reached." Jack watched as the inspector walked up the street to the police emergency telephone before going into the diner thinking that Cage's rank obviously came with a degree of privilege in how he conducted himself.

The Gripmans Bar and Diner was a narrow but long establishment with kitchens to the rear, both drinks and food were ordered from the waiters who were happy to recite the menu and drinks available from memory if required. The place was crowded, though less than half the clientele were cable car workers the remainder were the usual mix of office workers, with their wives or sweethearts, and the occasional group of men. The place had a vibrant atmosphere, neither too quite nor too loud for Jack's liking and he quickly found Boat in his usual booth at the rear.

"No Banjo?" Jack asked, seeing his old war buddy eating alone, giving his order to the waiter as he took his seat opposite.

"He cried off, chasing after some woman as usual." Boat, Hugh Phillip Partkis, to everyone else, except Jack and Banjo, was in his late forties, medium build with a square face, dark eyes black hair and a moustache of considerable thickness which he trimmed daily. Born in New York of Polish parentage, he had served in the Sharpshooters alongside Jack during the war. When mustered out he and Banjo had taken the train from Washington to NYC, but on meeting a pair of strawberry blond sisters travelling with their parents to Chicago had diverted to follow them. Boat, named partly because of the way he walked hunched forward like the bow of a boat breaking through water and partly because his rapid and accurate rate of fire, even for the sharpshooters, was likened to that of a gun boat, had married 'his' strawberry blond with whom he had two daughter's and a son and was proud to be a gripman driving the cablecars on the Chicago City Railway.

"You know Inspector Uriah Micajah O'Leary," Jack introduced Cage as he joined them. "This is an old friend of mine, Hugh Partkis, the best shot I have ever met."

"I have read about you, sir." Hugh extended his broad, strong hand for the inspector to shake. "Your arrest of the Post Office Raiders was most entertaining."

"As I'm off duty call me 'Cage'," the inspector smiled, remembering the extremely inept gang that had attempted to rob the Post Office and Customs House and he had 'single handedly' arrested. "Now Jack, the diary you purloined." Cage read through the notebook, skipping pages of the musical notes, as he slowly ate, whilst Jack demolished his chops, wolfed a double helping of pie, finished two beers and started on a bottle of whiskey whilst catching up with Boat on the week's events.

"Your wife and family are well?" Stevens asked with a full mouth.

"Mother is as hearty as ever, and busy enough for two now our youngest daughter is to be married," Boat smiled at the thought of how lucky he had been in his life; a son apprenticed as an engineer on the cablecars, his eldest daughter the personal maid of Mrs O'Shea and now his youngest, who had certificates to attest to her ability in the use of a typewriting machine as well as for her spelling, grammar and general mathematics, was engaged to be married to an up-and-coming young clerk who worked for DeWert Holdings.

"That reminds me," Jack smiled back, raising his glass, "I checked with my son about the young man in question and it seems he is an asset to the company and is due a promotion."

"Your good health, Sergeant Major," Boat clinked his friend's glass, knowing Jack had pulled a few strings but such things are expected of old comrades and Boat would ensure the debt did not go unpaid. "Here is to their future happiness, may it follow the path of your own daughter who has been much blessed." Boat was careful not to mention Jack's son, Andrew, who was married five years but with no sign of a child.

"Over the last two months or so there has been increasingly frequent mentions of an 'MW'," the inspector muttered, cutting through the others conversation.

"She first mentions him at a Knights meeting where her father is giving a lecture, she remarks on how she asks who MW is, having observed MW's enthusiastic and passionate agreement with her father's words, and how MW states, 'The Knight's political views are so clearly endorsed by the Bible, God's own words'," Jack remarked, then continuing. "It would seem that shy Philomena then attended more meetings, without her father's knowledge, and regularly commented on MW's passion for the cause, MW's drive and commanding ways, how MW speaks to her of a great future opening up and so on. The young woman seems quite taken with this MW and you should note her final entry is 'MW 4 o'clock GPH', which I assume is the Grand Pacific Hotel."

"You took in a great deal, given how little time you had to study the diary," Cage commented, making a mental note not to underestimate the elderly reprobate, whose face was often puffy and grey eyes bleary from drink. "A pity though she does not describe the excellent MW, but as a frequent attendee at Knights gatherings the list of possible candidates should not be excessive."

"If she has kept her feelings secret it might be because she thinks her family would disapprove," Jack speculated, sipping his whiskey.

"Knights, you say," Boat interrupted, "I'll have nothing to do with them. The rail company treats us well and I'll not have trouble stirred up where none is needed."

"The are many honest workers, both men and women, particularly amongst the Germans and Irish but coloreds also, who feel differently on the matter and not without reason," Cage disagreed. "Managers and factory owners across the city much abuse their power and demand a great deal for little in return from their workforce."

"I see you are a convert," Jack laughed, offering to top up their beers with a drop from his whiskey bottle. "It's possible that MW is a lowly labourer, below the status of the prosperous Blackstaffs, or perhaps he is white?"

"That is a possibility as the reverend, though an advocate of equality and peaceful coexistence," Cage returned his thoughts to the case, "is an equally vocal opponent of any mixing of the races. Though I do not see how her admiration for MW, white or colored, leads to the scene we witnessed earlier nor how it would include the other woman?"

"Speculation at this stage would be somewhat pointless," Jack observed. "Perhaps find MW first."

"At least we can rule out robbery, as we found both their purses and Philomena still had a locket around her neck, entangled with the garrotte."

"It's an awful day you have both had by the sound of it," Boat commented, frowning at the implications of what he heard.

Both his companions nodded despondently in agreement reflecting on all that had occurred that day before Jack, rather obscurely, stated, "There is something strange in this I can't quite fathom." Then, in a more cheery fashion asked Boat, "Do you remember seeing me yesterday?"

"It was the afternoon of the day before yesterday," Boat reminded him grinning, "we had lunch here with Banjo. Is the drink addling your mind so much you mix one day with another?'

"It seems so," Jack laughed, downing another glass and topping everyone up again. An hour later Boat had departed for the comfort of his home and Cage had wished Jack a good night and was donning his overcoat when Pinky and Pug barged into the Gripmans.

"Inspector, your precinct captain said we would find you hear." Pinky, or more formally Lucius Nathaniel Morgan O'Gail, a long serving Pinkerton, was a small man of Irish descent with slicked down hair, a thin moustache and missing the little finger on his right hand.

"O'Gail," the inspector stated without warmth, he was tired and dreaded this unexpected meeting would delay him further from his much needed rest, "I hope it isn't me you're wanting as I'm off to my bed."

"I'm afraid you will not get your wish just yet." Benjamin Elijah Raymond Burke, more commonly known as Pug, who was of Scottish descent, clean shaven, as tall as a tree and brawny as an ox and as quietly spoken as Pinky was loud, his trademark bowler hat in his hand as his large frame blocked the aisle behind his partner. "You should read this," he stated for explanation handing Cage a folded piece of paper.

"Stevens, you drunken bum, you need to beat it," Pinky commanded Jack, emptying Jack's bottle of its last mouthful and signalling a waiter for a replacement.

"Hello Jack," Pug said evenly, with a smile, hoping to quieten the sudden storm that flashed across Jack's face, as he pushed into the booth next to his partner. "Ignore this foolhardy soul, he means nothing by what he says. Though we will need some privacy to speak with Inspector O'Leary."

"Try the alleyway at the rear," the unsmiling Jack told them, taking possession of the whiskey the waiter delivered with a look that dared any man to try and take it from him.

"Jack, I am sorry but they are right," Cage told him. "This missive is from the chief himself telling me to treat with the greatest secrecy all this pair have to tell me and, worse still, I am to cooperate and work in partnership with them in solving the murder of the two women discovered this morning."

"The pair I found," Jack calmly stated, making no effort to move and pouring whiskey into everyones glass, which Cage wearily took as a signal to sit. "And, in which I remain a suspect."

"I remember that trading post where you cornered the Baynard brothers," Pug informed them all, as much to cover Pinky's cursing the day he had met Jack as for any other reason. "You sat down at their table and offered them whiskey, from the bottle you'd just bought, in celebration of something or other, then you gut shot the pair the moment they raised their glasses."

The two Pinkertons had known each other since growing up in neighbouring streets in New York and had enlisted together in the final year of the civil war in an infantry regiment. They saw little action but their sergeant was a Pinkerton and took them back to Chicago with him and had them enrolled as detectives. Over the years they had worked across much of the midwest, meeting and teaming up with Jack in the Black Hills, for a share of the proceeds they traced those with a bounty and sent Jack to 'retrieve' the quarry. It had proven a lucrative partnership until they returned to Chicago and Jack had left them still unable to face his family. Misunderstanding Jack's wishes they had told Martha that Jack was dead, something she had never forgiven them for.

"OK," Cage was too tired to play games, "he obviously isn't going to move so you pair have five minutes to tell me what is of such importance it can't wait until the morning."

"Well," Pug lowered his voice to a point where the others had to lean forward to hear him, "we have been informed that you found two women, a colored and a blond, we have this from our boss, WP himself, who got to hear of your find. Seems he was keeping close tabs on the blond and, not having heard from her at a prearranged time, is worried about her whereabouts. Putting two and two together, he sent us to find you with this photograph," the Pinkerton handed Cage the picture.

"I can't tell from that," Jack stated looking over the inspector's shoulder, "but she was a blond in her late twenty's, attractive, at least she would have been."

"I think this is her," Cage stated wondering what twist this brought to the case. "Certainly her general features are a match, though given the state she was in I can't be positive."

"Let's take it as a likeness until we learn otherwise," Pug had little doubt they were one and the same woman from what he had been told earlier in the day. "Her name is Mary Patricia Walsh and she worked for the Pinkertons, reporting direct to WP," Pug paused hoping for a reaction but Cage was too tired and Jack too drunk to register much in their facial expressions. "In fact he had hired her himself and was the only one, except his brother, who knew of her. She was working undercover to infiltrate the Order of the Knights of Labour, the agency had not had much luck in getting into the inner circle who run the show. We monitor their meetings easily enough but none, until Mary Walsh, have gotten beyond being a general member."

"As she was a woman," Pinky interrupted, "I expect they weren't as suspicious, plus she had played the long game, it seems, and had worked in a sweat shop for a couple of months and let them approach her. She gradually became an enthusiastic and active supporter, and was trusted more and more. Recently she had made friends with and was being helped by the daughter of Reverend Blackstaff, who 'certified her credentials', as they say."

"In her last reports," Pug went on as Pinky lit his pipe, "she was growing suspicious of the connection between the Knights and a newcomer, a man known only as 'Chicago Joe', who claimed he could get them protection from the street gangs."

"It's not a name I recognise," the inspector told them, his forehead furrowed, though he sensed his case would be solved in the next few sentences. "Though why should the Knights need to be protected from the street gangs?"

"It's true their membership has large numbers of Irish and Germans, as well as many coloreds, inevitably a number have connections with various gangs particularly the Dead Hands, Kings and Black Hawks and, for a relatively small fee, the local gangs stop any trouble happening at their meetings. However, this Chicago Joe seems to have suggested he could bring over entire gangs and whole districts of workers, starting with the Black Hawks. It would not only further swell their numbers but give them a *militia* that would stop violence at any meeting or march," Pug took a mouthful of whiskey, and peered meaningfully at his companions.

"In other words," the inspector elaborated, "a force large and violent enough to take on the police should they decide to intervene in a rally."

"Exactly so," Pinky confirmed, puffing smoke as he spoke, "relations with the constabulary not being so good recently."

"It's true," Cage, sadly confirmed. "Though many an ordinary policeman live side by side with members of the Knights and may in their hearts wish them luck against the bosses, we have had orders from the very top not to tolerate large gatherings and to be most vigilant, even excessively so, in upholding the law when dealing with them."

"Well," Pug took up the baton, "at her last report Mary, said she was looking more closely at this Chicago Joe and was deeply concerned about the man, his connections and what he was up to. She had a plan to get close to him and his organisation but did not want to say more until she had spoken with her friend, Miss Blackstaff, as she would need her help for her plans to succeed."

"Getting them both killed in the process," Cage concluded. "Your boss is an idiot beyond measure for involving a woman in such work, the dangers are too great as circumstances now show."

"You have no disagreement from us," Pinky told them, exhaling a large cloud of smoke as he did to emphasise the enormity of the error as he saw it. "Although WP said she was the most skilled operative he had ever seen who could even have put his father to shame. Believe me the father was as a god to the two sons, so it is not light praise he gave."

"We have evidence that Miss Blackstaff had befriended an MW whilst attending meetings of the Knights, we thought it might be a man but is obviously your Mary Walsh," the inspector informed the two Pinkertons, glancing at Jack who appeared to be asleep in the corner of the booth. "I take it that is not her real name but the one she used for cover."

"Yes," Pug stated, wondering what possessed a woman, an

attractive one at that, to take up such a calling. "WP would not give us her name until all is confirmed and he has spoken with the family, which he gave us to believe he knew well."

"It is late," Cage told them, standing, "and my bed beckons me. I will meet you both at the police station at seven o'clock, we will confer there with my sergeant as how best to proceed so we track down this Chicago Joe. Good night Gentleman."

But before he could go, Jack stretching himself awake said, "What doesn't make sense to me is why a *skilled* undercover detective, hand-picked by the top man himself, thought a shy, black, female piano teacher could help her in cornering a man she seems to have considered dangerous?"

Jack had left the others as they went their separate ways. He was still troubled by thoughts of his missing day and how his hip flask had found its way to the scene of a murder but on the positive side he was obviously no longer a suspect. It was too late for him to try and meet with Kitty, he would leave it until the morrow and would spend the day trying to trace his missing steps from yesterday. For now he would head home and hailed a cab on the south side of Rush Bridge; as he boarded he thought he saw, though only a fleeting glance, a figure in a brown check suit ducking down an alleyway.

3

DINNER PARTY

Day Two – Wednesday April 16th 1886

Jack solved the riddle of his hip flask whilst he waited for Kitty
outside a dime museum. He had unthinkingly reached into his
jacket for a drop to warm him on a chilly spring day then realising
it was Miss Blackstaff's notebook he had taken out he had carelessly
replaced it, only for it to fall to the pavement. It would have been
by instinct that he'd have had a fortifying drop before entering
the warehouse, the flask must have slipped to the floor, missing
the pocket in his absent-minded haste, and fallen amongst the
rubble. He was determined he could now legitimately retrieve the
flask from Cage and have the inspector send the notebook to Miss
Blackstaffs's mother with the rest of her daughter's possessions. It
was, therefore, a smiling and even-tempered Jack that a breathless
and late Kitty discovered waiting for her. Under the circumstances
she quickly gave up the pretence of having rushed to make up for
her tardiness and they entered the dime museum arm in arm.

Stevens rented a little apartment north of the river but they
only met there when they had sufficient time for a longer and

more intimate meeting, usually after a meal or before going out. Their other regular venue was the River Bar, though no more than a drinking den, it offered them privacy amongst the low class women and river men who frequented the place. Kitty, much to Jack's amusement, dressed in her oldest clothes when going to the bar, cussed a great deal and and comported herself like any of the other female customers who found the bar a profitable place to pick up paying clients. Kitty had a hankering for playing roles, some more to Jack's liking than others, and undertaking little adventures about the city. Today she seemed to be playing a shy and naive widow whom Jack was escorting to see the sights so that, as they sauntered through the museum, she was coy and reluctant to snatch kisses as they loitered in the darker corners.

At another time Jack might have enjoyed the game, forcing his attentions on the the 'unwilling' widow and, eventually, persuading her to accompany him to his rooms for an afternoon of debauchery; but currently he had other things on his mind. Hoping it would lead to some enlightenment about his missing day he asked Kitty if she remembered anything odd occurring at their last meeting.

"No, though you were quite drunk when I left you, I thought you were going to your home," was her unhelpful response, annoyed by his lacklustre enthusiasm for playing his part in her game; the exasperation in her face signalling she expected him to kiss her.

"Did you see the papers today?" he finally asked, releasing her as another much younger couple turned the corner, invading the privacy of the little nook they had discovered.

"The death of poor Philomena Blackstaff, you mean?" Kitty said, glancing over her shoulder to note the young woman was taking up her station so her man could steal a kiss or two before another couple supplanted them. "I wonder if the owners keep the lighting low to attract so many couples," she mused as they sauntered on, "it does little to help the viewing of the exhibits."

"Did you know Miss Blackstaff?" Jack ignored Kitty's comments on the establishment he had brought her to, she already knew he had suggested it for its reputation, knowing it would appeal to her adventurous nature.

"I knew of her, I went to one or two of her recitals for the working man and woman, and I spoke to her once," Kitty told him, twining her arm in his and putting her head, carefully so as not to displace her hat, on his shoulder as they stood before some exhibit of rather dusty Indian apparel. "It was a brief conversation, outside a hall she had played in down by the docks, it was of little consequence. However, she was respected and liked, the men and women of the area appreciated the time she gave and that she didn't put on any airs."

"Was she with anyone?" Jack wanted to know. "A blond woman in particular."

"The unnamed one found with her you mean?" Kitty told him, suddenly kissing him passionately as the other couple came up to view the exhibit, then quickly leading him away; she had it seemed found another game to play. "She was with her brother, I believe, he was speaking to a group of men whilst various people were thanking her, praising her playing, which she was modestly denying being anything exceptional. However, I considered her very talented and told her so. There were plenty of young blond women about but none seemed to be with her."

"You are a supporter of the Knights of Labour, aren't you?" Jack asked, pondering on the notebook entries about MW and how both he and Cage had jumped to the conclusion the young piano teacher was writing about a man.

"Supporter and recruiter, for more than two years now, I can go with impunity into any factory or business in the Dead Hands area of control. None would dare gainsay the sister of Mr Henry Tipwell, certainly not whilst some of his boys shadow my every footstep when I am about my recruiting activities," Kitty told him, all the while blatantly watching the other couple canoodle, then stating, "The hussy!" just loud enough for the woman to hear before Jack, tugging at her arm, pulled her around another corner.

"You saw nothing of Miss Blackstaff at meetings of the Knights, nor heard anything about her?" Jack asked, becoming irritated at Kitty's antics but allowing her to embrace him as they turned into a particularly dark corner.

"No," she gasped between kisses that were growing in passion, "I saw her father, the reverend, speak once or twice."

"Oh, the trollop!" the woman hissed, turning the corner and stopping to pull her own beau towards her by his lapels. The two men allowed their women their passionate and increasingly lewd embraces, the pair of women hissing insults at each other between kisses. Just how far things might of gone none could tell but the women suddenly took flight, pulling their men behind them, as voices could be heard approaching.

"I don't have time for this," Jack stated, annoyed though aroused by Kitty's wanton behaviour, pulling them up in front of another exhibit of a rusty looking machine of some type. "I have to see Hank and then get home to change, I have a dinner at my daughter's too get to."

"Oh, you might have said," Kitty scowled, watching the two young men that had interrupted her earlier game pass behind them, "I thought you brought me here for other reasons, you said I would enjoy it given its reputation for *public displays*."

"Still it is a mouldy dump and I am leaving," Jack started to pull her down the corridor, his voice rising in anger.

"Stop it, get your hands off me," Kitty kept her tone even but loud enough for heads to turn as they entered a more crowded area. Jack immediately stopped and looked around as if he was also searching for where the raised voice had come from.

"If I had time I would put you over my knee," he informed her, knowing it would cause her to smile again, she was far too adept at getting her own way for him to do other than placate her. "It was me that found the bodies yesterday and, frankly, I'm troubled by what I saw and look for answers as to why they were left the way they were."

"You are a strange one, Jack," Kitty smiled, knowing it was his curiosity, that led him into so many scrapes, that she liked about him best as she craved adventure herself, "most others would have run a mile," then laughing as she remembered the report in the morning paper. "So you are the, 'elderly gent, out walking,' who, 'discovered the mangled remains'."

"Yes," Jack snorted derisively, "and it is as accurate a report as their suggestion that the murders were done by members of the local street gang. The newsmen think these two are killed for the same reason there has been a string of vicious beatings across the city as the various gangs jockey each other."

"I'm sorry, Jack," Kitty purred, recognising from his tone that the killings meant more to him than ideal curiosity. "I can't help much, though I do now recall seeing the pianist at a recent Knights meeting and she was with a young blond woman, but I know no more about her. However, I do know someone who might, a woman on the Knights' membership committee I report to, if you promise to take me to the theatre afterwards I will introduce you to her tomorrow afternoon."

"It's a deal," Jack readily agreed his anger already gone. "Will it be 'The Bijou' or the 'Opera'?"

"I was thinking 'Hershey's', the music hall, would be more fun," she stated with a broad smile and a wink.

Jack knew exactly where Hank would be during business hours, at Brandon Edward O'Shea's side, and the great man would be in his normal place of business which was located in a corner of the restaurant in a hotel he owned. The hotel was discreetly located just off the financial district within the city centre, its entrance was down a short street that went nowhere. Jack had been there once before, many years previous, but he sauntered in as if he was a regular customer and approached the maitre d'hotel.

"Good day," Stevens responded to the quizzical smile, whilst wondering if this was the same impeccably dressed and barbered young man who had been here on his previous visit. "If I might ask that you pass a message to Mr Henry Tipwell, over there." He nodded to the group of men sat in one of the larger booths in the corner to his right, the booths either side being occupied by young men who were of an equal stature to Hank and were obviously there as guards.

"I am sorry, sir, but Mr O'Shea and Mr Tipwell are in conference with business associates and cannot be disturbed," came the polite and unctuous response. Jack smiled, expecting such a response, coughed loudly and dropped the revolver he had concealed in his hand, the crash against the polished wooden floor causing everyone to look up.

"Sorry," Jack exclaimed, bending to pick up the gun and making no effort to conceal it, "Brandon, Hank, my apologies for the disturbance." Then thinking he recognised one of the faces turned towards him as the eldest McCormick son, smiled broadly and nodded as he added. "Old age you know, I keep dropping everything."

"Good afternoon, Jack," Brandon, touching a finger to his hairline in the form of a salute that he'd grown accustomed to using on seeing Jack, in acknowledgement of Stevens being a veteran. "I am engaged at the moment but if you care to wait I will do my best to spare you a few minutes later today."

"No need, my dear friend," Jack courteously replied, neither man particularly liked or disliked the other, Martha having once been Brandon's mistress during the period she thought Jack dead, the men treated each other with cold cordiality when they met at some function or the theatre. "I see you have important and influential guests," he nodded at McCormick and received a hesitant nod in return, "but if you can spare me five minutes of Mr Tipwell's time I have a *personal favour* of his to complete." Jack returned to the hotel lobby, leaving Hank to deal with O'Shea's angry expression and spent a minute composing a note to Cage about the notebook and his flask, which he had a bellhop take round to the appropriate precinct station.

"He said he is dining with you tonight at your son-in-laws," Hank told him, not taking a seat and towering above him like a replica of the Home Insurance building. "Though he doesn't seem happy at your intrusion."

"My apologies, Hank, please explain to the estimable Mr O'Shea I only come here because it is urgent and about the personal favour you asked me to do for you."

"Very well," Hank sighed knowing Jack to be a man of good sense whom he trusted. "Though my intention was for you to report the find to the police, steer them away from jumping to conclusions and then walk away."

"Which is what I'm doing," it was close enough to the truth for Jack to consider that he didn't lie to his young friend. "But the police are on a path that brings them back to the street gangs."

"The reports in the papers this morning are erroneous, I can assure you, from what I know this is not the work of any gang," Hank was dismissive of the standard of reporting on the case. "There's been some trouble of late, not just round the stockyards where all the new Polaks and other immigrants fight for space, but here and there along a number of borders."

"Not between the Kings and the Dead Hands, though?"

"No, they are too evenly matched and the Kings profit from Mr O'Shea's goodwill," Hank told him, relenting and taking a seat, thinking Brandon would now want the full story from him.

"Rumour has it that the Kings have lost ground to the south of their territory," Jack queried, not certain what he wanted to know from Hank, still thinking about the way the women were posed and what the possible message they represented might be. "And, as you say, with all the immigrants coming into the city, the Italians and Greeks, could these attacks be the start of something?"

"Change is inevitable, especially west of the river," Hank

45

shrugged. "Each gang has it's own core territory, outside of that, it is a case of ebb and flow and the Kings claim too big an area for them to hold. The coloreds are pushing up from the southeast as they carve out their space, but it doesn't take from the Kings' home streets across the south river or there would be real bloodshed. There's room for them all, even the god-dammed Chinks are starting to hold onto a little space in amongst the coloreds. All of the recent beatings are of little real consequence just boundary markers to show where the lines are drawn."

"Hands and knees smashed, ribs kicked in, faces slashed, vitriol thrown; these weren't included in the Homestead Act as legitimate ways to mark out a territory," Jack pointed out.

"Maybe not, but hanging women from a rafter isn't a recognised way either," Hank stated, shifting himself in the chair, knowing he should get back. "Besides Reverend Blackstaff is respected for his work across the city. We may be Irish and the Kings German but we are all Catholics and religion binds as close as blood. What's more both Catholic and Protestant bishops speak out for the work the reverend is doing, so killing his daughter will anger a lot of people in all quarters of the city."

"You heard how the pair were hung up, does this mean anything to you?' Jack asked as Hank stood to leave.

"Sorry, Jack, nothing at all, other than it sickens me that any woman should be so treated. It is savage, something you read about that those heathens the Indians would do."

Jack could have told him otherwise but seeing his friend was already drawing away, settled on one final question, "The name 'Chicago Joe', does it mean anything to you?"

Hank paused, giving thought before he answered, "The only person I have heard of going by that sobriquet is real small fry, dabbles in whores and guns. Can't say the name has cropped up for a while, Italian I think, he worked north of the stockyards. More than that I don't know but I can get the word out and see what comes back, if it helps."

"It would. Thank you for your time Hank," Jack said, thoughtfully, to his friend's retreating back.

The dinner at his daughter's was large and formal, with a number of courses: duck liver, filleted fish, cutlets, various deserts, fruits and cheese each served with a different wine. Jack had to admit Abigail and Chester's chef was excellent, though he wondered how he might fare with a Dutch oven cooking on a cattle drive. The dinner was the centre piece in wooing McCormick and Deering to support Chester's campaign towards his goal for governorship. Neither man was quite in the league of Jason Gould but were big bugs amongst Chicago's elite. Nor were they naturally democrats, both being self-made men from 'humble' beginnings but neither of them particularly liked the current republican governor and Chester was looking to use their support and influence to his advantage.

Brandon O'Shea and Jacob DeWert, Chester's father, were also present and the three seemed to be getting along swimmingly with their two guests. Andrew, Jack's son, spent most of his time in deep conversation with McCormick's eldest son, whom Jack recognised from his interruption of O'Shea's earlier meeting. Whilst the former group talked politics, the younger pair, who in practice ran the businesses of each party, were hammering out the detail of the deal negotiated by O'Shea. The women, the wives of the illustrious men sat around the table, listened attentively and turned the conversation to fashion, theatre or social events whenever an otherwise unsuitable topic arose or during lapses in the conversation. Jack remained in happy silence throughout, nodding between mouthfuls of food or wine, he was so locked up in his own thoughts that he did not at first realise the elder McCormick had addressed him.

"Mr McCormick was asking about your time in the army, Jack," Martha came to his rescue.

"My apologies, Mr McCormick, I'm a little deaf, unfortunately it comes with old age," Jack stated, though he was many years younger than the man who addressed him. "What in particular did you want to know?"

"Actually, Mr Stevens, I wondered if you thought the lives lost and sacrifices made had been worthwhile or if the outcomes could have been better achieved through some peaceful solution?" It was not an uncommon question to be raised at dinner tables during recent years. Twenty years after the end of the war and, even with the Klan supposedly dead in the south, in practice the lot of colored folk had hardly changed since their freedom. With labour unrest growing in the great cities and railroads crossing the continent the country's focus was on its 'Manifest Destiny', to occupy and exploit the entire land from coast to coast. The United States was now expanding, far more populous and growing daily in wealth when compared with the Eastern Seaboard ideologies of twenty years previous.

"I'm not the person to judge the matter," Jack informed him. "My only concern was to get through the war alive and I have spent the last twenty years trying to put those times behind me." It had been at a large society ball a few months previous that Jack had bearded the governor on his role in the war. The man was heatedly debating just this question and was roundly chastising a number of young gentlemen on their lack of understanding that the war had brought, "this great nation into being."

Jack, rather drunk, had asked him, "What had a quartermaster, who never got within a mile of the front line, ever done for the union's efforts other than trying to save money on guns and ammunition?" Although Jack, at Abigail's and Chester's request, formally apologised for his remarks the very next morning, the press had a field day with the spat. It transpired that the governor had been one of the men who had blocked the introduction of the Sharps rifle as being too costly. A decision which the President overturned thereby providing the Sharpshooter battalion with a weapon that supplemented their skill and added greatly to their battle effectiveness. Despite Jack's apology, the affair had helped undermine the republican's position that it was the party that was making America 'great'; so it was possible that Mr Leander James McCormick, expected a more zealous response to his question.

"My father is a man of few words, Mr McCormick," Abigail, quickly turned the conversation, "being, like yourself, a man who puts action first. A sheriff who once worked with him told me he has never seen a man shoot so well as my father, to rival even Buffalo Bill himself."

Jack led the laughter at his own expense, enjoying his daughter's way of deflating a potentially tense situation, before admitting, "Truth is I could never hit a barn door from horseback nor had much inclination to shoot Indians or wild animals." Though he could have added that his toll of 'white two legged animals' was much higher than the showman's.

"The other men kicked you out?" Mrs O'Shea asked, turning a corner on a garden path and finding Jack lounging, whiskey bottle and glass in hand, on a bench. The women had withdrawn at the end of the meal, leaving their menfolk to discuss politics and finance over their drink.

"And, you?" Jack retorted recognising the short, stocky figure in the half-light of the chilly dusk. "No longer able to stand the tittle-tattle of the women?" Jack had met Mrs O'Shea, Nina, to a very select few, six years previous almost to the day, when she had knocked on his hotel room door.

"It began well," she stated, taking a seat unbidden at his side, remembering when she had first seen him and thought him nothing but a horned fool who was being deceived by his cheating wife. "With talk on how our various families would prosper through our now close connections, but then turned to discussion on children and how Sarah, Robert McCormick's wife, hoped for another child." Jack knew that Josephine Patricia O'Shea was in her late forties and childless. She had been born an O'Brione with four older brothers and a father all of whom were leaders amongst the dock, warehouse and transport workers of Chicago and were all now closely linked with the Knights of Labour. At twelve she had nearly died from smallpox but lived, scarred and barren, to be married at seventeen to Brandon O'Shea the rising star of the O'Shea, McGuire and Tipwell clan. Thereby cementing relationships between significant groups of workers and the city's political fixers and bosses of the criminal substrata. It was a marriage which brought great prosperity and influence to both families but neither love nor children to the two people locked together at its centre.

"I would offer you a drink, to commiserate, but I only have the one glass," Jack stated cordially enough, though he did not care much for Mrs O'Shea, "and it would be unladylike to drink from the bottle."

"Since when did you consider me a lady?" liking Jack less than he liked her. "And, given the intimacies once shared between your wife and my husband, I would think that sharing a glass should be the least of our concerns." When she had visited Jack at his hotel, unconcerned about her own reputation, she expected him to either be a weakling and too afraid to confront her formidable husband or ignorant of the affair. When she realised neither was the case she resorted, to taunts, threats and bribery which only served to anger Jack who defended his wife's honour and threatened violence in return. It might have ended in bloodshed, her own she suspected, had it not been for the presence of her companion, a heavyset black man, who had remained in the shadows of the doorway.

"I hold you in the highest esteem," Jack informed her noticing, as he handed her the refilled glass, her heavy make-up made her square, manly face seem like a mask through which peered two piercingly intelligent green eyes. "A harridan you may be but a lady all the same."

"And you? Still the cuckold?" she toasted him back.

"Dead men can't be cuckolded," he answered, her insult meaningless to him. She knew full well his wife, Martha, had thought him dead when she had become Brandon's mistress, and Jack would never have returned to her and his family had they not met by accident in a small out of the way town nearly 600 miles west of where they currently sat.

"As you are so unlike Lazarus of Bethany your resurrection must have been a shock to your *grieving* widow," Nina, commented, handing him back the empty glass. "Talking of the dead, I am given to understand that you were the one who found those two dead women."

"Did you recognise me from the description in the papers: 'elderly man out walking'?" Jack refilled the glass and swallowed the content, refilling it again and handing it back. "Or was it from Hank?"

"My godson informed me, though it must be a trial to realise how aged and decrepit you are becoming in others eyes."

"Yes, and this chill air is starting to creep into these old bones of mine," he stated, taking a swig from the bottle to keep the chill off and then offering to top up Nina's empty glass. "Did he tell you of the man I am seeking."

"He did, though the name means nothing to me. He also told me he is concerned about his sister, Kitty."

"What of her?" Jack yawned, doing his best to sound unconcerned.

"Only that since she moved to a place of her own, away from the family, he has seen so little of her and he is concerned for her."

"Hank is a good man and I assume a good brother," Jack stated, wondering why Nina, who never spoke without intention and rarely on any family matter, was telling him this. "If he'd like me to look into it I am more than happy to do so."

Nina paused before saying, "No need, I have the situation in my own sights." Then handed back the glass and rising to take her leave, added, "Do not stay out too long in this cold, less you catch something that takes you to your deathbed."

The next day Stevens met Kitty as pre-arranged outside the Grand Pacific on LaSalle and they hailed a cab to take them to the up-town address of her associate in the Knights. For a brief second Jack thought he spotted Martha on the opposite side of the street. But he quickly lost her in the crowd as the cab pulled away and then thought it was unlikely as she had told him she was visiting friends in Old Town.

Mrs Lenora Barry was obviously surprised to receive Mrs Kitty McGuire and Mr Jack Stevens in the early afternoon but being told her assistance in a important matter was sort, she readily did so.

"Mr Stevens is looking into the death of the two women mentioned in the papers," Kitty explained over coffee. "As they are linked to the Knights of Labour, I thought you might be able to help."

"I was asked, by a number of our senior members, to meet with the police only this morning," Mrs Barry informed them, somewhat suspicious that Mr Stevens might be from a newspaper, or worse as he had the look of a Pinkerton about him. "I have told them all I know and do not think it right to speak further on the matter."

"I take it that would have been Inspector O'Leary?" Jack asked, glad the police inspector was not dismissing the link with the Knights whilst he sought Chicago Joe. "He would have asked you about Miss Blackstaff and Miss Walsh, and perhaps a man known as Chicago Joe?"

"He did," Mrs Barry informed them, then felt compelled to continue as the silence between them grew. "Unfortunately I was not able to help very much, I have known Miss Blackstaff for sometime, mainly in connection with her father."

"I understand from her father that she was not that involved in the Knights nor in politics in general?" Jack asked.

"You know the family?"

"They are neighbours and, unfortunately, I was present when the inspector broke the news of Miss Blackstaff's death to them." Jack only stretched the truth by the slightest hair's breadth.

"It must be a terrible time for the family, I can't imagine what they must feel." Mrs Barry looked genuinely upset by the thought.

"Yes, devastating of course," Jack sympathised. "The family seems unaware of Miss Blackstaff's involvement with Miss Walsh, which naturally adds to their bewilderment."

"Their friendship did strike me a little odd at first, though it soon passed; they got on so well, you see," Mrs Barry reflected, rising to Jack's bait before swallowing it whole, to continue, "When Miss Blackstaff introduced me I thought it an odd coincidence that Miss Walsh had worked at the same sweat shop as I had. Some time ago I decided to undertake a first-hand exploration of the conditions for working women that had been described to me, unfortunately I discovered these to be accurate accounts. It was appalling, Mr Stevens, I worked in excess of 40 hours for less than a dollar a week; not enough to feed me let alone provide decent shelter."

"I believe Miss Walsh was an ardent supporter of the Knights and even spoke at meetings," Jack, redirected his hostesses thoughts back onto the path he wanted her to follow.

"She did, quite eloquent in her description of the conditions she faced and the stark choices these gave her in order to survive. Her determination to *hold the fort* inspired many others both to join and to speak of their own experiences."

"Whereas Miss Blackstaff was a shy, young piano teacher from a wealthy family of business owners, with no apparent interest in labour rights."

"Miss Walsh seemed to inspire her," Mrs Barry, smiled at the remembrance, "more recently she had become quite strident in her statements of support and that action needed to be taken to secure workers rights. Though of course, young women can often form friendships on the unlikeliest of grounds; I did not know them well but it struck me there was a loneliness in both that drew them together."

"There was never any suspicions about either of them, given Miss Blackstaff's sudden conversion and the coincidence of Miss Walsh having worked at the same sweatshop as yourself?"

"None, such conversions to the cause are not uncommon in our ranks. As Kitty will tell you our membership swells daily with men and woman from all neighbourhoods, backgrounds, trades and races; it will not be long before our voice can no longer be ignored by the wealthy and powerful," Mrs Barry explained, her voice growing in volume and ardour as she warmed to her topic, then pausing as a thought struck her. "The inspector asked a similar question, is there anything that we should have been suspicious of in either of them?"

"Not that I am aware of," Jack smiled, not wanting to give too much away assuming Cage had kept secret that Mary Walsh worked for the Pinkertons, "it is just odd that they should be connected to a man like Chicago Joe."

"I do not believe they were," Mrs Barry smiled back, relived that she had not wrongly put her trust in the two women when promoting them within the cause. "They did not seem to know him at all. They simply passed on a rumour they had heard that a gang leader, this Chicago Joe, was sounding out some of our more extreme supporters."

"Extreme supporters?" Kitty jumped in. "You mean those who advocate the use of violence to further our cause?"

"It is unfortunate that such hot heads exist," Mrs Barry, looked fleeting annoyed that Kitty had been so plain in her use of words in front of an outsider, "but as you know we do not agree with such views and any Knight espousing them is expelled," then for Jack's benefit, continued. "We believe in change through peaceful protest, though business owners have retaliated with violence and increasingly we are harassed by the police."

"And of Chicago Joe?" Jack asked, despite Miss Barry's views, he was well aware that the labour struggles were violent affairs on both sides.

"As I explained earlier, no one I spoke to knew the name and some thought the rumour was just one more of many circulated to discredit the movement. When I last saw the pair I told them this, though Miss Walsh seemed determined to pursue the matter as she had been told that Chicago Joe was a dangerous individual and we should be on our guard against him. Whether right or wrong, the pair will be sorely missed; as will Reverend Blackstaff who, understandably, has temporarily ceased public speaking. It is terrible times in which we live that two young women should have their lives taken in such a terrible way."

"Did Miss Walsh say from whom she had this information?" Jack asked, wondering how much of this Cage had discovered from his questioning of Mrs Barry.

"I did not think to ask," Mrs Barry stated. "Though as they were leaving Miss Blackstaff did say something to Miss Walsh about their needing to visit 'Ruby' again."

"Ruby, or Ruby's?" Jack asked, whilst there might be many people named Ruby in the city there was only one Ruby's no matter how unlikely a destination for the two young women.

"Now you say it, I believe it could be have been 'Ruby's' that she said," Mrs Barry stated puzzled that this seemed a significant difference, but then she did not know that Ruby's was one of Chicago's most secret and notorious of brothels.

"Hiding in plain sight," Martha Stevens had called it, when she explained her reasoning behind meeting with Ibrahim Minsky at the Grand Pacific for a late lunch. "If we are seen it will seem quite innocent, simply an eminent Chicago matron showing a newly arrived Russian count, a friend of a friend, the sights." Minsky had smiled at the idea especially as he was only to speak Russian to anyone else, though he was slightly annoyed that Martha had described his native tongue as 'jibber-jabber'. His revenge, therefore, was to speak at length to the waiter taking their order on what delighted him most about Martha's lovemaking.

"The Count will have… an omelette… with coffee… with cream not milk… and a brandy," Martha interpreted, scowling at Minsky and his endless stream of jibber-jabber. "Russian," she added for the waiter's benefit, "such an incompressible and long-winded language, so unlike our own succinct American idiom." The waiter, a native Greek and recent immigrant with only 'menu' American, nodded sagely and left the odd pair to their tete-a-tete.

"I have been giving our predicament some thought," Martha informed him, as she sipped her soup, "and I believe I have a way forward."

"It is not our predicament, but mine," Minsky interrupted, keeping his voice low so the other diners could not hear him speaking American, with only a light accent to betray his ancestry. "I have no intention of allowing you to participate."

"You are many things, my dear little Russian, but you are not a robber," Martha had every intention of helping her friend regardless of his objections. "You will be glad to hear that I have an almost complete solution. I know where O'Shea's safe is located, it is behind a picture in Brandon's study on the second floor, and I am attending a ball at the O'Shea's and will be able to get you access." Martha smiled triumphantly.

"Firstly, they would not keep the diamonds in Brandon's safe," Minsky poured cold water on the suggestions. "They will be in Mrs O'Shea's bedroom safe. Brandon's study is off limits to his wife as is her bedroom to him. Secondly, the entire first floor will be open to guests, and full of servants, both serving and watching that the guests don't pocket the silverware, so sneaking me up to the bedroom will not be viable."

"Neither problem is insurmountable," Martha was not to be put off, "dressed as a waiter and with a little help from me we will be able to get you to Mrs O'Shea's bedroom. As for the safe, well, it is about time there was a rapprochement between myself and Mrs O'Shea, given how close our families will be operating I will ask Jacob DeWert to speak with Brandon so that Abigail and I will be assured a warm welcome."

"How will that help me get into the safe?" Minsky asked, happy at Martha's desire to help him but thinking it simply a further delay and inwardly resolving to ask around for the name of a reliable housebreaker.

"Abby is bound to want a tour of the house and to see the diamonds, and no one refuses my charming daughter, even that pock-marked old witch," Martha explained, knowing her remarks were below the belt but her expression daring Minsky to suggest so. "It is at least worth a try before attempting anything else, so enjoy your cognac. Perhaps after our meal you will invite me up to your room, you do have a room here don't you?" she added with a most unladylike wink.

Jack had the devil of a job in putting off taking Kitty to the theatre as he had promised, "I need to confer with Cage, Inspector O'Leary, and you need to pay your brother a call."

"Why?" Kitty was annoyed at being let down, since moving away from the influence of her brother, which had taken a great deal of perseverance and determination on her part, she felt like a girl again; like the princess once locked in the tower who had gained her freedom.

"Mrs O'Shea said 'her godson was missing his sister' and that she intended to, 'keep the matter in her sights'," Jack explained.

"She dotes on him as if he were her actual son," Kitty scowled, she knew exactly what the old bat meant by, 'keeping her in her sights', she intended to make Kitty's life difficult and force her to move back home where she could be kept under lock and key.

"What troubles me is why Nina choose to tell me this," Jack puzzled. "If she had the slightest suspicion we are seeing each other she would have told Hank or caused mischief by now."

"She might suspect I am seeing someone, why else would I want my privacy?" Kitty stated sarcastically, then maliciously added, "though you would think she would have thought I had made the acquaintance of a younger and more handsome man."

"A younger man would indulge your whims and fancies to the extent that you would loose your reputation," Jack smiled, though he was only half serious; although he was pleased that a pretty widow like Kitty showed any interest in him, he knew her tendency to rush head-long into adventures would bring about her downfall unless some care was taken.

"Really? Perhaps I should try one or two, as I now have free time on my hands." Her smile gave no hint as to whether she spoke in jest or as a warning. "Of course you could send a note to the inspector's precinct and escort me home, under your watchful eye I can hardly get into trouble. Although I might do something rash when we are alone."

4

RUBY'S

With the aid of five dollars, left absent-mindedly beside the desk sergeant at Inspector O'Leary's precinct house, Stevens discovered that Cage was dining with Mr Benjamin Burke, the Pinkerton detective. Given that the two Pinkertons often had long periods of absence from the city it was unexpected to find that Pug had been happily married for twelve years to a petite, blue eyed, redhead who was still pretty, despite having given birth to four children. Whilst it was no surprise to discover that Pinky led a bachelor life. If the Burke's were surprised at Stevens' gatecrashing none expressed it and Mrs Benjamin Burke was particularly pleased at his coming as he brought candy for her and the children. The plump frame of each of the five showing her and her brood to have a sweet tooth.

"We considered it safe to meet here, in private, so as to be able to share confidential information without being overheard by unwanted ears," Pinky expressed his mild annoyance at Jack turning up unasked. Pinky had, eventually, forgiven Jack for once saving his life with a shot that passed within an inch of his head, but the diminutive Pinkerton had gained the habit of being unpleasant to Stevens and continued the practice with enthusiasm.

"I have only come to gloat at your collective floundering," Jack informed them with a smile whilst taking a seat, that Pug had brought him from another room, at the table. "Though I would never pass up on the opportunity of eating a plate of Mrs Burke's excellent roast."

"It's pork, Mr Stevens," Mrs Burke informed him smiling at the compliment. They all regularly dined at Jack's twice a year, along with Mr Hugh Partkis and his wife, and she was always made to feel comfortable and most welcome, though she still remained a little in awe of the grand surroundings, more so if the DeWerts or Mr Stevens' son was present, "and Nantucket Cranberry pie for dessert."

"To sum up," Jack said, after the meal they had moved to the small, neat parlour, for cigars and whiskey, "you have found nothing of Chicago Joe nor any other connections with the Knights of Labour. To be precise you are no further forward."

"There is one thing," Cage informed him, he was not worried at their lack of progress as he knew it was the way of some cases and detectives, above all else, needed patience, "as you have now owned up to being the owner of the flask it does make your finding of the bodies suspicious, especially as you cannot account for your movements of the previous day."

Jack turned the flask, Cage handed him, over noting that it was engraved with a coil of rope surrounding a well executed two-masted ship, "I expect it does,' he stated with a smile, handing Cage Miss Blackstaff's notebook which he still carried with him. Inwardly he was surprised the flask was not his; the one his son had bought him for his fiftieth birthday was solid silver rather than 'silvered' and engraved with crossed rifles beneath a triumphal wreath and the legend: 'To my father, who taught me the value of a True Aim in Life.' He pocketed it all the same, having checked that it smelt of rum rather than whiskey, a fact he thought Cage should have noticed. Though all the while the inspector watched him, wondering why Stevens did not state that the flask was not his.

"I take it from your tone, Jack," Pug surmised, "that you do have something."

"Only to report that the name Chicago Joe, means little to anyone I have asked, except being a smalltime whore-monger and gunrunner who has dropped out of sight for sometime," Jack explained with a shrug.

"We have heard the same," Pinky snorted derisively at the non-new news.

"Oh, and that he may be associated in some way with Ruby's, as the two woman were overheard talking about a visit to Ruby's in order to get more information about Chicago Joe," the silence which followed rather lessened Jack's pleasure in revealing what he had learned.

"There are many Ruby's in Chicago, and an equally large number of names for which it is a shortened version, so it could be any number of women they intended to visit," Cage informed him, between puffs on one of Pug's cigars. "Though as a possible name of a wife or girlfriend of Joe's it might be of help."

"No," Jack told them, annoyed at their missing the point, "Joe is reputed a whore-monger, Ruby's is not a woman called Ruby but the brothel that the women intended to visit to find out more about Joe. You see the link surely?" Even as he spoke he realised how thin his own reasoning was, but he had not expected the others to laugh at the idea; Pinky perhaps but not the embarrassed smiles of Pug and Cage.

"I have heard many a tale about the bawdy behaviour of many a minster's daughter," Pinky chuckled, "but, in reality, would two respectable young woman contemplate such a thing?"

"Joe's reputation was as a low class pimp north of the stockyard whilst Ruby's is a far more depraved house than any other in the city, and the perversions it reputedly offers come at a high price to an exclusive clientele," Pug informed them, "it is one heck of a jump to connect the two."

"It's a very thin lead," Cage added, his tone conciliatory given

Jack's scowling expression, "though admittedly the only one we have."

"You seem to forget that Mary Walsh," Jack decided he should flesh out his thinking for the others, "was an undercover operative for the Pinkertons, one you two described as very skilful. Such a woman might not baulk at going to Ruby's to follow up a lead and from what I have learned of Philomena Blackstaff she might be willing to follow her friend just about anywhere. Whilst most brothels would not admit a non-house female, Ruby's is more than likely to do so if they can afford the entrance fee."

"The fee, at least, would not be an issue," Pug interrupted. "Miss Walsh had money of her own to run her operation and spend as she saw fit, so the fee would be no obstacle."

"Perhaps they went there to bribe someone who was an acquaintance of Chicago Joe's," even Jack felt he was clutching at straws on this.

"I know little about the place or its staff and clientele," Cage admitted. "They seem to know the face of every cop in the city, whether on their payroll or not. They know of any raid that is planned in advance and have shut down their operation before we start. Unofficially, we haven't been able to touch them as they pay too many officials to keep them safe."

"It is true of the Pinkertons as well, though only in the sense that no one has ever wanted to pay us to look into the place and the agency has been threatened with having contracts cut with state and city government if a lead has ever taken us near the place," Pinky told them, as Pug nodded in agreement, filling the room with cigar smoke as he angrily huffed out smoke.

"I could go there, a man of my age and wealth would hardly be out of place," Jack smiled, raising his eyebrows as he raised his glass in mock salute to the others.

"It is $120 to get in, that is without the expenses incurred inside," Cage informed him. "I'd want a firmer lead than you have offered before I laid out such sums, even if I had them to hand."

"Who runs the place?" Jack asked.

Pinky and Pug both shrugged.

Cage pausing before answering, "Rumour has it that Black Rube does, he took it over about five years ago when the Black Hawks first expanded north."

"Black Hawks," Jack's smile grew, "and Chicago Joe offered their services to the Knights. Another possible link in the chain."

"Isn't he a Wop?" Pinky pointed out. "Don't they have their own gangs these days?"

"Some of the earliest Italian families to settle here fitted in where they could, with Catholic Germans and Irish mostly," Cage informed them, "but now they keep to themselves and these days the Black Hawks are exclusively colored, though they will do business with anyone."

"So they might do business with Joe," Jack theorised.

"Or Joe doesn't just have Italian heritage," Pug pointed out insightfully. "There are plenty of white men who have sired bastards with a colored woman."

"Whatever," Jack concluded, thinking the reverse of Pug's suggestion was also true. "But it's worth me having a look round to see what I can find out."

"I'll continue with my own enquiries," Cage told them enigmatically, then nodded at the Pinkertons and added, "Whilst you two need to find out more about who Mary Walsh really was, she may have been killed for a reason to do with her real persona."

Day Four – Friday April 18th 1886

Jack's first reaction on seeing Kit enter the River Bar was a disbelieving double-take. Kitty, dressed in a brown check suit, with her hair in a series of tight knots hidden under a cap pulled down over her left eye, was a passably handsome man who walked with the slight swagger of a typical young gent about town and whose only faintly feminine trait was the softness of 'his' countertenor voice. Jack's second reaction was anger, barely concealed as he called Kit to the seat beside him.

"I thought we agreed after last time you would not repeat this charade in public," Jack hissed into Kitty's ear, taking care not to draw attention to himself and his companion. "To dress like this in private is one thing but you risk too much to do so in public."

"You told me but I did not agree to abide by your instructions," Kitty informed him, she had artfully applied her make up so that it looked as if her chin had a light stumble on it. "Given how drunk you were last time it is a wonder you remember anything of meeting Mr Christopher Houston." Jack's face turned thunderous as a memory suddenly resurfaced at her words, reading his thoughts Kitty turned pale beneath her makeup and she pulled away from him, into the corner of the small booth in which they sat.

"You can strike me if you want, I can little defend myself," she stated fearfully, "but you will never see me again if you do."

"Hitting you is the last thing on my mind," Jack told her, pulling her back so they could talk privately, "but I do not rule out putting a bullet hole in your head to let a little sense in. Now, the truth, it was the night before my missing day when I last saw you dressed as Kit, wasn't it?" Kit nodded but kept 'his' silence.

"You scared me," Kitty eventually confessed as Jack glared at her, his anger not abating. "I know you will not hurt me, not intentionally, but on that night you were so drunk and in such a rage it scared me. It reminded me of when I was a girl and my father would come home drunk and beat my mother. Hank hid me behind himself but he was too small to stop my father's anger from reaching me."

"You say I beat you?" Jack was aghast at the thought, remembering his own unaccountable anger at Martha from the morning he had woken on the sofa.

"No, not much," Kitty confessed. "At first you dragged me from here saying if I'm to be a man I must piss as one, you took me to the rear and demonstrated how to do it. Then from there you took me to the alleyway behind and insisted we box like men, you made me put my fists up and told me to strike you. When I didn't, you hit me on my arms and it hurt, then you said, 'I snivelled like a girl, not a boy at all'. You sounded like my father when he beat poor Hank, who was just a child," Kitty paused, struggling to control herself as her voice rose and she clenched and unclenched her fists. "None, could prove it was my father that did for my mother but all knew he was to blame. Had he not taken a drunkards tumble into the river shortly after I dread to think what would have been our fate."

"Then the O'Shea's took you in and raised you as their own," Jack finished the story for her as she fought against her tears, screwing up her eyes to stop them.

"Hank was the favoured godson," she went on once in control of herself again. "I was just an inconvenience but a useful drudge for Mrs O'Shea, never *Mother* as Hank was privileged to use. Though Hank was always a good brother to me."

"What do you know of the day that followed your entrance as Kit?" Jack asked quietly, his anger gone now just curious.

"I tried to get away from you, but you followed me, raving. Then saying you'd teach me to shoot, as every man should be able to use a gun. You put your flask on a wall and tried to take aim at it, this was on Clark, and though the hour was late there were still people and carriages about." Despite herself she couldn't help smiling at the memory of it. "You were a damn fool, waving the gun about, staggering and ordering the shadows from the street light to get out of the way."

"I shot my flask?" Jack asked still having no memory of the events.

"No, you dropped your whiskey bottle, which you held in your left hand, then your gun and fell in a heap trying to pick up both,' she almost laughed. "As for the flask I have no idea, it stands on the wall where you left it still for all I know."

"I doubt that. A silver flask would not be overlooked by passers by," Jack stated, annoyed he had lost his son's present in such a ridiculous way. "However, this doesn't account for the following day."

"I could barely lift you," Kitty explained, with a shrug. "I hailed a cab and for a dollar the driver helped get you aboard, swearing he would kick you off if you were sick inside. I could not take you to our little hideaway, it is up two flights of stairs, so I took you home. Even so you made enough noise getting you up the front steps and into my door, fortunately the couple who live opposite are old and would be asleep and the only other occupant, the little Russian man who lives above, has a lady friend of his own. They make enough noise to wake the dead when she visits, so he could hardly complain. You would not think it from her looks, so well dressed and a wealthy looking matron. His exertions must more than compensate her for what she must pay him, for there is nothing else about the pair that they can have in common."

"So, I slept at your place, but what happened the next day?" Jack brought her back to the matter in hand.

"You slept through the morning and I had to go out to an appointment I could not miss," Kitty began to look shame-faced. "I didn't want you waking up still half-drunk and making a noise whilst I was out that would raise questions with the neighbours."

"And so?" Jack demanded as she grew silent.

"So I gave you some of the medicine the doctor had prescribed to me, after my daughter passed away, to help me sleep," she guiltily stated.

"That must have been years old, it could have poisoned me," Jack was incredulous.

"Obliviously it did nothing of the sort," Kitty stated in her defence. "Though you were still asleep when I returned and continued to snore through the evening and night. Past midnight you started too come to and eventually I was able to get you to stand, though you still didn't seem to know yourself or where you were. That is how I got you home, in another cab, and put you on your step," she concluded and, seeing Jack's look, further added in her defence, "What else could I do? Your family would have been worried and on the verge of calling the police."

"I don't believe they were," he scowled. "Did you go attired as Kit?"

"Yes," she admitted, "in case we were seen I thought it better you were accompanied by a man."

"Well at least that accounts for my whereabouts and my missing flask should Inspector O'Leary ever want to know," though Jack doubted Kitty would corroborate the story which would ruin her reputation. Then having a thought which caused him to smile said to her, "Though if you want to know what it is like to be a man, I have just the place to take you."

Jack had been in many saloons and bars where the favours of a dance hall girl could be bought, if so desired, but he had never been in a brothel. Ruby's was much as he expected such a high class establishment would be in terms of its plush decor, however, in all other respects it was unique. The unassuming entrance, a heavy, wooden door reinforced with iron bars, was off a dark, back alley somewhere between East 21st and 22nd streets not far from South State Street. In the reception area, guarded by members of the Black Hawk gang, he had handed over his guns and paid the entrance fee for himself and Kit. And, although he had brought a large sum with him, on paying for the drinks, he realised it would barely be enough if he were making a night of it.

Whilst the main room was unsurprising, although it boasted a small band and a well stocked bar, and the customers were served by both young men and women. The customers, usually in pairs or groups of three and four, were seated at tables and the majority were middle-aged men with the occasional younger man making up a party. There were two women, at least Stevens noted a woman and a man dressed in female garb, and a pair of young, elegantly dressed colored men. Their waiter, a youth in a very tight black suit, showed them to a table, brought them their drinks and a menu of the house attractions.

"Is this your first visit, sir?" the waiter enquired, receiving a nod from Jack and ignoring Kit, whose goggle-eyed stare clearly marked 'him' as first-timer. "Then pick your choices carefully from the menu, the time each show starts and the door to enter are clearly marked. You have the three tokens you were each given on entry and these give you access to three shows, if you want to see more you can buy extra tokens at $50 each," the waiter paused for a nod from Jack that he followed what was said. "If you want to attend the shows on the floor above you will need to pay a further $200 per show. I would not recommend participation in a show on a first visit, but the cost is shown against the name of each of the characters within the show. If you have any special requirements or would like a private performance simply let me know and I will ask the manager to speak with you to discuss these in detail and give you the cost." Again pausing to ensure his customer followed his description, ended with the question, "Is there anything else you require at the moment?"

Jack, who had been looking the menu over as the young waiter told them how the place operated, asked, "So, do I understand correctly that what we have paid only allows us to watch others and not to participate?"

"Participation costs extra, sir, but given the specialist nature of our performances it would be worthwhile to spend a token or two first in order to familiarise yourself. It is rare for any of our customers to express their disappointment in our services and then only to wish for more," the youth stated with a smile.

"And, do the waiters, like yourself, participate?" Kit wanted to know, warmed by the handsome youth's smile.

"For you, sir, I am certain they would queue to do so," the waiter's smile grew as he winked and left them. The low, reddish light of the shaded gas lamps hid Jack's blush but not his scowl.

"It seems I am a hit as a young man," Kitty beamed, ignoring Jack's despairing look. "What shall we see first?"

"There are two shows about to start: 'The young master is caught by his mother and chastised, the father watches then chastises and takes his pleasure of both', or 'Grandmother, mother and daughter accidentally become inebriated and take liberties of each other; the waiter who has tricked them joins in'," Jack smiled as he read the descriptions. "They both sound like plots from operatic comedy, don't you think?"

"What else?" Kitty wanted to know, taking the menu and casting her eye over it, whilst Jack looked the other customers and establishment over. There were four doors on one wall and a solitary door on another; the bar, band and entrance taking up the remaining wall space. Every few minutes a waiter or waitress would take up position by a door and allowing those inside to re-enter the main room and new customers to take their place, entry seemed to have been prearranged with a waiter. Only one man went to the solitary door beyond which Jack could see the stairs to the second floor.

"Well, the upstair specials sound awful. One is 'Street urchin soundly whipped by an official for stealing', and the other, 'Innocent young girl arouses her uncle's passion'. If you want to be the official or the uncle it will cost you $500." Kitty said, aghast, then continued, "However, in door three the next show is, 'The young mistress insists the two young grooms wrestle to determine which shall have her affection, but all three end up tumbling in the hay.' It seems they show variations of the same basic four or five scenes, the actors must be exhausted, and very sore, at the end of each day?"

"They will use different actors and much is likely to be faked," Jack explained. As she laughed at her own joke, his tone serious as he continued, "You will remember I am here to obtain information."

"For which you will need to mingle and there doesn't appear

to be much of that going on out here, so we should try one of the doors," Kitty pointed out, waving to the waiter. "We would like to try the next show at door three," she informed the waiter, holding up two of the entry tokens.

"An excellent choice, sir, a favourite of mine as it happens," he again winked as he turned away to add their table number to the list waiting for the show.

"Before you go," Jack stopped him, "do you get many women coming here?'

"A few, sir, though always with a friend or two," he stated, "though I should point out that guests do not tend to make themselves acquainted with each other."

"It is only that a friend of mine, who recommended this place to me, mentioned two young woman in particular; a blond and a colored woman," Jack put a double-eagle on the table, which the waiter dextrously scooped up.

"Such a pair would be memorable, I am here most nights and I'm sorry to say have no recollection of them," the waiter glanced round, ensuring his hushed tones were not overheard. "I am certain someone would have mentioned such a pair, if they had come in."

"I believe our show starts," Kitty pulled Jack to his feet, in her eagerness allowing her voice to rise to a more feminine register.

"So it does, sir," the waiter agreed, beginning to suspect the young man was more grass than hay. "Door three is now open."

Jack had expected to be shown to a seat inside the room, instead he found himself in a dark narrow corridor running along the side and rear of the room. In the wall on the room side six large slots were cut at regular intervals, so the customer could watch the show thereby giving the illusion that they watched without the actors being aware. As Jack was to quickly discover when the show began the darkness of the corridor also meant each observer felt himself alone and able to take some additional pleasure of his own.

"Jesus, Mary and Joseph!" Kitty exclaimed in a hiss close to Jack's ear as they shared the viewing through a single slot. "Would you look at the ginger haired fellow, the size of him." The two grooms had quickly stripped in order to wrestle and it was not the young man's stature to which Kitty referred; though in all fairness to his companion, who seemed unaroused by the proceedings, the ginger haired man had fully risen to the occasion. Kitty continued to whisper comments and giggled into Jack's ear as the wrestling quickly turned into a different game of one-upmanship. The men alternated in which gained the upper-hand, pinning his fellow down and seeming to take some physical pleasure from the position he placed his opponent in. Seeing things had started to go too far the young mistress watching the match intervened, tripped and falling between the men found herself, in a moment, stripped naked and taking part in the game.

Kitty, forgetting the role she played as Kit, began to impart kisses on her companion's cheek, then progressing to his lips. In the dark Jack also forgot himself and reciprocated, making her gasp as his hand slipped into her trousers, a gesture she was quick to return. As if choreographed, the actors inside the room reached the climax of their game, with many shrieks, oaths and groans, whilst the watchers, more discreetly, reached theirs. It was only as he buttoned himself that Jack noticed, the portly, grey haired gent at the neighbouring slot had been watching them rather than the show.

Whilst a somewhat gay and still excited Kit ordered another round of drinks and declared 'his' admiration for the show they had just witnessed to the handsome and fawning young waiter, Jack caught the eye of the portly grey haired gent who now sat on his own at a nearby table.

"Interesting show," Jack discreetly mouthed, leaving it to the other to decided which show he was referring to, the man raised his glass in salute and then, hesitantly responding to Jack's nodding smile, made his way to their table.

"May I join you?" the man asked, his voice tremulous if somewhat gruff, "My tokens are used up but I feel in the need of a further drink or two."

"Are you a regular?" Jack asked, then seeing the man's look of concern to be asked this he explained. "It seems a sensible idea to ration oneself to the three tokens, otherwise the visits could become quite a financial drain."

"Indeed yes, you are both newcomers I take it?' he responded smiling as he relaxed in their company.

"We are," Jack began to introduce himself, "I am… "

"No!" the man interjected, raising his hands in a gesture to stop Jack, "Remember the house rule, 'Neither ask for nor give a name.' We are a secretive club you understand, all are friendly and accepting of each others tastes but outside we are strangers to each other."

"I understand, forgive the habit of a lifetime," Jack nodded and smiled away his faux pas.

"Of course, easy to forget," the other man agreed, waiving the waiter back to the table. "May I buy you both a drink? Champagne?" Given that the usual topics of small-talk such as work, family, etc. were unfitting to the venue they began to ask about the shows, about which the man seemed to know a great deal.

"Forgive me, young sir," their guest addressed Kit, "but you seem to have a smudge on your cheek." Kitty nodded her thanks, her stubble make-up had smudged when kissing Jack earlier and was now a grey patch and she began to dab at it with her handkerchief, which was a somewhat lacy affair.

"I see the young man attempts to make himself look older than he is," their guest gave them a lop-sided grin and a wink. "You should not worry too much as *youth* is greatly appreciated here and you are, young sir, most becoming."

"Actually," Jack explained, as Kit smiled 'his' thanks at the compliment, "I thought to bring my nephew here to introduce him to two women I had heard of that frequent the place."

"That would be such a waste," the man commented, winking at Kit. "There are more pleasures to be had in this life than can be found beneath a woman's skirts."

"It is a matter of experience," Jack elucidated, "a variety of diet one might say. A blond and a colored woman who come here together they would, I thought, offer a different variation to our usual practice."

"You must mean, 'the piano teacher and her pupil'," their guest snorted a laugh. "Unfortunately, I am afraid you are mistaken to look for them here. They are amateur performers but I am given to understand they will not perform again."

"They are performers?" Jack had previously considered this but had dismissed the possibility.

"Yes, though only twice, I missed their first exhibition but was here for the second," the man finished his champagne before continuing. "Not usually something I would take an interest in but the place was a *buzz* of expectation, the intensity of a real amateur performance is always worth a token or two. They performed 'The teacher chastises then comforts the errant pupil' a vigorous and heartfelt performance, to be sure. Despite the popularity of the unique combination of two females from different races performing together it is rumoured that the second show was their last."

"When was this?"

"Three nights ago, in the early part of the evening, the place was crowded in anticipation despite it being the hour to dine," the man waved the waiter to bring another bottle, whilst Jack ruminated that the pair had gone missing the same night as their last performance and, coupled with the waiter's emphatic denial of their having been at the club, wondered what had occurred here to bring about their deaths'.

"Why," Kitty asked, "if they were popular aren't they coming back?"

"For some the invigoration that performing before others brings wears off," their guest shrugged.

"Did you see them leave?" Jack asked, noticing their waiter was watching them.

"No, all the staff and performers come and go by another entrance, the former are not encouraged to fraternise with customers and the latter want their privacy," he stated with a smile, emptying yet another glass. Jack deciding it was his turn to buy the drinks and, having disliked the taste for the watered-down whiskey, waved the waiter to bring another bottle of the champagne.

"Do you know a 'Joe' who works here?" Jack asked as the waiter served the drink, "I think my friend said he went by 'Chicago Joe'? Is he the manager or something?"

"The name is not familiar to me, sir," the waiter stated, his face a picture of suspicion, "but I can ask the manager to speak with you if you wish?"

"It seems I have been given poor information about this place but I have to say the service is excellent," Jack laid out another double eagle, which disappeared as quickly as the last. "You are sure there is no 'Joe' here?"

"I will ask the manager to step over, sir," the waiter informed him, once again smiling. "That you might pay your compliments direct." Jack nodded and waited patiently whilst their table guest flirted with Kit, who obviously enjoyed the attention, if not the hand that wandered freely on 'his' leg. Stevens did not have to wait long as a tall, thick-set colored man wearing a tailored suit and spats, his face set in an impassive cold stare, approached.

"You asked to see me?" the man's voice was deep and neutral, Jack noted the lack of any 'sir'.

"Why, yes, thank you for your time," Jack affected a slight slur as if drunk. "I wanted to compliment you on your establishment and to apologise?"

"Apologise?" the impassive face creased in puzzlement but the coldness of his eyes did not change.

"I was given to believe the manager of the establishment was called 'Chicago Joe'."

"That is not a name I recognise," the puzzled expression abated but the coldness of the stare grew icier.

"Again my apologies, I should have realised that an establishment run by the Black Hawks could only be managed by Black Rube," Jack smiled, dropping the slur, he only had a vague description and many suspicions about who Black Rube was but knew enough of him that he would not be stood before him now. "Give him my regards when you next see him, I am sure he will remember me, when you describe me to him."

The man paused for a moment, then stated, "Enjoy the remainder of your stay," and left them, as did their table guest who was obviously put out by the manager's words more than Jack was. Though Jack only waited for the manager to leave the room before heading for the exit, pulling Kitty behind him, he had no intention of giving the manager time to decide on what action to take.

A few minutes later, with both his guns retrieved and away from the alleyway entrance he relaxed, believing the coldness of the manager's stare was confirmation enough of a connection between the mysterious Chicago Joe, the Black Hawks and Ruby's. The excursion had cost him dear financially, though he could afford it as his investment in the River Bar gave him ample private funds not only to pay for the apartment where he met with Kitty but also provided him with money enough for the odd extravagance such as he had had that evening.

The pair had emerged from Ruby's into heavy rain and Jack did not have to persuade Kitty to take the first cab they saw home. He told her to change cabs halfway so her journey home could not be traced and gave her sufficient change for the cost. Fortunately her kissing him as they parted was not noticed by the cabman or her leaving might have been more memorable. Despite the late hour and the rain, Jack then set about finding the second exit from the club, which proved less difficult than he expected. He walked around to the street where a row of shops ran along the back of the club and even as he spotted what looked like a heavily reinforced door between two shops, the door opened to allow two men out.

One of the men was the manager, wearing a black overcoat, the other was a slim man wearing a rain slick. A carriage was waiting for them in the road but despite the rain and the driver's glances, the men paused to light cigars which struck Jack as an odd thing to do in the rain even if they waited on a companion. As a flash of lighting streaked the sky and thunder cracked, Jack's head suddenly exploded into a shower of stars and he fell into darkness.

When he came to he was without his jacket or hat, his collar hanging from his shirt. He was tied to a chair, blindfolded, with a head that was filled with the stabbing pains of many hot needles. Realising he could see through a slit below the blindfold's material he tilted his head back, immediately regretting he did so as the pain in his head shot down his neck and the room swam, nauseously around him.

"He's awake," the voice of the manager informed someone. Jack could see a wood floor, table, chair legs and two pairs of feet obviously belonging to those who sat at a table a few feet in front of him. The spats worn by one pair of feet seemed to confirm this was the manager from Ruby's, whilst the other pair, wearing a smaller pair of ankle boots, got up and almost danced towards him. The hand that reached out and slapped his face, making Jack's head spin with pain, was white and almost delicate, like those of a piano player.

"So he is," a light, almost laughing voice confirmed, as Jack groaned. "What's your name?" the man had bent close, though not so Jack could see his face, and raised his voice, the tone now harsher.

"Jack," Stevens mumbled, surprised at how weak and tremulous his own voice sounded.

"Speak up!" the man shouted in his ear, causing Jack to jerk away.

"Jack, my name is Jack."

"There are a lot of Jack's about," the manager said, his voice as neutral and unconcerned as it had been in the club.

"What are you doing nosing around our club, Jack?" the white man punched him in the stomach as he asked, leaving Jack gasping for breath and wanting to be sick at the same time. Despite his delicate hands and thin arms the man was strong and knew how to punch, so it was a while before Jack could answer, not that he rushed to gain his composure as it gave him time to think.

"Perhaps, we would get on quicker if you hit him only when he fails to answer," the manager pointed out.

"Maybe, maybe now he knows to answer quick without thinking," again the white man's voice went from a light, mocking tone to an angry, harsh shout. "I'm waiting, Jack."

Jack had been wondering whether his jacket and guns were on the table but quickly responded, "I was looking for Chicago Joe, I have a business proposition for him."

"Oh, a *business proposition*," the light, mocking tone had returned, then the man bent to ensure all his strength went into the blow he gave to Jack's left knee with the cosh he now wielded. The pain rippled up and down Jack's leg, shooting even into his guts, as he tried to double up pulling against the ropes that firmly bound him to the chair. After a pause for Jack to regain his senses the light voice continued, "You a friend of Chicago Joe?"

"No, never seen him," Jack managed to explain as he struggled to control his breathing so he could speak, "for all I know, either of you could be him. But, I have information for him," Jack went on, knowing his best way out was by talking and the closer he stuck to the truth the easier for him to lie.

"Now, why would Chicago Joe be interested in hearing what you have to say?" the light tone remained but less mocking and more inquisitive.

"The police are looking for him," Jack thought he was on the right line, the man hadn't struck him and was curious enough to suggest that either he was Joe or he knew him. "They think he murdered those two women, found down by the river the other day."

"That's a lie," the man almost struck him again but held back as the manager stood and intervened.

"Hold up," his voice commanding, suggesting he was more in charge of the situation than the other man. "Why would they think that?"

The question alone suggested that the manager knew nothing of the deaths, "They have found a link between the two dead women and Ruby's, I thought Chicago Joe would be interested to know or at least Black Rube might."

"What's the link?" the white man shouted, slapping Jack though without the force of previous blows.

"A young black woman who is a piano teacher and a blond woman, her pupil. Does that sound familiar at all?" If Jack hadn't been in so much pain he might have smiled. The two men moved out of the limited amount of the room he could see and muttered angrily to each other in the corner. Whilst they talked Stevens got his breathing under control and tested his bonds, which were tight, even if he got loose he doubted he could walk, let alone run, given the pain still throbbing up and down his left leg. "Look," Jack, deciding that talking was still his best chance to get away, raised his voice to attract the men's attention. "You both obviously see some value in what I have told you, so doesn't it make sense for us to do some business, just tell me what you want in exchange for the message you want me to deliver."

There were sounds of a slight scuffle which Jack took to result from the manager holding the white man back, before the manager asked, "What do you mean by, 'what we want'?"

"This works in a simple way," Jack began feeling himself closer to safety with each word. "You probably want to deflect suspicion away from Ruby's by letting the police know what you know, or suspect about the murders," Jack explained, taking his time so tempers cooled. "You won't want to give-up that information for nothing, not if you want the police to believe you. And, to reduce the risks associated with dealing with the police, I act as the middle man. It is a role I play on behalf of many of the top men in the city."

"What will this cost..." the manager started to ask when a door, to Jack's left banged open and, what sounded like two men came in. Only one man advanced into the room and if Jack had not been able to recognise him from his voice he easily did so from the man's well tooled foot wear and stylish trouser legs. Only Jaunty Tipwell spoke with such a nasal twang and wore such flamboyantly fashionable suits. Jaunty must have recognised him and, keeping his voice low so Jack could not hear his words, had pulled the other two into a corner to explain the error of their ways in harming a friend of Hank Tipwell's.

After a brief pow-wow the white man, recognisable by his ankle boots, approached Jack, who half-expected an apology and his bonds loosened to release him. Instead Stevens saw a thousand stars quickly fade to blackness as his head exploded.

5

DIAMONDS AND DEATH

Day Six – Sunday April 20th 1886

Minsky cursed in a mixture of Hebrew and Russian, throwing the small key-like piece of metal across the room.

"Although I don't understand your jibber-jabber," Martha told him, trying to play down the latest setback in their plans, "I am sure you should not be using such language in front of a lady."

"You are right," Minsky took deep breaths to calm himself, it would not be fair to lose his temper with Martha after all she had done for him, but he had spent more than a hour crouched before the duplicate safe she had procured for him and, despite the instructions and tools he had purchased from the housebreaker he had consulted with, he had not managed to do more than jam the lock. The safe, a heavy cubic foot of metal, refused to open even when he now tried the keys that came with it and for all his efforts his only achievement was to give himself backache. "However, with only a day to go before the ball I despair of being able to open this infernal device."

Martha had not wasted time in arranging a meeting with Mrs O'Shea for Saturday morning and, with her daughter, had not only been shown the O'Shea's house, off of South Prairie Avenue below East 14th Street, from attic to cellar, but also her 'fabulous' diamonds and, most surprisingly, the safe in which the diamonds were kept.

"It is the latest design," Patricia O'Shea, enthusiastically told them, she seemed inordinately proud of every item in the house, including the doorstops, though she obviously considered the safe and its contents as her crowning glory. "The key," which she kept in a pocket below the waist of her inner skirt, "operates a double lock, an anti-clockwise turn releases the mechanism, then push in and turn clockwise to open. We are assured that it cannot be opened with a false key and there are only three keys to it in existence: mine, one in Brandon's safe and one at our bank."

It was disconcerting for Martha to see Mrs O'Shea, "Please, call me Patricia, I would say Nina but only your husband and Brandon call me that, and I shall call you Martha," smiling and chatting so happily. However, Martha had achieved her goal more easily than expected and, with Minsky, had visited the safe makers that afternoon and purchased a safe of exactly the same design.

Martha had left Minsky to take the safe to his home whilst she had returned to see how Jack was doing. Despite her husband being carried home, grievously injured and near dead late on Friday, she had blamed him for the state he was in and the upset it caused her. Her blood boiled all the more heatedly when she heard him repeatedly muttering, "Ruby, Joe," Joe obviously being short for Josephine. "If he must consort with harlots from the docks," she thought to herself, taking the word of the two men who had found him, associates of Mr Tipwell, as they styled themselves, "then he deserves to be attacked and robbed."

She was not mollified when the doctor arrived and said the blows to Jack's head were severe but should not prove fatal. Nor did it help when Inspector O'Leary arrived, the police having been informed by Andrew after Martha had sent word to her children, and after a few moments explained he knew the meaning of Jack's words and told her, "Your husband has done the police force great service," and had then dashed off again. The doctor left, having given Jack a draft to send him into a deep sleep, giving instructions that he would send a nurse to tend the patient who should stay in bed for a few days, kept from alcohol and fed broth and plain food only until the swellings on his head and left knee went down.

Whilst Martha and Abigail visited Mrs O'Shea, Inspector O'Leary was putting in motion a series of events that would lead to an 'unplanned' police action. The Pinkertons, as yet ignorant of Jack's plight, were in a tense meeting with the head of their agency. And, poor Kitty having learned of Jack being attacked had spent all of Saturday worrying and concerned about how her lover fared. All the time wondering at the strange noises coming from her upstairs neighbour and hoping, though failing, to get a better look at the face of his mysterious lady friend who now seemed a frequent visitor. In the end she resorted to spending Sunday morning at church service, praying fervently for divine intervention to bring about Jack's swift and complete recovery. Through it all, Jack swam in the deep, dark, cold waters of an uninhabited sea, with some unseen and dread being grasping at his feet with icy fingers, his only thought to follow the small ruby red glow that danced before his eyes.

"Every minute I spend in the house is a danger," as Sunday afternoon drew towards evening and a squall of rain pattered against the windows, Minsky reviewed the obstacles they faced to successfully complete their plan. "The safe's hinges would require a sledgehammer to break, even if I had the strength of Hercules, the noise would alert everyone to my presence. The darned thing is too heavy to carry, I had to pay the cabman to help bring it up here, and it can hardly be concealed under my jacket. My only hope was the skeleton keys I purchased but either I am an imbecile in their use or the makers' claims about the lock are true."

Martha contemplated her lover's despair; she had once held a passion for Jack's best friend, who had subsequently died so tragically in the war, but it had been a largely platonic and girlish desire. Whilst for Minsky, she felt an earthy, physical passion that encompassed laughter and joy as well as a bond of friendship; she did not like to see him in despair and defeated as he currently was. Jack, however, she knew could not be defeated, as the black rage that stormed beneath his placid outer shell drove him relentlessly to complete any task he started regardless of cost.

"I dare say if Jack were here he would simply suggest blasting the safe with dynamite and shooting his way out," she had meant it light-heartedly but Minsky did not smile as he stood with one foot on the safe, staring down at it in thought. "I meant it as a joke," she assured him, wondering if she had hurt his feelings in bringing up Jack. "I know you can't blow it up."

"Perhaps I can," Minsky mused, "I remember Brandon once talking to his cronies, years ago before I left his employ, about a substance called night… nitro… nitro something. If only I could remember."

"Not Nitroglycerin?" Martha stated, remembering Andrew had recently informed them that the DeWert mines were starting to use army ordnance made of the strange sounding chemical, instead of dynamite.

"Ha, you are a wonder and a wonderful woman," Minsky shouted with delight, pulling her to her feet so they could do a wild, laughing jig around the broken safe. "Now," he crowed as they danced, "if only I can buy some before tomorrow evening then, like Cendrillon, I will go to the ball."

"I may yet lose my job but I have achieved what no other police officer in the city has," Inspector O'Leary informed them, raising his glass to toast himself. "To my success!"

"What is it that you have achieved that threatens you so much?" Jack wanted to know, taking a sip of whiskey, his first in virtually two days. Martha had rationed him to one glass and despite his initial intention to make it last the evening he downed it in one after the first sip.

"I will not be pouring you another," Pinky told him, sitting opposite Jack in another of the padded armchairs that made their late night meeting in Jack's parlour, with its fire chasing away the chill, damp spring air, so much more comfortable than a bar. "Your wife was very specific on the matter and neither Pug nor myself want her angry with us again."

"She has only recently forgiven us," Pug confirmed his agreement with Pinky's position, "for passing on your message about being dead, and that was years ago and hardly our fault.'

"I did not mean for you to relay that message, only that I would not be returning," Jack defended himself.

"You clearly said that the money you had paid into the bank on your family's behalf was their *inheritance*, how else should we have taken it?" Pinky raked over the old argument once again.

"Nor will I intervene," Cage told them, "Mrs Stevens seemed unhappy enough with me when I told her you had gotten your injuries by helping my investigation, though I thought it better than the story those pair of layabouts told when they delivered you to her doorstep."

"I do not know what the world is coming to when a man is treated so in his own house," Jack bemoaned. Stevens was propped up on cushions with his left leg supported on a low table to ease the pain of his knee, he had managed the stairs with the aid of a stick and, having been fussed over by so many females for the past two days, was glad to come down for the masculine company. Being comfortable and his leg still smarting from his recent exertions he decided not to try and retrieve the decanter of whiskey by his own efforts, instead he would bide his time. "You haven't told us your news yet, Cage," he reminded the inspector.

"The words you muttered in your delirium, 'Ruby and Joe,' set me thinking," Cage explained, making a show of enjoying his whiskey as he spoke. "It caused me to make up my mind to put a plan I had already formulated into action."

"Without even informing us," Pug pointed out.

"Only my sergeant and a few other trusted officers were summoned to a bar," Cage continued, "and then taken by cab to their unknown destination. Only at the last minute did I reveal we were to raid Ruby's. I had already had an iron bar prepared so the rear exit could be secured from the outside, cutting off any retreat, and I sent the youngest cop to the nearest emergency telephone to say an officer was attacked and injured by Black Hawks in the back alleyway. Then the sergeant and I sauntered down to the entrance and held it open at gunpoint whilst our men, took down those guarding outside. As reinforcements arrived, to help their fellow officer in distress, we pushed on into the main room and the new arrivals swarmed in behind; after that it was plain sailing."

"Rumour has it," Pinky put in, "that two officers were wounded, though not seriously and a number of the staff were injured resisting arrest."

"It was a little *hot*," Cage agreed, "for the first few moments. Though once those inside realised the net was closed on them they gave up quickly enough."

"Did you bag anyone of significance?" Jack, wanted to know, judging whether his desire for another whiskey yet outweighed the pain in his leg and deciding it did not, simply stared ruefully at the decanter.

"The manager, who claimed the name Ruben, though all the guests and most of the staff gave false names. But, my sergeant recognised, amongst other personages, Mr John Wesley Blackstaff."

"The brother of the murdered girl?" Pug knew enough of the Blackstaffs to wonder why such a man should be visiting Ruby's. "An odd coincidence?"

"Despite his father, the reverend, the son is a bachelor of some wealth," Cage added, "so his attending such a club might seem natural to some and simply a coincidence, although it is a strange one given his sister's connection to the place."

"Which certainly seems beyond doubt from what one of the customers told me," Jack informed them. "Although from the way the manager and his friend, the pair that did this to me, talked, I don't think they had anything to do with killing the girls. Certainly the manager seemed surprised at the allegation." Jack had decided to keep Jaunty's role in the affair secret for the moment, partly as the the man had saved Jack and partly because he wanted to confront him himself; if Jaunty Tipwell had visited the Black Hawks without Hank's knowledge he would be punished.

"Everyone at Ruby's denied knowledge of any Joe, Chicago or otherwise, and of the Misses Blackstaff and Walsh. Although I suspect they lied as we found some old menus which included a description of the *piano teacher and her pupil* that seems to fit our murdered pair." Cage told them.

"They must have died within a few hours of their last performance there, yet there doesn't seem a direct connection with the place," Jack pondered the point. "Although I have no proof of it, I suspect the slim, easily angered man who enjoyed using his cosh on me is Chicago Joe."

"You now that description sounds a lot like Joseph Mannheim, the second-in-command of the Kings," Pug stated, to nods from Pinky and Cage. "Although I have never heard him called 'Chicago Joe'."

"This makes my brain spin, and it aches enough as it is. I could do with a whiskey to clear my head," Jack said wistfully, only to receive shakes of the head from all three of his companions. Jack had slept for much of the previous day, the doctor giving him a sleeping draft, but he had been plagued by his old nightmares, whether as a result of his injuries or the shock of the attack he could not say but truth was he felt far from well and believed in the maxim: 'Whiskey, the cure for all ills'.

"At least, we can rule out anything in Mary Walsh's real life to warrant her being killed," Pug explained. "Our boss was reluctant to say anything about her but we did get sufficient from him to rule that avenue of investigation out. It seems she was from the New York City branch of a well known Chicago family, she was well educated having a degree in Classics." Cage and Jack both raised eyebrows at the unusualness of this. "How exactly she became involved with the Pinkertons is not clear, but she was wealthy in her own right and seems to have been investigating abuses in the factories she and her family owned here in Chicago. It was suggested that she already had connections to the Knights and may have approached WP directly herself about concerns that the organisation had been infiltrated by extremists."

"Whatever her background and intent," Pinky said, helping himself to another glass of Jack's whiskey, "the risk she took in going to Ruby's was too great, WP had too much faith in her abilities and gave her too great a freedom of action."

"As performers they are likely to have been safe enough, it also gave them better access to the staff and won their confidence more easily," Jack pointed out.

"Undressing in front of so many voyeurs, must have required courage, especially for the the daughter of a minister," Cage surmised. "Although, in reality, they were protected from any unwanted advances and, in their innocence as unmarried young woman, to kiss and caress each other may have seemed a trivial thing. It certainly would not have raised any passion in them that might have have been lasciviously dangerous had a man been involved. Though it is not *how* they gained entrance to Ruby's that should concern us but *what* they discovered, or they were thought to have discovered, that should lead us to their killer."

"On that we are no further forward," Jack pointed out, he was waiting for the whiskey decanter to reach Cage, who sat closest to him, before making a bid to claim it. "If you have Ruben under lock and key perhaps you will sweat the answer out of him."

"I don't have him under lock and key anymore, they were all released yesterday."

"The heat was turned up, I expect," Pinky grinned at the inspector's predicament, though he felt sorry for the officer, O'Leary could not have expected anything else to have resulted from the raid.

"Inevitably my unauthorised actions annoyed my superiors, both the innocent and corrupt," Cage explained, laughing at himself for the situation he had gotten himself in. "I barely had them in the cells before a judge was lined up to release them. I held Ruben, or whatever his real name is, for as long as I could before letting him go although he said nary a word the entire time we had him. None believe my story that I, like those with me, was responding to the emergency call; at least the others will be given the benefit of the doubt as they acted on my orders."

"If you are kicked out," Pinky said, "our agency would take you in like a shot, the office has talked about nothing else today other than your raid."

"And," Pug chimed in, "the pay would be double what you currently receive."

"You should take the offer and resign," Jack watched the decanter as Cage helped himself to another.

"Perhaps," Cage smiled, sphinx like, "but when I released Ruby's manager I had hints dropped that he had talked, not least about the boxes of guns and sticks of dynamite we found. What is more, I have set officers to watch both entrances to Ruby's as well as follow the manager and other members of the Black Hawks. If I keep stirring the pot something will jump out, either the killer or something leading us to him." Jack had stood as Cage talked and, ignoring the shooting pain in his leg, secured the decanter.

"Jack! How could you?" Martha's reprimand, catching him with a half-filled glass and decanter in hand. "The doctor said, 'sleep, no alcohol and plain food,' and you three sit by and allow him to act so foolishly." The Pinkerton's and Chicago's finest beat a hasty retreat under Martha's polite but insistent goodbyes, which made it clear they had outstayed their welcome. Jack, at least, had the satisfaction of downing the half-glass he had managed to pour, though the nausea and dizziness he felt afterwards he put down to his tiredness and the pain in his leg.

Day Seven – Monday April 21st 1886

The funeral of a young person or child always seems more poignant, as in old age death is expected, and to watch parents bury a child, even an older one, is particularly sad. The funeral of Miss Philomena Blackstaff was no different. The father, Reverend Blackstaff, tried to look dignified and comforted by his spiritual beliefs, though for much of the service, which he did not officiate at, he looked frail, broken and without hope. The mother, Mrs Blackstaff, was blank and unresponsive, like some automaton, so deeply had she fallen into her grief she could not feel nor comprehend what was happening. Whilst the brother, Mr J W Blackstaff, did his best to bear the burden his parents could not shoulder and listened to the condolences and thanked those present for their kind words. Although his eyes flashed angrily every time he caught sight of Inspector O'Leary, the sergeant and Jack Stevens, leaning heavily on his stick, standing at the rear of the crowd.

The sergeant, Magnus Magnuson, with shining blond hair, bushy beard and blue eyes that sparkled with vitality, could not in his youth, fully comprehend the depth of pain the family felt, but smilingly offered his condolences, nodding as if to assure them of his intentions to ensure the killer brought to justice. Inspector

O'Leary was more direct, grimly assuring all three that the police would use all at their disposal to bring the deceased justice and that he would work tirelessly in helping to do so.

"I can offer you nothing that will replace the light and love you have lost," Jack told the parents, "I hope through prayer you will find some comfort and understanding."

"I pray for the soul of the man that did this, for his soul is the black of hell," the reverend told him in a voice that was only a feint echo of its former self. "My daughter marches at God's right hand under his benevolent gaze."

"Amen," Jack and the preacher's wife both whispered in response.

"I will not rest," Jack stated more firmly, having moved on to the brother and shaking his hand whilst he looked him steadily in the eye, "until those responsible are brought to the noose. Whoever they are, they shall pay for this crime." There could be no doubting the absolute assurance of his words.

"The orchestra is easily as good as Lounsbury's," Abigail enthused, ensuring her father was settled in the O'Shea's downstairs parlour, which had been cleared of its usual furniture so it could be used as a recital room for the various singers and pianists the O'Shea's had retained. "Are you fine? Mother will be along shortly." Jack told her he was quite content to sit and listen to the recitals, sipping his champagne, along with the others who had no inclination or ability to dance. Stevens smiled, as Abby left him, despite being the mother of two, at times like this she still seemed a young girl eager to join in the quadrille that the orchestra was playing.

The O'Shea's house was large with a ballroom down one side of the first floor, with a number of french doors that opened out onto the garden allowing the cool spring breeze to waft in; the scent of the early blooms mingling with the pomades and perfumes of the men and women present. Opposite was a large dining room where, those who needed refreshment, could find liquor or cold food, there was also a billiard room, its door shut as Mr O'Shea and Andrew competed with the elder McCormick and his son. The kitchen ran along the outer side wall with a short corridor to link it to the large entrance hall which was a bustle of servants and guests, crossing from one activity to another.

"Sitting this one out?" Mrs O'Shea asked taking the seat beside Jack. Three or four matrons who were trying to engage her in conversation followed her into the room but Mrs O'Shea, seating herself next to Jack in a solitary chair at the rear, left them floundering.

"I like to dance," Jack ruminated, still with an ear to the singer's reasonable attempts to execute, 'Where my Love lies Dreaming'. "I cut quite the figure in a cotillion and when I was sheriff I was known for my square dancing as much as my waltzing."

"Really, Jack, I had no idea you were noted for your terpsichorean ability," Mrs O'Shea's tone showed not the slightest hint of sarcasm or disbelief at Jack's statement. "I am certain Kitty will regret missing seeing you perform, perhaps even to waltz with you."

"A touch of gout, brought on by old age will keep me from the floor tonight, I am afraid," Jack lightly touched his aching left leg with his stick, ignoring Mrs O'Shea's comment about the absent Kitty.

"Gout?" Mrs O'Shea observed, her tone now sympathetic. "I should seek a second opinion, if I were you, bruising about the head is not a symptom of gout that I recognise."

"It is Canadian gout," Jack informed her solemnly. "It causes the swelling of the head as well as the leg."

"Really, I am sorry to hear it. Though it relieves me to know that the rumours that you had been half-seas-over and had fallen down the stairs of a brothel are unfounded. Your dear wife must be so relived to avoid yet another scandal," Mrs O'Shea stated with considerable compassion.

"Nina," Jack said, finishing his champagne, "you should not bait me whilst I have a stick in my hand."

"So charming to talk to you again, dear Jack," Nina told him, "but I must circulate amongst my guests, if there is anything more I can get for you, given your decrepitude confining you to your chair?"

"That is most kind of you," Jack said with a cordial smile, "so few woman these days pay heed to the needs of their *elders and betters*. More champagne, would not be amiss, and a request for the singer, if she knows 'San Antonio Rose' it is an old favourite of mine."

Nina was as good as her word, sending a servant in with more drink and asked for his song to be sung, but the singer not knowing the words agreed that 'Wait for the Wagon' would do instead. Jack, having given his word to Martha to keep off whiskey and other strong drafts, at least until he was recovered, was happily making do with beer and champagne as both lifted his spirits and were refreshing to his palate. He had never been partial to city water and the scare last August, after a particularly violent storm, that the town's sewerage had once again flooded the drinking water he had sworn off it for ever; unless boiled for his coffee. Like many of the wealthier Chicagoans he had quit the city for a few weeks to 'summer' further south along the river but he had heard rumours that many had died, amongst the poor, of cholera. Fortunately no one he actually knew had contracted the disease but he heard innumerable tales in the bars on his return.

Fellows, the O'Sheas' English butler, brought over from London many years previous, gently shook Jack awake from his reverie. "I am sorry to disturb your concentration on the entertainment, Mr Stevens, but your wife has asked for you," he stated in the clipped tones of the Queen's English.

"What?" Jack asked, puzzled by how he had missed the end of 'Wait for the Wagon' and there now seemed to be a pianist in place of the singer giving the audience a spirited rendition of 'Camptown Races'.

"Mrs Stevens, sir, has asked to speak with you in the drawing room upstairs, she has received a communication of a private nature which she has found upsetting," Fellows explained as he helped Jack to his feet, across the hall and up the stairs, making Jack feel like an elderly invalid but as he was feeling dizzy, from having sat so long in the stuffy recital room, he readily accepted the butler's solicitous support.

"I am so sorry to trouble you," Martha said to the pair as she met them at the top of the stairs, "but it was quite a shock," she explained, starting to usher them both back down. "But I am fully recovered and we should return to the party, it is really nothing to worry you about."

"What?" Jack grimaced as he spoke, his leg had stiffened as he rested and the sudden climb up the stairs had caused his knee to protest painfully.

"It is nothing," Martha stated, a little irritably at Jack's lack of compliance, "simply a message from a friend that her daughter, who is with child, has been taken ill. Silly of me to be so affected but I only spoke to her recently and she was so happy at the prospect of her first grandchild."

"I'll come down at my own pace," Jack informed the butler and Martha.

"Should I have your carriage brought up, Mrs Stevens?" Fellows asked, sounding genuinely concerned at events.

"No thank you," Martha replied. "My friend has gone to her daughter's bedside and there is nothing I can do."

"Very well, ma'am. The gentlemen who brought the message, does he wait below?"

"I sent him away," Martha explained. "Please do not let me detain you further from your duties, my husband and I can manage now. And, thank you once more," she said slipping two dollars into his hand, "you are truly a gentleman of the first water."

"Thank you, Mrs Stevens," the butler smiled and left her, passing back through the hall, checking that the small knots of guests had drinks and the servants circulating amongst them were doing so with a purposeful air.

Jack had only been to the second floor of the house once before, having been invited up to Brandon O'Shea's study, his inner sanctum, and knew he had an excellent whiskey there. So Jack tried the door as the champagne had obviously upset his stomach and he needed something to calm himself and clear his head. Unfortunately, the door was locked and, cursing his luck, he turned to go back downstairs as he did he thought he heard a thud from the floor above. He knew there were only bedrooms up there but wondered if a servant had dropped something heavy.

Minsky was feeling inordinately pleased with himself, he had purchased a set of secondhand clothes that he thought a man of the working classes might wear when out and, ensuring he had a large cap which obscured his face, had made his way to the O'Shea's front door. His disguise was helped by the fact that the young men, members of the Dead Hands, standing guard at the door and the butler who met him were all tall and, therefore, tended to look down on his cap rather than his face. He had met Fellows before but the normally astute butler did not recognise him nor his feigned New York accent. Martha had done her part, acting upset at the news Minsky had brought, and having the two men escort her to somewhere private, inevitably that being on the second floor, then asking Fellows to fetch her husband whilst dismissing the fake messenger. Minsky, however, as planned had gone to the third floor and Mrs O'Shea's bedroom, it was locked but easily forced.

Once in the bedroom, Minsky had lit the small bullseye lamp he had brought tucked inside his jacket, and quickly located the safe hidden inside a false cupboard built to hide it. He had struggled with getting the heavy mattress off the bed and covering the safe, realising too late this might have been better done after he had set in place the nitroglycerine, just three drops from the

94

small vial he cautiously carried in his breast pocket. However, he managed to do this and fit the small percussion detonator over the lock, setting the clockwork mechanism going and pushing the mattress back in position. Having only thirty seconds before the detonation he rushed to shelter in the wardrobe at the other end of the room.

Having reached a count of fifty he stuck his head out wondering if the mechanism had jammed, it would be just his luck to pull back the mattress and have the safe blow up in his face. However the slight smell of burning sent him rushing back across the room. He pulled the heavy mattress, which was smouldering on the inner side from the small blast, and sent it toppling, with a crash, to the floor. Momentarily annoyed that he had made enough noise to alert the household by dropping the mattress, he was pleased at having achieved an almost silent opening of the safe, its lock mechanism destroyed by the small but powerful blast. The boxes containing the jewellery were all damaged but he emptied them out into the long, thin bag Martha had sown for him.

The gems glittered in the light of his lamp, the slithers of blue-white light making him laugh to himself at the riches they implied. Two large necklaces, four earrings, three bracelets, three brooches and six rings, went inside the bag which he then tied around his waist and under his shirt, but the tiara was unexpected and, for a moment, stumped him as he did not want to break it to secure it in his bag. Then he hit on the idea of putting it around his upper arm and squeezing it tightly in place, the silver of its mounting being pliable enough not to snap.

With his jacket back on he made his way downstairs to the second floor, where he could hear the strains of a waltz from the ballroom. In their planning he and Martha had decided it would be dangerous for him to leave by the front door as he would look out of place in his street clothes amongst the guests in their formal wear and the servants in their uniforms. Instead he went into the small dining room on the second floor, which though called the breakfast room was used for the family's more informal meals, opened a window and climbed out onto the kitchen roof and, from there, down onto a water barrel and the safety of the dark, crescent-moon lit garden. Careful to avoid the couples walking the paths and standing in darkened corners, and the occasional guard, he crept from bush to bush until he found a tree that allowed him to clamber over the wall.

He was surprised to see, on checking his watch he had been less then forty minutes, from starting up the drive until dropping into the alleyway outside the rear of the extensive gardens. It had felt like hours and he was sweating profusely but now the weight of the world had lifted from him and his step was light and smile broad as he sauntered out onto the main road, a quite if unlit residential street. A few steps further on he broke into a whistle, an echo of the waltz he had heard earlier, unaware of a large, broad shouldered shadow tracing his steps.

Day Eight – Tuesday April 22nd 1886

They were awoken early by Gideon, their colored man-of-all-works who was a very early riser, knocking on their bedroom door.

"What?" a bleary headed Jack called out. They had not left the ball late yesterday, Martha had seemed unnerved after receiving her message of ill-tidings whilst Jack's leg and head had ached and left him feeling tired and more morose than normal.

The door opened the merest crack, allowing Gideon's stage whisper to reach the couple without allowing him to see in the room, "There are two gentleman downstairs insisting on speaking with you, sir, a Mr Burke and a Mr O'Gail from the Pinkerton agency, sir."

"Very well," Jack sighed, knowing the pair would not be about at this hour if it were not urgent, some breakthrough about how the Misses Walsh and Blackstaff had died no doubt. "Tell them I will be down shortly and offer them both coffee."

"Really, Jack, at this hour? If you would only consort with men of reputable standing or at least men who knew the bounds of decency by not calling on their friends at such an hour as this." Martha, who had shown no sign of being woken by the knocking, said the moment Gideon had silently closed the door.

"Perhaps they have come with good news," Jack informed her, struggling to dress as his aching limbs stiffly fought against him. "Though at this hour it had better be along the lines that the City Fathers have decreed that, 'hence forth whiskey will be free and water will be one dollar a quart'." Jack decided he must have misheard as he assumed a woman of his wife's matronly ways would not have told him to, 'go to the devil', though he smiled all the same as he clomped down the stairs.

"Leg still hurt?" Pinky asked, peering at Jack over the coffee cup he held in both hands.

"No it's fine," Jack informed him, "I just like walking with a limp."

"Inspector O'Leary, sent us," Pug intervened before the pair could get started on their usual swapping of insults, "there has been a robbery at the O'Shea's house."

"Really?" Jack was too tired to think of any cutting remark to make about this and didn't even wonder why Cage thought it necessary to let Jack know.

"Unfortunately someone was killed during the robbery," Pug went on.

"By *killed* you mean they are actually dead, attested so by a doctor and the inspector and not just your usual wild surmising?" Martha demanded entering the room, an elegant dressing gown covering her night-attire. "After all, the last time you told me of a death, my husband's, it proved to be far from the truth."

"We cannot apologise any more than we have done for that misunderstanding," Pug went on, standing and indicating that

Martha should take a seat, whilst Pinky looked increasingly embarrassed and apparently hoped his coffee cup hid him from view as he refrained from lowering it, "but this is a real and most unfortunate circumstance. I am sorry to inform you that Mrs O'Shea has been shot during a robbery."

"What?" both Jack and Martha asked at the same time, both looking shocked and puzzled at the news.

"Mr O'Shea," Pug continued, "has asked for you both. Despite his confused and shocked state he has had the presence of mind to ask that you go with us to inform his godson, Mr Henry Tipwell."

"Of course," Martha quickly took on the mantel of feminine practicality in such matters, "I will finish dressing, Jack you should prepare yourself as well.'

"How are you two involved in this?" Jack wanted to know as he stood to follow his wife.

"We had arranged to meet for an early breakfast with Cage and his sergeant," Pinky explained, more comfortable now Martha had left. "He wanted us to look more closely at how the Kings and Black Hawks seem involved in working together and the link with the murdered women. We had just started when a message came for the inspector and we tagged along."

Martha broke the news to Hank and his wife, they had been married two and a half years, Jack and Martha having attended the lavish wedding, and the young woman was heavily pregnant with their first child. Martha was quick to get the woman back to the comfort and rest of her own bed after the shock of the news they brought. Jack had known Hank, who was normally calm and thoughtful regardless of the situation, long enough to have seen him violently angry and despairing in his frustration at events beyond his control but he had never known him to be so totally bewildered. Hank repeatedly asked Jack if there was any possibility of a mistake having been made. Jack waited patiently, ignoring Hank's repeated questions and wishing for his whiskey flask, whilst his wife made arrangements for the care and wellbeing of the mother-to-be, then he went with her and Hank to the carriage and waiting Pinkertons.

Hank continued to state, "There must be a mistake," and, "It makes no sense, are you sure it is mother, I only spoke to her yesterday?" The Pinkertons, squashed in with Jack on one seat of the carriage whilst Hank and Martha sat on the other, told Hank what they had already told Jack, then went quiet. Hank, eventually turned his face into the corner of the carriage, Martha who had held his hand from the moment they had sat in the carriage, stared stonily ahead, while the three men opposite stared at their own feet trying not to hear the muffled sobs of the muscular, young, Irish-American who controlled the largest gang in Chicago.

6

MISSING

The O'Shea's house was set further back from the road than it's neighbours. The long drive and the large spacious gardens filled with trees, coupled with high walls, afforded the house some privacy. There were a number of uniformed police on the front gate, and a few onlookers, and at the door there were more officers and a group of young men, members of the Dead Hands Jack assumed. The heavy clouds, rolling in from Lake Michigan, cast a natural mourning shade over the house and its now subdued atmosphere greatly contrasted with the glittering, noisy gaiety of the previous night. Jack and the Pinkertons alighted first and any intention that the officers or waiting men had to speak with them died as Hank dismounted and turned to help Martha down, then taking her arm led them all inside.

The butler, Fellows, was waiting in the hall but hardly had time to offer Mr Tipwell his condolences when Brandon, hair disarrayed, unshaven and wearing a smoking jacket with his dress trousers from the night before, came out of the parlour to meet them. Brandon, his once muscular frame, now running to fat with a jowly face, embraced his godson who returned the embrace, still needing to bend over his tall godfather. Inspector O'Leary and Sergeant Magnuson followed behind, then stood to one side with the others of the party, giving the grieving pair a moment to console each other.

"Has Hank's sister been informed?" Jack asked, thinking it a natural enough question to ask under the circumstances.

"A messenger has been sent to notify her," Fellows explained, adding, "These tragic events have shocked the entire household. I was wondering if it would be possible, Inspector, for you to continue your questions using Mr O'Shea's study? That way the the servants can begin to tidy the house, the routine and return to work will help them achieve a degree of normality at this time."

"Once each room has been searched they can begin work, though I want an officer in the room in case anything is turned up," Inspector O'Leary informed his sergeant, nodding to the butler. "Though I want you, Fellows, to accompany us all to the study." Brandon led the way, followed by Hank, having taken Martha's arm, the Pinkertons, the sergeant and butler, with Jack limping heavily alongside the inspector.

"What exactly has happened?" Jack asked, grimacing as his mounted the stairs. "And why are the Pinkertons here?"

"They didn't tell you?"

"Some half-baked story of an early meeting with you," Jack informed him.

"I would like to see my mother, that is Mrs O'Shea," Hank stated, turning to the inspector outside the study.

"Later Hank, when the time is appropriate to do so," Martha told him, noticing how both Brandon and the sergeant had looked askance at the words, giving the still befuddled Hank no option but to continue into the study.

"Use your noodle," Cage told Jack, "Mrs O'Shea is an O'Brione, her family run the unions and workers in many areas, particularly around the docks and city railroads, they are also heavily involved with the Knights of Labour."

"You think this is linked with the two murdered women?" Jack stated in surprise.

"Not in the least," Cage almost pushed Stevens into the room, his voice barely a whisper, "but they will not leave any stone unturned and the tenuous link gives them the opportunity to poke their nose into this case."

"I will not detain you all long," the inspector told them once they were seated; Mr O'Shea, looking crumpled and crestfallen behind his desk. Hank had pulled a chair next to him and Martha sat upright, staring coldly about her at the end of the desk. Jack perched on the arm of her chair as it gave the greatest ease to his injured leg. The Pinkertons had sat in chairs at the opposite end of the room, whilst Sergeant Magnuson and Inspector O'Leary stood. "I realise you have family to speak with and to comfort in this hour but for my investigations to go ahead I need to clarify a few points."

"We realise this," Brandon, muttered, his tone becoming more authoritative whilst sitting in his own inner sanctum, though he was still pale and his demeanour confused. "If you can get this over with quickly I would be grateful, I… " he paused glancing at Hank. "That is, we have much to do."

"My understanding," the inspector spoke from memory whilst the sergeant kept an eye on his notebook as his senior colleague spoke, "is that one of the maids, who sleeps directly over Mrs O'Shea's room, says she heard what she thought was a muffled explosion just after three o'clock in the morning from the room below. At first the maid thought she had dreamt this but hearing other noises, as if someone moved around and realising this must be her mistress, went downstairs to see if she needed anything. Finding the door unlocked, she knocked, then looked in and found Mrs O'Shea."

"Her screams brought myself and the other servants to the scene," Fellows interrupted, his eyes on Henry Tipwell rather than the inspector.

"You tried to raise Mr O'Shea," O'Leary went on, "but he remained asleep?"

"Yes, Inspector, I had to shake him awake and he was quite confused at first," the butler explained. "I took it upon myself to send for the police."

"When we arrived, the doctor was already here and had treated the maid and had spoken with Mr O'Shea," O'Leary paused for Fellows to state he was correct. "No one other than yourself, the maid and the doctor had been into Mrs O'Shea's room?"

"That is also correct, Inspector."

"The party last night, the last of the guests left just after one o'clock and no guests stayed the night?"

"That's right, Inspector," it was Brandon who spoke. "Nina had said she did not feel like entertaining guests, she found that organising the ball was tiring enough and she did not wish to have to entertain houseguests the following day as we normally did. Neither of us are as young as we were so… " his voice trailed away as he glanced at the ashen faced Hank.

"And, she did without her personal maid that night, Miss Beatrice Partkis?" Fellows confirmed this with a nod. "Isn't that somewhat odd on the night of a ball?"

"I thought so, but Mrs O'Shea did not consult with me on the matter, she always dealt with Beatrice herself," the butler explained his face neutral, which in itself suggested he found the situation unusual.

"Beatrice has been with my mother for some years," Hank finally found his voice, "and my mother had grown indulgent of her, though finding her indispensable. I have no doubt that she would have agreed to her having the night off no matter how inconvenient to herself."

"Beatrice would not have asked for such unless it was important, she was quite devoted to Mrs O'Shea," Fellows said.

"She has yet to return?" O'Leary asked, though he knew the answer, as Fellows shook his head.

"Last night, was there any reason for any of the guests to come upstairs?" both Brandon and Fellows shook their heads. "Apart from Mr and Mrs Stevens are you aware of any others coming up here?" Both Brandon and Hank turned puzzled faces towards the Stevens' but the inspector continued. "And no one, other than invited guests, were admitted to the ball apart from the messenger who came for the Stevens'?"

"That is correct, Inspector," Fellows confirmed, "Mr Tipwell undertook to ensure the house was policed around it's exterior and I kept a watchful eye on the servants. Of course it does not rule out the possibility that someone gained entry either during or after the ball."

"Though the house was locked up as the guests left and Mr Tipwell's private force continued to patrol the grounds," O'Leary summed up.

"Yes," Hank confirmed, "though I left early, to attend my wife as we expect the birth of our first child any day, however, I trust all of the men I left here to keep things secure."

"The man who brought you an urgent message?" the inspector asked Jack and Martha, his face decidedly professional and unsmiling.

"He was the friend of a woman I know, a charity case I am working with," Martha explained, her voice and body quite rigid, as she struggled to control the turmoil of emotions that raged within her. "He followed Fellows downstairs and did not return, I saw him from where I sat."

"You had not seen him before?"

"No," Martha wondered if she should tell more of the story Minsky had prepared, if she was questioned, then remembered his injunction to, 'volunteer no more than what was asked'.

"You did not see him leave?" O'Leary asked Fellows.

"I did not, it was quite crowded downstairs but, frankly, given his dress the man would have stood out had he done anything other than leave," Fellows clarified for the inspector. "I was but moments in returning with Mr Stevens and Mrs Stevens was already coming downstairs."

O'Leary looked at Martha but Jack went on with the description of events, "Martha went down with Fellows, I loitered a bit outside here, to stretch my leg and then followed them down. Everything seemed as quite as a… church midweek," Jack realising the inappropriateness of using the word 'grave' changed his metaphor as he spoke it.

"When did you and Mrs O'Shea retire for the night?" the inspector asked Brandon.

"Almost immediately after the last guest departed," O'Shea explained, his normal somewhat florid colour had returned to him, no doubt the shock was passing, "Fellows brought us both a last glass of champagne and I wished my wife good night at her bedroom door."

"Her glass was left untouched on her bedside cabinet," O'Leary informed them. "I take it you drank yours?"

"I did," Brandon readily confirmed.

"Had you already drunk a great deal?"

"No, no more than I usually would at such a function, perhaps even a little less as I wanted my wits about me with McCormick about," Brandon elucidated readily enough. "I spent much of the evening playing billiards with Andrew, Jack's son, and the McCormick's."

"Yet you slept through the shot that killed your wife, which woke the maid above, the maid's screams, which woke the rest of the servants, and Fellows still found you fast asleep?'

"One moment, Inspector, you said the sound that woke the maid was an explosion not a shot?" Hank asked, despite his bewildered expression never having left his face throughout the inspector's questions, had obviously been following what was said in minute detail.

O'Leary paused, then gathering his resolve to describe the details of Mrs O'Shea's death, explained, "The noise the maid heard, we believe, was the sound of a shotgun, the weapon used to to shoot Mrs O'Shea. It would appear someone entered the room, forcing the lock, a fact we find at odds with what the servants have told us as it was not usual for her to lock her room at night," both Hank and Brandon nodded their heads to confirm the point. "It can't be ruled out that it was two people though one man on his own could have managed had he tied up Mrs O'Shea, for which we have found no evidence, or she was knocked senseless allowing him time to break into the safe. The method used to get into the safe, to steal the diamonds, was quite professional and would have made little sound, no more than dropping a heavy boot upon the floor."

"Why was she shot?" Jack asked in the silence that followed, as Hank and Brandon absorbed the meaning of the inspector's words.

"Perhaps she had seen their faces," the inspector explained, refraining from smiling at the question only Jack and himself would think to ask, "or perhaps it was the intention from the first." Jack would have asked more but Cage's expression caused him to keep quiet.

"My mother's injuries... ?" Hank's voice was low and hard, the anger behind them clear for all to hear.

"Were extensive," O'Leary hurried over the fact. "She would have felt little and death would have been instantaneous." Martha's sigh and stifled cry caused them all to give a brief, silent prayer for the departed.

"There is one other thing," the inspector finally stated, after a pause to allow them all a moment to compose themselves. "Do you recognise this?" O'Leary handed Brandon a small filigree of silver holding three or four small diamonds.

"It looks like the clasp off of one of my wife's diamond necklaces," Brandon confirmed as Hank peered over his shoulder and nodded in agreement.

"And this?" the inspector pulled a blood-stained handkerchief, with an embroidered 'B' in one corner from his pocket and held it before O'Shea. "Can you explain how this handkerchief, which matches newly laundered ones in your room, and the broken clasp from your wife's stolen necklace come to be in your bedroom?" O'Shea sat, mouth working but with no sounds expect spluttering coming from it, uncomprehending and confused, his mind trying but failing to connect the facts of what he had been told with what he thought had occurred. It was, however, too much for Hank to bare.

"What do you imply, Inspector?" Hank leapt from his seat, banging his right fist on the desk with force enough to make it jump and sending some of its contents to the floor. "Answer him Father, tell him what you know and send him packing with his twisted, lying words."

The Pinkertons were quick to their feet and the sergeant stepped forward, but O'Leary remained where he stood, impassive and unmoved, Martha remained rigid in her seat and Jack, who had instinctively reached for his gun, eased his posture on the chair arm.

"Can you answer, sir?" the inspector quietly asked again, though Brandon's mouth worked still he made no sound. He looked wildly around the room, his eyes avoiding his godson who stood at his side towering over him and came to rest on Martha's rigid, staring face.

"Tell them, Brandon," Martha's voice was small but insistent. "Tell them what you know, what has occurred here with your wife." Of all the people in the room she alone knew with certainty the robbery and murder were not linked, she was equally certain that Brandon would not murder his wife no matter how much he may have wanted to.

As he looked into Martha's eyes it was if the years fell away and he remembered telling her how he wished his wife dead so he could marry the 'widowed' Martha. However, it had turned out that Martha was not a widow and years had passed during which he had learned to be content with his lot. His faith would not have let him divorce and his sense of honour would not of allowed harm come to his wife, though he thought nothing of betraying her with a number of women. It was to Hank he gave his answer, standing to look his godson in the eye and putting his hand on his shoulder, "I cannot explain how those things came into my room," his voice was even and controlled, "the clasp looks like the one from your mother's necklace that she wore at the ball. The handkerchief is mine but I do not know how it became stained. I can't explain how I slept though what occurred here last night but I can tell you, on my oath, that I am not involved. I slept, as Fellows found me, a deep and restful sleep. Beyond that and the wish that this was nothing but a nightmare part of that sleep, I can add nothing."

Kitty arrived just as O'Leary and Magnuson were taking Brandon O'Shea, arrested for the murder of his wife, to the police station. Beatrice Partkis had still not returned and was urgently being sought, suspicions growing every moment she was absent. The Pinkertons had slipped away to report back on events to their boss, though they could see no connection with the death of Mary Walsh news of O'Shea's arrest would be of considerable interest to the detective agency. Fellows went to see to the servants, the ordering of the household and lunch for the four that remained.

Hank railed and fumed, unable to take in all that had occurred, whilst Jack brought an increasingly disbelieving Kitty up to date.

"This is madness," Kitty clearly told them as Jack completed the story, "why should Brandon steal his own jewels? Though they were gifts to Josephine, everything in the house is his property?"

"I will not stand for this," Hank stated, bounding out of the room as he spoke, "we have lawyers, I will have them go to the station to obtain my father's release."

"You see, Hank thinks so to," Kitty concluded.

"The police think Brandon staged the robbery to make it look as if his wife was killed by persons unknown, his sleeping through the whole thing is an unconvincing alibi and the finding of the bloodstained handkerchief and the clasp in his room is evidence of his involvement. They have established that it would have been difficult for someone else to have entered the house and, frankly, housebreaker's may carry guns in their pockets but rarely do they lug shotguns along."

"You consider yourself an expert no doubt," Kitty was disdainful. She did not yet know how she felt about Mrs O'Shea's death but she liked Brandon, he had always been kind to her, and she did not like to see Hank hurting as he obviously now did.

"My husband simply means to explain things to you, they are not his thoughts but those of the police," Martha told Kitty, who was not so many years younger than her but seemed most girlish in her ways. Kitty scowled in return, she did not like Martha, for one thing she was far too attractive for a woman her age, though at the moment she was pale and drawn, and hastily dressed. She had seen Jack's wife a number of times, though usually at a distance at a ball or social gathering. Now close up, there was something in her expression that sparked a memory in Kitty's mind that was immediately extinguished as Jack spoke.

"The police may jump at the obvious but Inspector O'Leary is no fool," Jack explained. "Given the circumstances he had little choice but to arrest Brandon. It is Hugh's daughter, Beatrice, I am concerned for as her absence implicates her and adds weight against Brandon's side of the scale. Although, I expect she will appear at any moment with a completely innocent explanation."

"I have sent word to our lawyer's insisting they go to my father urgently," Hank burst back into the room, his anxiety and frustration exhibiting itself in his need for action. "I am going to the station myself, but you are obviously welcome to stay here."

"You should go to your wife first," Martha told him. "Rumours spread like wildfire and she should hear of these events from you."

"You should leave going to the police station," Jack informed him, "your presence won't help, only the lawyers can do that. I am going to visit Hugh Partkis, Beatrice's father, and will then visit the station on my way home. You need to stay calm, look after your wife and see that the family business continues."

Hank looked as if he very much wanted to smash something but nodded at Jack's words, "You are right, before word spreads out of control I need to see a number of men, make certain they do not jump to unfounded conclusions. Then there is mother's family to be told and our own clan, a funeral to be arranged… " Hank's voice trailed off.

"Go with him, Kitty," Jack told her, as they said their farewells, Martha noting the fleeting and appreciative smile the younger woman flashed at her husband, but then they were parted. Leaving the big O'Shea's mansion empty, apart from the servants who, under Fellows' watchful eye, were quickly restoring it to its normal pristine condition.

"If you drop me anywhere near the city centre I have errands to run and people to see," Martha informed Jack once they were settled in the cab.

"Could you let Andrew know, if I drop you at DeWert Holdings on LaSalle? I suspect he will want to know as might Chester. O'Leary will have made himself a legend by arresting Brandon, on top of his raid on Ruby's, even if he is released," Jack would have laughed at the thought, if Martha had not seemed so upset.

"Do you think him guilty?" she asked. "I know Brandon is capable of a great deal but even if he could do the act the manner of it seems wrong."

"Most men are capable of anything and sensible men will do stupid things," Jack stated, unhelpfully, but added, "although I agree with you that it is not so much Nina's being killed as the odd way it was done."

"It makes no sense, Jack," Boat, the epitome of a worried parent told Stevens for the fifth or sixth time. "If she were going off somewhere for the day, certainly for the night, she would have told us, wouldn't she Mother?" Mrs Partkis again nodded in agreement, biting her lip with her red-rimmed, teary eyes fixed on her front door and praying her eldest daughter, Beatrice, would enter the next moment.

"Hugh, sit down, your striding back and forth is not helping," Jack almost ordered the ex-trooper to do his bidding. He was watching the worry eating away at the pair from the comfort of an armchair in his war buddy's front parlour. The police had been and gone by the time he had arrived, Hugh had been on his way out to work and had sent a message to say he would not be in that day. The couple had done their best to answer the uniformed officers questions:

"Do you know where your daughter is?"

"Did she tell you she had the day off yesterday?"

"Do you know when she is expected to return to work?"

"Have you seen her at all this week?"

"Is she stepping out with anyone?"

"Have you any idea where she might be?"

"Does she speak about Mrs O"Shea?"

"Is she unhappy working for the O'Shea's?

"Does she ever talk about Mr O'Shea?"

The answer to each question always being a variation of "No", though Mrs Partkis was able to give a fuller answer to who Beatrice's friends were.

Finally Hugh's temper snapped when the elder of the two officers asked, "Has she ever talked about her relationship with Mr O'Shea, has she found him particularly friendly or more informal with her than might normally be expected?" It was only too evident why his war comrades had nicknamed him 'boat' as he tore into the enemy all guns blazing, demanding to know what the officer meant by such a question and how dare he imply such a thing about his daughter who was a reputable and hardworking young woman.

"Now, Mr Partkis, please keep calm, we are here only… " the officer began, taking a step back from the still muscular and imposing if older Boat.

"Only here, it would seem," Boat interrupted, his voice a quite roar, the father bear anxiously defending his cub, "to impugn my daughter's reputation. She would not steal from her employer, if she were given the day off she would not be present to have participated in the theft. She is no longer a child and lives her own life; she is not expected to tell us all that she does." The latter of course was a lie, their daughter though in her mid-twenties and living away from home most of the time, her servants room at the O'Shea's being larger and more private than her bedroom at home, but she was still expected to ask her parents permission to step out with anyone. Neither father nor mother could envisage a situation where their daughter would take a day off work and not tell her parents.

"Boat, sit down," Jack stated firmly, as Hugh hesitated thinking himself master in his own house, but Jack was still his sergeant major and, without murmur, he seated himself in the armchair opposite, his wife on the sofa between them her eyes still fixed on the front door down at the end of the small hall. "I realise how you both must feel, I have a daughter myself and, though she is married and a mother, if she went missing I would be as concerned as you are now. However, let us be sensible and acknowledge that youngsters can act without thought."

"Not my Beatrice," Hugh stated empathically; daring Jack, sergeant major or not, to contradict him.

"Beatrice being the daughter of the young man, who was then the age she now is, who diverted his journey and life to follow a pretty young woman from New York to Chicago," Jack pointed out. "She being as pretty as the woman that young man followed and, we must be honest, the pretty young woman made no objection to being followed from New York to Chicago; I even hear she spoke with and encouraged the young man in his wilfulness."

"Times were different then?" Hugh stated, though his tone was calmer and Mrs Partkis took here eyes off the door to look at Jack, her face softening at the thought.

"It is still by far the most likely explanation that her going off is completely innocent and simply a coincidence," Jack told them, the tension in the room easing with each word. "You can be absolutely assured she was not harmed or they would have found her alongside poor Nina." The thought of this causing Mrs Partkis to start, Jack quickly went on, "As you have said, she was not in the house at the time." Jack did not say that the police would be thinking she had got back into the house when the others were asleep, bringing the tools that her accomplice, Mr O'Shea, needed and taking the diamonds away with her when she left. If either of her parents thought this then they could not accept it as a possibility and made no mention of it nor allowed themselves to dwell on it.

"You are right, Jack," Hugh acknowledged, looking at his wife, who nodded her agreement, though neither looked less worried. "It is those darned police getting us worked up over nothing."

"You have given them the names of all her friends and the places she is likely to visit?" Jack asked. "You have not thought of anyone else since they left?"

"No," Mrs Partkis found her voice for the first time since the police had left. "Beatrice would not go to the theatre without a friend and there are few she would stay the night with, all of them girls of good family you understand."

"Banjo and my son are visiting all those we named, as are the police," Hugh explained. "We thought her friends might talk more openly to her brother than those heavy booted imbeciles the police…"

"Father, please," Mrs Partkis quietened her husband's flaring temper. "The main thing is they are looking for her and pray be she is quickly found to put an end to this nonsense."

"Of course, Mother, I apologise," Hugh stated, chastised.

"What sort of theatres does she go to?" Jack asked, hoping that the more questions he asked the more likely they might remember something that had not yet come to mind.

"Oh, nothing too high-brow nor anything unfitting," Mrs Partkis said. "Her favourite is the 'The Bijou' on Jackson and Halstead."

"I believe she last went in January, to 'Haverly's Theatre', she spoke of it often," Hugh told Jack with a slight smile at the memory of his daughter's enthusiastic retelling of what she had seen there.

"And, apart from visits with her friends is there anything else of note she does?" Jack asked, wondering if there was a man anywhere in the story, "Anything at all she does or visits for entertainment?"

"She regularly attends church, of course," Hugh said, "she has friends there and occasionally they meet to read and discuss passages from the bible."

"There are also the recitals and lectures, many from the church go," Mrs Partkis explained. "You will have heard of them, it was the family of that poor girl who was killed the other day who gave them."

"You mean the Blackstaffs?" Jack asked, knowing he should not be surprised at this given the growing popularity of the reverend's lectures and Miss Blackstaff's piano recitals.

"Yes," Hugh nodded, scratching his head as he strove to clarify a memory, "she was quite taken with it, something on the 'Understanding the Symmetry of God's Great Work'. I didn't really understand but it seemed to be about how music, poetry and the bible are all expressions of God's love, how everything He created works like a clock."

"It included numbers, 'mathematics', she said," Mrs Partkis actually smiled at the thought of her daughter struggling to explain what she had heard. "How numbers are the key to all things. She likes numbers, she cannot spell, unlike her sister who is better than any dictionary, it is why she became a maid as she could not pass the certificates her sister has to use the typewriting machine."

"I did not take Reverend Blackstaff as a man much interested in numbers," Jack said, before the mother's reminiscing became too broad. "He seemed more a man of words."

"It was the son who gave these lectures not the father," Mrs Partkis explained.

"It'll be a long shot," Jack told them as he left, though Boat winked at the reference knowing Jack was an expert on long shots from his days in the Sharpshooter battalion, "but I will make a few enquires myself. With the police and Beatrice's brother visiting her friends, including those from the church, you'll soon be scolding her for having forgotten to tell you she was staying with a friend as part of some outing or party."

Martha had strolled up and down LaSalle and then Jackson for over an hour, expecting at any minute to see Minsky appear outside the Grand Pacific, she had even gone inside to check that he had not arrived already. They had agreed to meet an hour before, after he had passed on the diamonds and received his IOU's back thereby clearing his debts, but she had been delayed at the O'Shea's. She knew her Ibrahim, her darling Minsky, could not be involved in the murder of Josephine O'Shea and, despite what her heart told her, she suspected that act had been committed by Brandon, at least done by his orders. Perhaps, she thought, after the theft had been discovered Brandon had finally had enough of his wife, perhaps even suspecting her of stealing her own diamonds to pawn, and that was that.

She was beginning to think she was attracting notice by constantly walking up and down the streets near the hotel entrance and there was still no sign of Minsky, her worries and concerns multiplying by the moment. He had assured her that he had already agreed a safe way to contact and meet with Black Rube, Minsky had also assured her he had no intention of going anywhere near Black Hawk territory and the meeting to exchange 'the goods', as he termed them, would be done somewhere public. She gave up her vigil and had the hotel doorman hail her a cab to take her to Minsky's apartment, if something had gone wrong then he would have returned there.

As much as she tried she could not help but dwell on the worst. Minsky was experienced in crooked deals and criminals but, even so, the meeting might have gone wrong. Worse still she could not keep the thought out of her head that he might have simply absconded with the diamonds. He had talked of his plans to put his disreputable past behind him, that great fortune meant little to him now and he looked only for a comfortable life which might allow him to occasionally meet with Martha. He spoke of using the small cut of the proceeds he would be paid to purchase a tobacconist shop with a room above, smart enough that he could take tea with her on occasions. The diamonds, however, were worth a fortune and he would know how to dispose of them and with the money sail back to Russia to live the life of a grandee.

She knew she risked embarrassment going to his apartment like this, having perhaps to explain herself to his neighbors, but as it turned out none of the residents were home. After a moments reflection she had the cab take her to her daughter's, she knew Jack would be out late, going wherever his curiosity led him, and her grandchildren would distract her. Minsky would contact her as soon as he was able, she knew it in her heart, and he would send a message to her home pretending to be one of her female friends.

The precinct station had the feeling of a fortress under siege with uniformed officers bustling about and a number of shady looking men, who Jack assumed were plain clothes detectives, wandering in an out. In the street outside a number of men stood about in knots, watching the precinct doors, with carriages lining the street

116

on either side, looking very much as if they waited for a signal to storm the station doors. In the middle of it all Jack sat calmly on a bench just inside the door waiting patiently to ask O'Leary's permission to speak with his prisoner. He suspected that any past misdemeanour Cage had committed in his superiors' eyes had been washed away by O'Shea's arrest, given the increasing number of authoritative and commanding men that breezed into the station causing the coppers present to bustle about even more in pretence of being fully occupied.

Arresting O'Shea and bringing him to the station in handcuffs had shown that the great man was vulnerable, in a way no one had previously thought possible, and even his friends in high-places, at least those he paid to be his friends, were taken by surprise and thought carefully about which side to take and were currently applauding O'Leary. It would change quickly enough, Hank would see to that; he would pull in favours, lean on those who vacillated and make examples of anyone who stood in his way to secure Brandon's release and have the charges dropped. O'Shea could have been discovered, shotgun in hand standing over his wife but he would never be convicted. Though what Hank would do if he ever came to believe his godfather was responsible for his godmother's death was something Jack would not have cared to bet on.

As he thought of Hank, Jack heard an office door crash open somewhere on the floor above; a heavy tread thundered down the stairs and Hank, a volcano on legs, followed by three smartly dressed, sour-faced lawyers, tore through the throng and out of the precinct door. Within seconds the street emptied apart from two groups of watchers, one the press and the other Dead Hands. Shortly after the senior officers also left the station and O'Leary came down to check how things stood with the duty sergeant, who pointed over to Jack.

"Why are you here?" Cage wearily asked.

"To report my missing silver hip flask, in the hope it has been handed in," Jack responded in all seriousness. O'Leary's loud belly laugh not only cleared the tension but also the area of uniforms, who took the cue that normality had now been restored to the station.

"I can't let you speak with O'Shea," Cage eventually stated, dropping on to the bench next to Jack, his weariness suddenly engulfing him. "He is to be transferred to County for the night, to appear in court in the morning. He will be released after that I have no doubt."

"Hank will ensure he is set free with no charges," Jack commiserated, though he knew the inspector realised there was never the possibility of any other outcome. "Though, if you can find conclusive proof, justice, of a sorts, might happen."

"The maid is still not found," Cage explained, "at the moment the lawyers are pointing the finger of suspicion at her. So I am putting everything into finding her, she is either an accomplice, a witness in hiding or dead, either way she is key to proving Brandon O'Shea is guilty."

"You think he killed Nina?"

"You know his reputation for being a womaniser," O'Leary had heard rumours of Martha's prior involvement but, like most others these days, had dismissed them as scuttlebutt, "and their dislike for each other is readily talked about. Talk is that with the growth of the Knights of Labour his wife's influence, through her family, over the city's workers has been greatly diminished; so she has lost her use to him. In all, I think he came up with this story of a robbery, as much to convince Henry Tipwell of his innocence as anyone else, and had her killed."

"Possibly," Jack could not counter the logic of Cage's thinking as being off the mark.

"I would put money on another body turning up soon, that of some hard man, who was brought in to do the killing," Cage posited.

"Let us pray you find the girl shortly, if nothing else it will bring ease of mind to her parents." Jack was beginning to doubt she would be found alive as each hour passed, though he still prayed it was a coincidental elopement that was the cause of her being missing. "If I can have five minutes with him I might be able to elicit something to help you."

"We have been sweating him all afternoon to no avail and you think you can do better in five minutes?" With anyone else Cage might have been angry enough to kick them out of the station but it was more to see the smug grin that crept onto Stevens' face wiped away that he said, "OK, five minutes, go leave your guns at the desk." As Cage had not said anything about knives, Jack kept his hunting knife, with which he could dismember a bear, tucked in his boot top.

Brandon sat on a stool in a small cell he had to himself, the other prisoners being held were all in a larger common cell. He still wore his smoking jacket and dress trousers, his hair tousled and face unshaven, his eyes, however, were full of fire, focused and ready for the fight. Though overall, Jack thought, he looked older and more diminished than of old; his flabby frame no longer up to the exertions demanded of a man in his position.

"I have only been given five minutes so I must be direct," Jack explained, he had been told he must stand, though could keep his cane, nor touch or pass anything to the prisoner, the cell door would remain open and the guarding officer stood outside. Brandon looked up but said nothing in response. "Did you kill Nina?"

"You of all men, Jack, should know the answer to that is no," Brandon barely moved or changed his tired expression but his voice still carried its old tone of authority. "You and Martha remain together, do you not? Bound by the same oath that bound me and Nina. Yet you have more cause to break that oath than I did."

"You and Martha both broke that oath long ago," Jack responded, now was not the time to rake up the past and the fact was he had put those days behind him, "though I hardly, 'forsook all others' and Nina did not exactly 'honour' you; so none of us have anything to be proud of."

"But not reason enough to kill," Brandon told him, his eyes steady as Jack's gaze bore into him.

"Do you have any idea what has happened to the maid?"

"None, it is a mystery to me," Brandon shook his head, causing his jowly face to tremble. "My suspicion is she has nothing to do with this and her missing is an unfortunate coincidence, though your inspector friend thinks otherwise."

"How do you explain your sleeping through all the commotion?"

"I cannot explain it," Brandon, shrugged. "I sleep soundly but even I believe I should have been woken by a shotgun blast in the next room. Before you ask, Fellows poured my nightcap himself from a freshly opened bottle, he handed them to Nina and she passed my glass to me. It was something of a ritual after we had been out or had a party."

"Fellows would be the last on any list of suspects I might have and it hardly seems plausible that Nina should have drugged you," Jack mused, glancing at his pocket watch.

"I did not watch that closely, nor had any suspicion that might give me cause to do so, but I would more believe I did these deeds in my sleep than Fellows being involved," Brandon smiled at the thought. "No, this is the work of someone who wants to send me a message, a revenge for some past action I have taken. Hank will get to the bottom of it and as soon as I am out of here I will ensure whoever is responsible will get their reward, one that will be spread equally across their family."

It was as much the murderous intent that flashed across O'Shea's face as anything else that convinced Jack he was being told the truth. At that moment the Brandon of old, the clever, wily thug who had clawed his way to the top of his clan and the dung heap that was Chicago's corrupt darkside, flared back to appear on the old man's flesh that sat huddled before Stevens.

"I never got the chance to thank you and Martha," O'Shea stated halting Jack as he turned to leave, the guard having called, 'time up'. "Of all the people I know, those I employ, those who owe me their position and loyalty, even my family, it was you two I first thought of to ask for. I could trust no one else to bring Hank to me, to help him with those first few hours. I thank you for it and tell Martha I owe her a great debt as well." Jack paused but could think of nothing appropriate to say so nodded and left.

Back in the lobby O'Leary was standing by the duty sergeant's desk, barking orders to various uniformed and plain clothes officers. As the men all started off to complete the tasks they had been given O'Leary caught sight of Jack, leaning on his stick, watching the proceedings.

"Damnation! You are convinced O'Shea is innocent aren't you!" the inspector exasperatedly said, just how he read this in Stevens' face he could not say but it was as clear to him as if printed in ink on the other's visage.

"What's happened," Jack nodded in response, his curiosity roused at the station's sudden purposeful activity.

"A body has been found," Cage explained, handing Jack back his guns, "a patrolman has just telephoned it in, a large colored man with half his face burnt off, found in an alleyway just three blocks north of the Black Hawks territory. Any bets on who it is?" Cage waved Jack to follow, wanting to know what had been said in the cell and knowing Jack would have tagged behind in any case.

7

SEARCHING

Day Nine – Wednesday April 23rd 1886

Stevens finally clawed his way out of the pit of mutilated corpses and into Martha's arms as he awoke early the next morning.

"You were tossing an' turning, muttering in your sleep," Martha told him, holding him tight and brushing back his thin, grey hair, knowing her touch would help calm him after his nightmare. "After all these years the war still haunts you."

"I think the recent drama and deaths have brought it back to mind," Jack told her, longing for a whiskey to clear his head and to stop his body trembling, his voice horse. "Another was found last night."

"Another woman? Or a man?" Martha asked, tense despite herself, suddenly concerned it might be Minsky.

"A colored man, found on the edge of Black Hawk territory," Jack explained, sitting up and disentangling himself from her. "Cage thought it was the manager of a disreputable house called Ruby's and possibly the leader of the Black Hawks, though truth be told I doubt if his own mother could have recognised him.

Whoever killed him did so by pouring vitriol over him, much of his face was burnt away.'

"Dear God in Heaven protect us," Martha blasphemed, shocked at the thought but glad it could not be her Ibrahim. "What terrible times we live in. No wonder your nightmares have returned." Jack did not admit that his nightmares rarely left him, they were less vivid than in earlier years but only when he was in his cups did he sleep soundly enough that he would wake with no recollection of having dreamt.

"I should see Boat and his wife this morning, do you want breakfast or should we lie a while?" Jack asked; glad that she opted to get up and eat, neither had much inclination to 'lie awhile' as both had their worries and concerns foremost in their minds.

Stevens had no luck at Boat's.

"Hugh has gone with our son to search for our Bea," Mrs Partkis, who looked as if she had not slept since they had last spoken, told him. "They are trying everywhere they can think and showing a photograph of her to anyone who will look. They are going to the stations and docks in case she has eloped," the mother caught her breath as she spoke the word, partly from disbelief that her daughter would do such a disreputable thing and partly out of hope that she had. "And will also try again everyone who has already been spoken to."

Jack left telling her he would try his contacts along the river and docks and that, if it helped, they could offer a $100 reward for information leading to her daughter being found. She thanked him if somewhat unenthusiastically as each minute that passed brought her nearer to hearing news she dreaded and the thought of offering a reward seemed an act of final desperation.

Blackstaff's Chandlery was one business amongst a number of manufacturing and mercantile establishments, in a wide and busy street just off the river. Like its fellows it was built of brick and stone and had a solid appearance with the firm's name chiselled in the lintel over the door. However it was the old wooden sign, hung on the wall, depicting a coiled rope with an old fashioned two masted ship at its centre, that arrested Jack's attention as he went inside.

"This is an impressive place you have here," Jack stated, taking a seat once he was eventually shown into John Wesley Blackstaff's office.

"It is our main office, the site of the original chandlery," John Wesley informed him, polite though obviously surprised and not too happy by Jack's visit. "Our main stores and place of sales are up by the docks, fewer and only smaller craft come this far up now, as the merchandise goes straight from the ship onto the railroad for distribution."

"Is that why the warehouse you own on the riverfront has fallen into disuse?" Jack asked, still looking around the office at its many seafaring related decorations and memorabilia, hoping he gave the illusion of being out of his depth in a place of such high finance.

"In part, it was our oldest building quickly if cheaply rebuilt in wood after the Great Fire, but we still own property along the river built in brick, so the older building seemed the most obvious to sell. A consortium of speculators has purchased the site and intends to build offices rather than wharfs along there."

"Talking of business that reminds me of mine, I believe this belongs to you," Jack reached forward and put the hip flask on the desk in front of Blackstaff. If he had hoped the brother of the dead woman would act surprised and defensive at the revelation, Stevens was disappointed as John Wesley looked decidedly unconcerned and barely glanced at the flask.

"Yes, it is one of ours, we have a number made up and they are given to our better clients, we have a range of gifts we use to reward our most loyal customers," Blackstaff explained, picking it up and placing it in a bottom draw of his desk, "unfortunately they are not always appreciated though."

"Is there anyway of knowing the name of the customer you gave this to?" Jack noted that Blackstaff neither asked where Jack had found it or why he was interested in it.

"No, they are given out by our senior staff and managers, including myself, all of the flasks are identical," John Wesley glanced at the large clock on the wall, checking it against his pocket watch to emphasis he was a busy man who could not afford to waste time in idle chat. "The police sergeant who asked me about the flask took a list of our best clients away with him but, as I explained, I could not say that others had not received the flasks."

"The flask was not the main reason I came here," Jack said, annoyed to realise that Cage had been one step ahead of him and had not, as he thought, missed the clue of the flask. "A girl has gone missing, and though we pray there is no link with your sister's death and that she will be found alive, it is possible she knew Miss Blackstaff, and attended lectures given by yourself."

"Really," Blackstaff seemed to be coming increasingly annoyed. "Large numbers attended my sister's recitals, so I doubt they knew each other."

"The young woman's name is Miss Beatrice Partkis, in her mid-twenty's, medium height a little on the stout-side..."

"Actually I do remember Miss Partkis," Blackstaff interrupted, his annoyance dissipating momentarily, "she was one of a small group of Catholics that attended some of the seminars I gave recently. Her parish priest was concerned about the content of the talks and, at first, forbade them to attend. Miss Partkis asked me to intercede and, after a meeting with the priest, he dropped his objections."

"She knew you well enough to ask for your help on the matter, did she also know your sister?"

"It was simply a matter of a misunderstanding about the content of my lectures," John Wesley explained, the note of irritation in his voice returning. "I do not speak against or for any religion but simply hope to demonstrate how mathematics can reveal the inner beauty of God's creations, that many things, including music, art and poetry, can be reduced to numbers. I cannot say I knew Miss Partkis, she spoke with me on behalf of her group, as for her knowing my sister I would consider it unlikely. As I remember it was Mrs Katherine McGuire who introduced her to me."

"Mrs Katherine McGuire?" Jack puzzled for a second, then could have kicked himself for his stupidity; McGuire was Kitty's married name she had dropped it, in favour of using Tipwell, once her son had gone west and she had moved away from the O'Shea's, as she thought herself truly single once again. "Mr Henry Tipwell's elder sister?"

"I believe so," John Wesley confirmed, his irritation with Jack now blossoming.

"Thank you," Jack said, despite the denials and obvious coincidences, he could not help feeling there was a link between Miss Blackstaff and Miss Partkis though he could not say what or even why he thought so. "I will not take up more of your time."

"I suppose now a white woman is missing and Mr O'Shea arrested and released for the killing of his wife, that my sister's death will fall by the wayside," John Wesley made no attempt to hide his anger.

"The police continue with their enquires and take all their cases equally serious," Jack said, hoping to reassure the dead woman's brother. "As for myself, though I give priority to the missing woman as she may yet be alive, I have not forgotten my oath to you and I still pursue the killers."

"Though neither you nor the police seem any further forward," John Wesley sated disdainfully. "For all your supposed efforts you might just as well have used my grandfather's tarot cards."

"I do not know what to tell you," Jack had stood to go, he kept his voice calm and face neutral realising how frustrating the situation must be for the family, they wanted the tragic events explained and put behind them so they could grieve for their loss, "your sister's movements have been traced to the point of her death, and there are suspects and possible motives but as yet little hard evidence that will give the police the proof they need to make arrests. However, they continue with their enquiries and, I am sure, will bring things to a conclusion."

If John Wesley Blackstaff was reassured in anyway by Jack's words it wasn't evident, he did not rise nor shake hands with Jack but returned to reading the papers on his desk; perhaps he was simply too angry to respond. Jack, hesitating for a moment, obviously dismissed but wanting to send his 'thoughts and prayers' to the Reverend and Mrs Blackstaff, simply opened the office door to see himself out.

"I'm sorry," Stevens paused, turning in the doorway, his curiosity getting the better of him, "you referred to your 'grandfather's cards'?"

"He was inordinately superstitious," Blackstaff, literally speaking through clenched teeth though as calmly as his anger would allow him, pointed at the highly decorated playing cards framed and hung on the wall behind where Jack had sat, "he would consult his tarot cards, expecting to be told his future, on every important decision he made."

"Oh… I see. They obviously worked for him given the success of the business," Jack said but getting no further response simply added, "Good Day," as he closed the door behind him.

Jack had already been to the main docks and spoken with the two senior Dead Hands who oversaw all the activity there, explaining about the missing Beatrice and the reward for information about her. Both of the men told him that Hank had already put the word out but neither were hopeful for any return, there were hundreds of women moving around the docks each day, some plying their trade others simply passing through, the chances of Beatrice, if she had passed that way, being noticed were slight. In return Jack had been told that Brandon O'Shea had been released and he and

Hank Tipwell were at O'Shea's hotel, their usual place of business, consulting with lawyers and various big bugs.

Stevens was having a hard time trying to find Jaunty Tipwell, who ran the north side of the river front. Jack had been in various eating and drinking establishments around the area and left word he was seeking Jaunty but no one knew or admitted to knowing where he could be found. It was at the currently little used and near deserted fork of the river, by the bend where it's northern and southern branches met, that he saw the man he was looking for. Jaunty always wore the latest of styles in the boldest of colours and was easy to spot, despite his average stature and build, sandwiched between the two taller men who were his perpetual bodyguards. The elegantly moustachioed Jaunty, who smoked a continuous stream of cheroots, smiled, joked and talked endlessly was also a sadistic thug who took offence at the slightest insult, intended or not, and would take heavy-handed and violent retribution without warning, often simply for the pleasure of it or because he could. Jack knew Hank did not like his cousin but he was a Tipwell and, provided he followed the clan's code and his victims were not blood related, a blind eye was turned at his excessive behaviour.

Stevens was less than impressed by the trio's sauntering along, deep in conversation without the least concern or wariness of their surroundings; it was not until they were well within pistol range that they noticed his presence and he could, if he were an assassin have blasted all three. Of course they were well inside their own territory and perhaps understandably of the view they would not be accosted but Jack was more used to Hank, Brandon and the wary, ever-alert bodyguards who protected the pair.

"Hello, Jaunty, a good day to you," Jack, putting on a friendly air greeted the local gang leader. Jaunty's first reaction was obviously to wonder who would dare address him in such a familiar way, then recognising Stevens, someone who was on first name terms with Hank and Brandon O'Shea, he responded in an equally pleasant tone, thought obviously not remembering Jack's first name addressing him as "Stevens'."

"Jack, you must call me Jack, no formality between close associates," Jack smiled, aiming to keep the upper-hand. He stopped a few paces before the three, his hand on his pistol in his pocket whilst his colt was plainly in sight in his shoulder holster. "I have been looking for you all over," subtlety suggesting that Jaunty was not where he should have been, "as I have important questions I need your assistance with." Jaunty, already sensing that Jack was possibly baiting him or at least was being overly familiar, remembered he had last seen Stevens when he had stopped Joseph Mannheim using his cosh on Jack.

"Not now, Stevens, I'm busy perhaps catch me later at Welsh's," Jaunty told him, he'd be surrounded by his own Dead Hands there and could better decide on how to treat Stevens.

"I understand, Jaunty, what with Brandon's predicament all the Dead Hands and their senior men must be busy at the moment," Jack, made no attempt to step aside thereby calling the obviously *unbusy* Jaunty's bluff. "Unfortunately, I need to take up five minutes of your time on urgent and confidential matters." There was a small part of Jack, the part of him that grew and gnawed away inside him at each hour that passed without a glass of whiskey to sooth it, the part that released more tension and rage to heat his blood, that would have been happy for anyone of the three men opposite him to make a move. As his own gun was ready to fire and aimed at Jaunty's guts he would easily kill two of them before they could pull their own guns and he doubted if the youngster on the right would have kept his wits about him sufficiently to take aim, so Jack felt little for the odds against him.

"Is it about the personal favour you did for Mr Henry Tipwell?" the youth on Jaunty's left piped up, causing both Jack and Jaunty to turn to him in surprise.

"Of course," Jack remembered, "you are the young man who found me at the Gripmans. Yes, it is related to that and the situation Brandon finds himself in." Realising Jack had accosted him on clan business Jaunty's demeanour immediately changed, he thought the riverfront territory allocated to him was, in every sense, a backwater and he looked for any opportunity that would promote him in the eyes of his superiors so was more than ready to assist Jack.

"Come Jack, you have my ear and my help in all you need," Jaunty stated, motioning his bodyguards to remain where they were as he took Jack's arm to lead him down an alleyway to the very edge of the river's mud and to a point where only the murky, foul smelling water could observe them.

"It is basically two things, Jaunty," Jack explained, leaning on his stick and putting his back to the river so he could still see the two bodyguards and keep Jaunty covered by the gun in his pocket, "the first is about the girl who is missing, Mrs O'Shea's maid, that the police seek."

"As does Mr O'Shea and my cousin Hank," reminding people of his close blood relation to Hank was something Jaunty commonly worked into every conversation as he knew the weight it would carry, "they have had the word spread for any information about her."

"I take it you have nothing to help with on that score or you would already have passed it on, but did you know she attended the the lectures the Blackstaffs put on, especially those of the brother of the girl found hanging in one of those old warehouses just a couple of blocks down?"

"She and a lot of people," Jaunty pointed out realistically if unhelpfully, "though I will pass it on as it is better information than none at all."

"And you might get more," Jack played on the theme that Jaunty might benefit by helping him, "if you were to set a watch on the younger Blackstaff who runs the family business." Jaunty nodded and looked as if he was going to do so without delay, so Jack quickly moved on. "But, on a more important note about your future wellbeing, does Hank know of your meetings with the manager of Ruby's and Joseph Mannheim?" Jaunty looked both panicked and angry at the same moment, like a hyena disturbed at its meal, and was about to do something he might regret when Jack pulled his gun out; the two bodyguards blissfully unaware of the tense situation playing out behind their backs. "Now, think carefully, Jaunty, I don't accuse you of anything and even if Hank doesn't know it doesn't mean you betray him."

"I do no such thing and I would call you a liar for saying so, gun or no gun," Jaunty sounded sufficiently outraged for Stevens to suspect he told the truth. "The territory I hold borders the river on two sides and a parcel of the Kings territory runs alongside the river on the west bank. It has long been the case that the man in charge of each side will meet to settle disputes, in recent years the meetings have become frequent and regular as it helps us keep the peace. There is little profit in our fighting and the Kings are under pressure on their other borders so want things kept secure with our clan. I might not like Joseph Mannheim, he is quick to anger and acts without thinking," 'There is the pot calling the kettle black,' Jack thought at Jaunty's words, "but his father is getting old and fat and Joseph is taking on running more of the Kings' operations. Unfortunately though his elder brother is in line to take over and this doesn't sit well with Joe."

"It sounds like it is a good alliance to keep, as in the longer run it might help split the Kings or even put their future leader in your debt," Stevens surmised, lowering, though not re-pocketing his gun in acknowledgement that he believed what he was being told, as Jaunty nodded in conformation. "Where does the manager of Ruby's come into this?"

"You mean Hermes Ruben, nephew to Black Rube who is leader of the Black Hawks? Not that anyone sees very much of Rube, but his hand is felt on everything that is South of 22nd Street and west of Michigan. However, if it weren't for Ruby's the Hawks would be of no account, that place brings them money and influence to almost rival the Kings, though nothing as great as we have," Jaunty swelled with pride at the thought of his clan, the power they wielded and wealth they gained from their criminal activities which made the lives of so many of the ordinary folk who lived in their grasp so fearful and unpleasant. "Since Ruben took over, some months back, as Ruby's manager, marking him as heir to Black Rube, he let it be known he would be interested in taking part in our meetings."

"How did he know about them. I take it they were not advertised for public invitation?" Jack asked with a smile, finally pocketing his gun.

"No, they were not," Jaunty explained, becoming noticeably less tense himself, "but Joseph was a regular customer at Ruby's and it seems they had gotten to know one another. However, it benefits us all as we trade information and, from time to time, help each other out."

"So, Joseph Mannheim, is Chicago Joe?" Jack wanted to know, steering Jaunty to his next and most important question.

"No, not as such, it was a name he made up when at Ruby's, a passing joke, but he seems to have used it at times, when doing something he didn't want his father to know."

"Like running guns and girls in places he shouldn't?" Jack guessed.

"Yes, he does a good Italian accent," Jaunty grinned.

"So, our two dead girls connected him to Ruby's somehow and he killed them?"

"Not that I know of, him and Ruben thought you were deranged at suggesting such a thing," Jaunty said, looking pretty much as if he did not care one way or the other. "Neither of them seemed happy that the girls were dead, one because they had brought in customers and the other as he liked to watch them. The way Joseph talks he is partial to dark meat, whilst Ruben favours only what is green and folds."

"You have heard about Ruben today?" Jack asked, but seeing

Jaunty's face crease in puzzlement went on, "He was found dead late yesterday with his half his face burnt off from having vitriol poured over it."

"Vitriol, you say?" Jaunty, not unfamiliar with doling out violent retribution himself, seemed shocked at the thought. "That's a weapon Joseph has been known to use; his cosh is for light work," Jaunty nodded at Jack's cane, "a heavy hammer for something more lasting and vitriol if he is really upset."

"Sounds to me like 'Chicago Joe' is the result of Joseph and Ruben working together, to sell guns and dynamite to extremists in the ranks of the Knights of Labour. It also looks like Joe might have done for Ruben to keep him quite about their bit of business on the side, which is likely to have included killing the girls."

"Whatever you think, Jack," Jaunty shrugged, unconcerned, "it is possible and I wouldn't put it past Joe to kill for pleasure. Though to me I think you have it wrong, the fact is Ruben wanted to take over a number of the other colored gangs so it could be one of them that did for him."

"Then I need to speak with Joseph himself, to see what he knows. How do I get hold of him?"

"You don't Jack, this side of the river we have taken a liking to you and your eccentric ways; like your pulling a gun on me just now, we know you don't mean anything by it," Jaunty informed him with confident grin. "But Joe doesn't take to such things or being called on informally and is likely to resort to his heavy hammer, assuming he is in a good mood, if not he'll think of something worse."

"Let me worry about that, I just need to know where he holes up."

"Very well," much to Jack's surprise, Jaunty pulled a notebook from his pocket and scrawled an address on it. "I can't say where he will be at any particular time but this is where he sleeps, when he sleeps. I wouldn't let the local coppers know what you are up to in case it gets back to him. Word is some Pinkertons tried to pick him up a little while back and they got a beating for it, fact is I doubt if even Hank would be able to help you if you put yourself in Joe's hands."

"That's good of you to say, Jaunty," Jack thanked the other, knowing what he wanted in return, "I will put in a good word for you with Brandon and Hank, assuming this all goes OK."

"How'd you get so close to them?" Jaunty asked, his curiosity getting the better of him. "You aren't family, not even by marriage, not even Irish or Catholic."

"Partly through some financial deals made by O'Shea on behalf of my family," Jack said, then adding with a wink, as he sauntered off. "Though mainly because I killed a couple of Tipwells some years back."

If Martha had ever doubted it she now knew that Minsky was right in his assertion, 'she had no shame'. She had had a cab drive her back and forth across Chicago, stopping at every haunt she could remember Minsky ever mentioning, sending the cabman in to ask if her diminutive Russian friend had been seen recently. Twice she had asked to be driven to his apartment and had gone inside herself but finding only the elderly couple at home.

"The Russian gentleman who lives upstairs?" the pair, seemingly ancient, grey and garrulous with each other but pleasant to their unexpected visitor, echoed each others words. "No we haven't seen nor heard him for a few days since," the man informed her.

"Such a gentleman, always pleasant and so busy," the woman explained. "In and out, day and night, such a gallant man of the town. No, we have not seen him."

"Not like the woman who lives opposite, going out on her own," the man informed Martha. "A pleasant sort but not respectable."

"The woman opposite, what can I say? We had a word for her sort when I was a girl but I would not use it now, no matter how well it fits," the woman told Martha, her voice dropping conspiratorially as she confided in another woman of refinement. "Out at all hours, unaccompanied and living on her own, goodness knows what her family must think."

At the end of each visit Martha escaped as quickly as she could, declining offers of coffee and cake and, on the second occasion, avoiding stepping over the threshold when invited. Her worries mounted, she stopped caring what the cab driver might think of her, she had tipped him often enough after each place they had visited and he must have made more that day than he normally did in a week. She had concluded that Minsky was in hiding, the exchange had gone wrong and he was unable to get word to her because of his current circumstances; she could not, no matter how low she felt, entertain the thought he had run off and left her.

Though she had only eaten a light breakfast with Jack and had missed lunch she had no appetite and her head ached with worry, she sat in the cab whilst it waited in a side street trying to work out her next move; she needed help but her options were few. Under the circumstances she could hardly go to the police. She could approach Jack but was too tired to do so, he would want to know every detail and would wheedle it out of her. Perhaps she could pay a Pinkerton detective to seek out the missing Minsky, but she was fearful Pinky and Pug would hear of it and she could not face them knowing. Nor would she go to Brandon, it would be too much, he would guess her motives and she would not subject herself to being in his debt, it was all too complicated as things were without adding that burden. That only left one possibility: Hank.

She had been told at his home, where she had visited only recently to give him such terrible news, that his wife, Mrs Henry Tipwell, was at her mother's house until she gave birth. The maid who answered the door remembered Martha and had told her Mrs Tipwell would be in good hands as her mother had given birth to seven children herself. Whilst Mr Tipwell was helping his godfather, Mr Brandon O'Shea, and was being the 'good husband' by staying out of his wife's way. Martha, put two and two together and had the cab take her to O'Shea's hotel, a place she knew and was known. She waited in the cab whilst the doorman took her note in for Mr Tipwell, she did not have to wait long.

"Is it news from Jack?" Hank asked, causing the cab to sway as he got inside.

"No, though I believe he is out searching for the Partkis girl," Martha hesitated, knowing Hank had enough to concern him what with his wife about to give birth whilst his godmother was murdered and his godfather suspected of the crime.

"I hope he is having better luck than I," Hank stated, sounding tired and down-hearted. "I would like to question the girl before the police find her." Then in a more upbeat tone asked, "What can I do for you? I have not thanked you for your help and kind words of yesterday."

"It seems so long ago," Martha still hesitated, but unable to think of any other course of action took the plunge. "It seems a time of troubles as I am very worried about a friend of mine who has also gone missing."

"Another woman missing?" Hank was perplexed by the thought.

"No, a man this time, you would have known him in the past," Martha struggled to keep her tone neutral and her breathing easy as she spoke, "do you remember Minsky, the Russian that worked for Brandon?

"Yes, terrible fellow, I was glad when Brandon gave him the boot," Hank had never been happy with the string of dancers and actresses that Minsky always seemed to find for Brandon whenever he tired of his latest conquest, it all seemed very disrespectful of Hank's godmother. Though when Martha became Brandon's mistress Minsky had all but disappeared from the scene. And, Martha had been a respectable widow, or so they all thought at the time, and she had a steadying affect on Brandon. Everyone respected the genteel widow and the respect Martha seemed to demand rubbed off causing Brandon to act the better gentleman for it; he had even started to treat his wife better as a result.

"Well, he has returned. I recently bumped into him and we began to talk of old times, he seemed down on his luck…"

"Ahh… I see," Hank jumped to conclusions. "So, he borrowed a sum of money from you and has disappeared.'

"No," Martha said, firmly but without rancour, "he refused my help but told me he had some dealings with Black Rube, Jack has mentioned the name and I believe he is an awful fellow.'

"Of the worst kind," Hank muttered.

"To cut a long story short," Martha continued, "I insisted Minsky meet with me after he had concluded his business as I wanted to know how he fared. He promised faithfully he would do so but I have not seen him nor had word from him."

"He is hardly reliable nor a man of his word," Hank could see Martha was plainly worried and tried to reassure her.

"No doubt you think me foolish," Martha knew she sounded it, "but my instincts tells me his is in trouble and… well… he was part of our lives all those years ago. I would not want to see him hurt."

"I will see what I can do," Hank stated solemnly, no matter how wild the goose was he had to chase he owed Martha a debt and would run after a whole flock if it were demanded. "I'll have someone run down to where the Black Hawks hang-out and see what they can pick up. A white face won't be out of place at this time of day, though as it gets dark they will have to take care fortunately I have a man suitable to the task. If there is any word or sign of what has happened to Minsky he will sniff it out."

"Thank you, Hank," Martha smiled, gripping his hand in earnest relief and gratitude, "it will be a weight off my mind. And, please, be discreet; Brandon and Jack have enough to concern them without being troubled by my silliness."

"It will be done as you ask and as quickly as I can manage, so have no more cares on this point," Hank reassured her, as he got out of the carriage.

"I hope everything goes well for your wife," Martha told him from the window as the cab set off to take her home. "My prayers are with her."

Hank smiled as he watched the cab turn in the street to leave by its only exit, "The world," he thought to himself, "needs more women like Martha Stevens; so loyal and caring of others."

Jack sat in his usual seat in the corner of the River Bar, behind the door, where he could not be seen but could see all that were in the place. The small bar was full, as was normal at almost any time of day, with some two dozen patrons. Jack had arrived, having eaten a late dinner alone at the Gripmans, and had steadily downed a number of beers and a half a bottle of whiskey. A regular had produced a squeeze-box and began to play tunes in exchange for drinks, he was soon accompanied by two female songsters and an unknown man who played the harmonica passingly well. The remainder of the patrons, except Jack, joined in the choruses or took the lead in the songs as was their individual want or degree of inebriation.

Depending on how you read a clock the hour was very late or very early when Kitty arrived, dressed as Kit, arm-in-arm with a Canadian sailor, at least Jack assumed him such from his rolling gait and accent. The night was a balmy one and the door stood open but most of the men still wore their jackets, the Canadian however wore only a tight shirt that showed off his muscular frame. As the pair entered, deep in laughing banter, most turned to watch them, the women smiling in the hope the handsome pair might be looking for company though quickly realising they would not attract such a pair they returned to their current escort or lonely drink.

Jack scowled unhappy at the laughing pair: seeing 'Kit' where he wanted 'Kitty', frustrated by the length of time he had waited to see Kitty and, most of all, infuriated by the incessant caterwauling of the other customers.

"Hello, Jack," Kitty hailed him, working to keep her tone gruff and manly. "How are you, old man? This is my new friend Bartholomew, say 'Hello' to Jack, dearest Jackson, Barty my boy." Whether it was Kitty's attempts to sound the 'Hail fellow and well met' or her use of his full and formal first name, that was only ever used by his wife when she was angry with him, that grated most on his nerves but Jack's scowl deepened and he clamped his jaws shut as he attempted to keep his rising anger inside himself.

"Good evening, Mr Jackson," the Canadian comically bowed in acknowledgement to Jack, then began to pull Kit to the bar for a drink.

"Kit, a word," Jack almost spat the command out, his frustration evident to everyone expect the pair at whom it was directed.

"Yes, yes, Jack my lad, a drink first," Kitty and her friend hauled up to the bar, banging down some coins and ordering beers. The bartender, who ran the place on Jack's behalf, glanced over at Jack who had stood, swaying, as he glared at the pair, wondering what he should do; if the barkeep was aware of Kit's true identity he was keeping it a close secret as he wanted nothing to do with Jack's private life. "Beers and quick about it," Kitty insisted, laughing at her own bravado, drunk on the game she played.

"Come on man, we have a raging thirst to quench, two beers," the Canadian, Barty, laughed, enjoying the ruckus they were creating. The shot from Jack's gun crashed into the ceiling sending plaster and splinters to rain down on his table and the surrounding floor. The stampede that followed cleared the bar, knocked over tables, chairs and sent glasses crashing. Dust and gun smoke swirled round the small bar, Kit and Barty sprawled for cover on the floor unable to comprehend what had occurred, and the barkeeper had ducked out the small door to the rear.

"Another word or screeching cord and I would have killed someone," Jack resumed his seat and placing his gun on the table in front of him, his head feeling clearer and calmer than it had for many days. Perhaps if Joseph Mannheim or Jaunty Tipwell had been present he might have shot them simply for the pleasure of it, though equally the presence of John Wesley Blackstaff could have tipped him over, but he would not suffer Kit's insolence. Kitty's game galled him too much and as for the idiot with her who had fallen for it, it was simply too much for him to bear. "If you pair of wallpapered deadbeats will join me, I'll buy you both a beer."

"God, Jack, you are in a foul mood," Kitty said, making little effort to keep up her pretence, as Barty helped her from the floor. "You'll have the coppers down on us."

"Is it true that you introduced Beatrice Partkis to John Wesley Blackstaff?" Jack showed no concern about his actions, he was tired and fed-up by his apparent lack of progress on the cases he followed and, more than anything else, was angry that despite her disguise he still felt a pull of attraction for Kitty.

"What?" Kitty took a seat opposite Jack, waving her friend to join them and, though he seemed reluctant to do so, he took the seat next to hers. "Ohh... yes, Beatrice knew I support the Knights of Labour and recruit for them."

"Knights?" the Canadian puzzled, though the other pair ignored him.

"What does that have to do with it?" Jack asked, replacing his pistol in his pocket as he noticed Barty eyeing it.

"Blackstaff is considered a model employer," Kitty sounded exasperated at such an obvious answer and was clearly annoyed at Jack's mood. "He is a keen supporter himself and has brought other employers over to his way of thinking, to treat a worker well is to get the most from them and the better profit. Unfortunately he is in the minority and none of the bigger employers support his methods, naturally I do all I can and have asked that, where possible, his good works are supported by the Dead Hands so that his business does not suffer."

"What's all this talk of a black staff, dead hands and knights?" the Canadian laughed, thinking the other pair spoke in gibberish, rolling up his sleeves as he did so as if preparing for a fight.

"What's that on your arm?" Jack asked, noticing a crudely drawn tattoo of what looked like a compass on the other's forearm, it reminded Jack of one of the picture cards framed on Blackstaff's wall.

"It brings good fortune," the Canadian told him, his head swimming by the ever changing direction of the conversation.

"It is the Wheel of Fortune," Kitty explained, "from the tarot cards."

"Tarot cards, how do you know of them?"

"One of the O'Shea's colored maids, an old woman, would read the cards and tell my fortune," Kitty revealed. "It was quite a thing to behold and had taken her a lifetime to learn, she said she had it from her mother who was a slave, brought over as a girl from darkest Africa."

"I'll lock up then, now you have driven the customers away," the barkeep emerged from the rear, having judged that it was now safe to return.

"Good idea," Jack told him, "then bring a couple of bottles over and and a pack of cards, we will have a party of our own. You two young men are up for a drink or two and a game, aren't you?" Jack smiled, winking at Kit to say, "You are not the only one who can play games."

8

CONFIDENCES

Day Ten – Thursday April 24th 1886

Jack awoke, having slept the sleep of the dead with his head cushioned on his arms and sprawled across the table top. He was stiff and his left knee still ached, though not as badly as his head, which both hurt and swam at the same time. His mouth was dry, strange tasting with a fur-covered tongue. He found it an effort to sit up, eventually realising he was still in the River Bar, though alone except for empty glasses and bottles which littered the place. There also seemed to be a pack of cards strewn about but nothing that gave him a clue to a memory of the previous evening, the last thing he had in mind was eating alone at the Gripmans.

The barkeep, who lived in the attic with his latest paramour, as the floor between was used for stock and various items of broken furniture from the bar below, was happy to provide Jack, whose appetite increased as his nausea declined, with coffee and breakfast. As the hot black cups of Arbuckle percolated through his soul, so Jack's memory returned. Barty's confusion had increased as the night had worn on and Jack had drunkly called 'Kit', Kitty. Although the Canadian seemed less disturbed than he should when Jack and Kit exchanged kisses as payment for losing a hand of cards. Jack had eventually fallen into a stupor mid-game and had not seen the going of Kit and Barty.

Feeling better for the coffee and food Jack left the barkeeper to tidy the place, in readiness for a new batch of customers, and headed for the small, private apartment he kept for his liaisons with Kitty; where he could also get a change of clothes and a clean shave. He then intended to hunt out Cage in order to swap notes on how they both progressed.

Martha, on the other hand, had spent the previous evening alone and worried, had slept badly, risen early and had eaten virtually nothing once again. She had hired a cab for the day and they were slowly patrolling around the north side river front, just how this helped to find Minsky she did not know but she had to do something and could not remain inactive at home. She was surprised to catch sight of Jack, walking unsteadily and leaning heavily on his cane, going north. Her first thought was to hail him, assuming he was heading home, but as she thought to do so he turned west and, on impulse, she told the driver to, "Follow the gentlemen with the stick." The streets were already busy: men on business hurrying along the sidewalks, women walking with their friends, carriages, cabs, horse riders, men pushing carts all filled the thoroughfare with noise and bustle. The chilly, damp laden breeze doing little to clear the smoky air; instead it only added to the discomfort of both animals and humans.

Jack, despite his limp, ploughed on and made better time than most through the throng. The cab driver kept his distance and occasionally lost sight of Jack as he cut down some back alley too narrow for the cab but always picking him up a few blocks away. On the whole they moved north and away from the busier thoroughfares and into a quieter, residential neighbourhood. An area where prosperous and skilled craftsmen lived in dwellings subdivided into family apartments. Without hesitation, obviously on familiar ground, Jack turned and went into a building. After a few minutes wait outside, asking herself why she should be spying on her husband, Martha told the driver to wait and followed Jack into the building. A central stairs, with a family apartment on each side, led up two flights to the third floor and a door with the name 'Stevens' tacked to it.

Jack's response of, "Who is it?" was more cautious than Martha had expected when she knocked at the door and the pause at her response, "It is your wife," was considerably longer than she thought appropriate.

"Hello," Jack greeted her, opening the door a crack, standing in his shirtsleeves. "So, it really is you."

"Perhaps you thought it another of your wives?" Martha asked.

"Now why should you say that?" Jack scowled, the door remaining a barrier between them.

"If you let me in and offered me a seat we can discuss it," she motioned with a fluttering wave of her hand that the door should be fully opened to allow her entrance. Jack, obviously uncomfortable and annoyed, complied and quickly closed the door behind her. The place was smaller than Martha had anticipated, consisting of a parlour combined with a dining room and two small bedrooms behind. The apartments would all share a kitchen and laundry room at the rear of the house with a yard and privies out back, requiring the families in each building to find a common accord to avoid any conflict over the shared arrangements.

"Hmm… nice," Martha commented, glancing around at the sparsely furnished room: a sofa, table, two chairs, coal for the grate in a large scuttle, a small carpet. "Through there is your bedroom I take it?" Jack nodded, following her gaze and becoming increasingly annoyed at his wife's intrusion, "Quite the bachelor's home from home."

"It does, when I am out on business and the hour too late to return home," Jack stated, knowing that if Martha asked to see the other rooms she would see Kitty's things.

"And so convenient, being just ten minutes by cab from where we live," Martha blandly observed, making no effort to move and seemingly engrossed in looking at the small, plain brown mat.

"What does that mean?" Jack snapped. "I slept here last night and was dressing before returning home."

"Was that after your morning constitutional along the river?" she asked, looking up at him, a smile on her lips tinged with disdain for his lie.

"What business is that of yours?" he demanded, his voice rising in anger, as he swept up his stick, which was laying across the table. "Well? It is you I think who should explain why you are here." For a moment they glared at each other, the pause allowing Jack's temper to cool so it did not boil over into words or actions he would regret but long enough for Martha to remember past grievances and the many times she had backed down to save them both from angry words.

"As you ask," she told him, her voice even though resolved to have it out, "I was out looking for my lover when I chanced to see you entering this building."

"What?" the word coming out sharp like a small dagger thrown between them.

"I was looking for a man, a close and intimate friend whom I love, who has gone missing…"

"You dare come here, accusing me…" Jack had no idea what he was saying and resorted to throwing his stick against the wall, the clatter it made did little to satisfy the rage that now gripped him, he instinctively pulled his colt out of his shoulder holster. Martha did not flinch, did not murmur, but waited serenely for her husband to put a bullet between her eyes. She was surprised to watch him reach back and hurl the gun with all the force he could muster at the wall behind her, the crash was loud and followed by

145

a further crash as a portion of plaster followed the gun to the floor. Jack stormed into the bedroom that overlooked the street, kicking the door shut behind him with force enough to almost start it from its hinges.

Martha waited a few moments, wondering if he would return with his second gun the one he habitually carried in his jacket pocket, but deciding from the silence that he was not she got up to follow him; for better or worse she intended to complete what she had begun. Jack was laid on the bed his hands behind his head staring at the ceiling, his face hard and angry. A glance told her that a woman had, at times, shared his bed. She went to the chair at the foot of the bed, lifted the dress and female undergarments that would have fitted a tall, slim woman, held them pointedly for a second, then dropped them on the end of the bed and sat down.

"I have been worried out of my mind… "

"What is that to me?" he had meant it to sound unconcerned but it came out as a harsh shout instead.

"My friend has been been missing for two days now," she went on, her voice even, she stared fixedly at the washstand with its bowl of water ready for Jack to shave, the cut throat razor open beside the lather brush. "It may not seem a long time but we had agreed to meet the day before yesterday and he would not have missed it or, at worst, would have sent me word. Since then I have looked everywhere I can think of but with no sign nor word of him."

"I knew you for a loose woman," Jack suddenly sat up and spat out the words, "but this is beyond the pale," throwing himself back down, his face now turned to the wall, though this was no defence against the worm of curiosity that began to burrow into his mind.

"He has been involved in a business undertaking, not of his choosing, with the Black Hawks and Black Rube in particular," Martha now struggled to hold back her tears, she could think of nothing worse than to cry now, having come this far she was prepared to beg for Jack's help, pay whatever forfeit he demanded but she would not cry, not resort to the blackmail of womanly tears. "I understand from what I have heard you say about that person that he is a dangerous fellow and I am terrified by the thought of what has become of my friend."

"Your *lover*," Jack interjected, his voice harsh but no longer a shout, "that is how you styled him, not *friend*."

"Yes," Martha agreed quietly, though not timidly, she wanted him to understand it was his help she wanted, not to hurt him, "he is my lover. A Russian by origin, still with a slight accent to his voice, shorter than average for a man he would only reach to your chest even in your stocking feet. You will have heard me speak of him once, many years ago when I told you of my time here in Chicago, after you had sent me away and I thought myself a widow." Jack punched the wall at this, startling her, reminding him of his past wrongs did not improve his temper. "His name is Ibrahim Mikhailovich Minsky, a few know him as Karl, though almost everyone calls him Minsky."

"The fat, little rat that sold your paintings to O'Shea and DeWert?" Jack said, with a snort of derision.

"He is of a stout build, but not fat," Martha stated a little too defensively.

Jack did not want to swear at Martha, nor use the words he knew many would throw at her to describe her inexcusable and lewd behaviour, as he thought to do so would be undignified and he would not stoop below the standards of a gentleman. "You know,' he told her, turning over and propping himself up on his elbows, scowling at her, "Nina said you would make me wear a cuckold's horns again and I'd be fool enough not to be aware of it."

"Strange you should mention Nina." Martha, a carter's daughter, was more than happy to revert to her class and describe that 'loathsome woman' in terms she thought fitting. "But it is that bitch's diamonds that Minsky has stolen. That was the business he was forced to undertake by Black Rube and it is why I am so worried that my darling Belorussian is missing."

Jack's face screwed itself into a knot as he went over Martha's words in his mind as if they were some code he was attempting to decipher, his mouth opened and shut again; then he swung his legs round so he could sit up on the edge of the bed. "Your fat, little Russian stole Nina's diamonds?" he finally worked out.

"Yes,"

"Then he blew Nina's head off?"

"No," Martha firmly stated, even without proof she was certain on this point, "he was not a fighter. If he had been caught he would run but not fight to save himself, he simply wasn't the type. Besides," she added conclusively, "where would he have gotten a shotgun from?"

"You knew what he planned beforehand?" Jack asked, still incredulous at what he was hearing.

"Yes, I helped him plan how to do it and then helped him get into the house," she tried not to sound pleased at her part of the venture but still it crept into her voice. "He was disguised as the man who brought me the distressing message."

"About an hour before midnight?" Jack spoke more to himself but Martha nodded to confirm the prearranged time of Minsky's charade. "Did you see him leave?"

"No," Martha admitted, remembering the last time she had seen him was walking up the stairs to Nina's bedroom, "though he would not have stayed much beyond midnight, we agreed he should not spend longer than an hour."

"It makes no sense," Jack muttered after a few minutes thinking, Martha had sensibly kept quite but was intently watching her husband as he thought. "If he had been caught an alarm would have ben raised, at the absolute least Fellows and Brandon would have been called on. So why should either keep quite about it the next morning when Inspector O'Leary questioned them? It is also beyond all reasonable belief that Nina would have gone to bed ignoring the open safe and, of course, her mattress would have been on the floor."

"Brandon must have killed her,' Martha calmly stated after a further pause as Jack muttered to himself.

"Had she been strangled or bludgeoned to death then I might agree, there was a revolver on his bedside table and he might have used that. But a shotgun? No I can't see Brandon doing it like that," Jack informed her. "Nor do I believe he had a motive, not anymore as he grows old and looks for companionship not excitement."

"How can you be certain of all this?" Martha wondered, they had not been allowed onto the third floor of the O'Shea's house, where the bedrooms were.

"After Cage left I had a look around, whilst you and the others talked. I have also spoken to Hank, Brandon and a few others since then," Jack informed her, standing as he did and wincing at the ache in his knee. "I will shave and finish changing then we must go to Cage, as this information changes everything."

"I will not publicly attest to being an adulteress and an accomplice to robbery," Martha emphatically stated, she could stand much but public humiliation was beyond reason. "Think what it would mean to our children," she began to plead.

"We will not tell him the truth," Jack told her, annoyed once again. "I will tell him I have looked into your story and believe you were duped into helping the *messenger* gain entry to the O'Shea's house. I will also say that I have learned that the man's name is Minsky but that I haven't been able to trace him. The inspector may not fully believe us but with no other evidence he will have to take us at face value. You," he looked at her sharply, his tone that of an irritated sergeant major, "will say as little as possible and we will go over the story a few times before leaving."

Jack returned to his shaving, fiercely lathering his brush, and cursing under his breath as he waited for his hand to stop trembling before putting the razor to use. Unable to sit still, Martha put herself to use in tiding the small apartment, scooping the broken plaster into a bin, replacing the gun and stick on the table, straightening the furniture and picking up clothes. The female attire she bundled into a ball and dropped in a corner beside the wardrobe in the second bedroom. She hung up Jack's dirty clothing and laid out fresh for him in the room where he still shaved, taking exaggerated care so as not to cut himself, as she did so she noticed a brown check suit she did not recognise and, on closer inspection, realised it was far too small to fit Jack.

"What is this?" she asked, showing Jack the suit she had straightened on its hanger.

"Put that back, it is nothing," Jack told her as he started to dress in the clothes she had set out for him. "Let us concentrate on learning the story we are to tell Cage."

"Who do you think killed Nina O'Shea?" Martha asked from the other room, as she hung the the small sized suit back in the wardrobe, sniffing the fabric as she detected the smell of a woman's scent and wondering which of Jack's friends owned it. Pinky she guessed from the size, he probably made use of the rooms when Jack wasn't there. "Men," she thought to herself, "are like dogs in a pack when it comes to helping each other. They will fight over every scrap they find but close ranks against any outsider; females, of course, being considered outsiders."

"It's the method of her death that is the clue," Jack called back. "A shotgun has two attributes: it is noisy and messy. It is not the sort of weapon one uses for a quiet, neat job that an assassination at night requires."

"Then why use such a weapon? Whoever did it brought and took the weapon away," Martha asked, returning to help him with his shirt collar and cravat, he did not need the help but it was their habit when he dressed in the same way he would help her with her buttons and hooks. "It seems a cumbersome thing to carry especially if breaking into a house."

"Exactly, so it was brought for a reason, one not linked to the robbery or Minsky," Jack stated, patiently waiting for her to finish.

"It was meant to raise the household and to, literally, blow Nina's head off."

"Dear God, why do such a thing?" Martha demanded, her face sorrowful and puzzled as she stepped back to admire her handy-work, "I did not like the woman but to kill her in such a way beggars belief."

"Whoever did this planned it thoroughly in advance so their exit was swift and undetected, as the gunshot would have had the household up in moments," Jack pointed out. "What's more blowing her head off did not disguise Nina's figure nor what she wore. Cage told me that Brandon identified her more from the rings she wore than anything else."

"That is… " Martha began, then stopped dropping into the chair and shaking her head in despair. "It wasn't Nina was it?"

"No," Jack said quietly, his own voice and expression despondent. "It can only have been Beatrice that was killed. Which is why we must tell Cage and also I need to find out what he has discovered about another man, one linked to the killing of those first two poor women," Jack paused, his voice catching, "then I must go to visit Boat and his wife." Jack waited for Martha to finish the prayer she gave up for Beatrice's soul, though his own prayer for a shot of whiskey was to remain unanswered for some hours.

"Beatrice was a similar height and build as Mrs O'Shea," Jack continued to explain as Inspector O'Leary and Sergeant Magnusson listened, Cage noticing that Mrs Stevens discomfort rose the longer Jack spoke. The inspector believed what Jack was telling him but was certain that things were being distorted or left out to the story, "admittedly she was much younger and a great deal prettier but even her hair was a similar match."

"The medical examiner barely looked at the body," the inspector informed his sergeant rather than Jack or Martha, "just took Mr O'Shea's word for it that it was his wife."

"Understandable," the sergeant sympathised, "given the number of bodies he deals with the cause of death for Mrs O'Shea was hardly in question and… "

"His slipshod methods have put us on the wrong track, spending days looking for the maid and hauling Mr O'Shea into custody. Who do you think will get a kick up the… " Cage paused remembering Martha's presence. "Who do you think will carry the can for that?"

"You agree then that Brandon is innocent?" Jack asked.

"It seems likely, but I will rule out nothing at the moment," was as much as Cage would concede. "As far fetched as it appears, the most likely suspect is that Mrs O'Shea orchestrated her own fake death, propably to discredit her husband and make off with the diamonds, she would have had help from a lover perhaps."

Despite her obvious embarrassment and upset at the situation Martha could not help giving a short derisive laugh at the suggestion, "You obviously did not know the woman. She had many faults," Martha informed the inspector, "pride, arrogance, even vanity of a sorts, but she was a devout woman and would not have contemplated taking a lover, even if anyone would have had her." Jack scowled at his wife to keep quiet as they had agreed, whilst the inspector and sergeant exchanged glances.

"It is equally possible she was abducted, removed from her room and the dead girl brought in and then shot to… well you understand my meaning," Jack offered an alternative.

"It is possible, but why?" the sergeant asked.

"To put the police off the scent and extract a ransom from Brandon," Jack smiled, sitting back in the wooden chair and stretching his aching left leg.

"There are many new threads to pursue in this," the inspector concluded. "We must seek out this Minsky, and ascertain his exact role in this affair," the inspector did not fail to notice Mrs Steven's glance at Jack, who was studying the knob of his cane. "Though first I will go to the morgue, the body is not yet released so there is still time for it to be properly examined. Jack, Mrs Stevens, I would be grateful if you can give a detailed description of Mr Minsky to the sergeant and he will arrange to see if the Russian can be found."

"I should go to Boat's, that is Mr and Mrs Partkis, to inform them of what has been discovered about their daughter," Jack said, as grim and as unwanted the message might be he was determined to be the one to deliver it.

"It would be better to wait," Cage disagreed, "until I have a more detailed knowledge and description of the body. I would hate for that information to be given to the parents and then it prove false. However, if you wait at home I promise to accompany you should it prove necessary."

"That is very sensible," Jack agreed, happy at the stay of execution as it would give him the opportunity to fortify himself for the task. "Before we go, has there been any news of Joseph Mannheim?"

"None," the inspector informed him, "I have had the address you notified me of watched. The place is used by the Kings and is obviously a disorderly house but there have been no sightings of any of the Mannheim's. I have also spoken with the Pinkertons who have been looking for Joseph for some days but they have had no luck and few recent sightings."

"We will get him, you can be assured of that," Sergeant Magnusson assured them all and Jack in particular, as he had been detailed to oversee the operation.

"When you do track him down, take care as he carries vitriol, as well as a cosh and probably a gun," Jack emphasised the dangerous nature of the man they sought. "I doubt he will talk without persuasion."

"Once he is in our care, he will sing," the sergeant stated confidently, tapping the desk with a balled fist.

"I might be of further help," Jack went on, realising that he might be pushing his luck, "if I speak with Hank and Brandon first about our recent… "

"No," Cage snapped, "the information you have given us is of great help and, whilst I appreciate what you have done to get it, it is not to be shared; not until I say otherwise." The inspector did not want O'Shea, with all his resources at his disposable, getting hold of Minsky before the police. "Do I have your word on this Mr Stevens?"

"Of course, Inspector,' Jack smiled, he would have offered his hand had Cage used his first name, however, he recognised this was more than a friendly request but a formal police warning that the inspector would act on if Jack ignored his injunction.

They did not have to wait long for Inspector O'Leary to call for them, Jack had used his time to catch up on reading the papers and taking a drink whilst Martha had knitted.

"It is as we feared," O'Leary informed them, on being shown into their parlour, though he did not take the offered seat, "it is a young woman in her mid-twenty's, there is little to identify her by other than three large moles in a form of a triangle below her right knee."

"I would like to go with you," Martha stated rather than asked as Jack stood to accompany the inspector. Neither of them objected, neither of them wanted the task before them and Martha's presence could only help.

The Partkis' guessed why Jack, Martha and the inspector were visiting them together, they could see their worst nightmare coming true in the drawn and grim faces of their three unlooked for guests. The bereaved parents held each others hands as they listened to Jack's explanation, with O'Leary nodding to confirm the truth of what was said.

"Three moles below her right knee," Mrs Partkis echoed, her face already wet with tears and her voice quavering, "that is my Bea." For a few minutes the room was quite apart from the subdued sobs and intoned prayers of those gathered there. It was

Martha who suggested sending for the Partkis' son and younger daughter and perhaps notifying their parish priest.

"I wish to go to her," Hugh stated, standing looking down at his wife who nodded that she also wanted to see her daughter, though could not for the moment find the strength to rise.

"I will see to the arrangements," O'Leary muttered, glancing at Martha hoping she understood that a delay was needed.

"Perhaps you should wait until the priest can go with you," Martha hesitantly suggested, "to lead the prayers." Hugh nodded his thanks at the suggestion and sat down heavily, his eyes on Jack.

"Do you know who did this?" he asked Jack, expecting nothing but an honest answer from his old sergeant.

"The case is much clearer now," Jack said as earnestly as he could manage, "the police have leads to follow up and will soon have answers for you."

"The O'Shea's, was our Bea killed because of them?" Hugh demanded.

"Mrs O'Shea is still missing, there is nothing to show that Mr O'Shea is involved," Jack recognised the other man's tone, his demand for vengeance was clear. "Those involved, Hugh, will be caught and brought to justice, it is but a matter of time."

"Justice? For the rich?" Hugh's voice rose in anger.

"She loved her work and was devoted to Mrs O'Shea," Mrs Partkis told them as she dabbed at her tears, not understanding what was being said or inferred.

"I will have the truth of this," Hugh muttered, placing an arm gently round his wife. "They will pay for what they have done, an eye-for-an-eye."

Martha and Jack waited until the priest arrived, shortly followed by the son and daughter. Inspector O'Leary had left to make the necessary arrangements and though he did not tell them he had to visit O'Shea and inform him that his wife still lived and ask what he knew of this already. When they parted, Martha implored Jack not to stay out late as they still needed to talk and resolve much but, even more than this, she could not bear the thought of another night alone. Jack gave his word, though neither felt it stood for much as they both knew it was a bottle he would be meeting.

Jack waited at the corner of the short dead end turning in which O'Shea's hotel stood until Inspector O'Leary emerged, having guessed the inspector would be there.

"Cage!" Jack called as O'Leary was about to drive off in the small police carriage. "Was Hank with Brandon?"

"Yes and the sister," Cage told him, obviously impatient and none to happy that Jack was there. "They all seemed surprised at the news Mrs O'Shea was alive, Tipwell looked ready to tear my head off whilst O'Shea seemed completely stunned."

"Nina could be cold-hearted and ruthless but it is difficult to believe even she would act a part in this pretence of her own death," Jack pointed out, holding onto the carriage's window frame so O'Leary could not have the driver move off. "It seems too complicated a way to get revenge on O'Shea and the facts would have come out eventually."

"Perhaps, but they admitted to nothing, no knowledge of a ransom nor any idea of a reason as to who might or why she may have been abducted. Finding Minsky holds the key, and we now also search for Mrs O'Shea, they will have accomplices and eventually a lead will come to light that will take us to them," O'Leary informed him. No longer in a humour to wait he called the driver to, "Move on," and Jack had to release his hold. Stevens waited for a moment or two then decided this was not the time to speak with the family and left to find a drink.

The River Bar was packed, as always, but the noise inside dropped as Jack entered and from the look the barkeeper gave him he knew he was not welcome their either. Remembering his promise and unable to think of an alternative he bought a bottle and took it with him, not that he was short of a drop at home but the cool, smooth, roundness of the bottle offered him a comfort of sorts on the cab ride home.

Day Eleven – Friday April 25th 1886

"Is there anything in the papers about either Beatrice or Mrs O'Shea?" Martha asked Jack over breakfast. They had spent the previous evening quietly: they ate dinner together, Jack drank, Martha knitted. They went to bed relatively early and at sometime in the early hours had made love, though somewhat lacking in passion it helped reinforce the bond that was their marriage.

"Nothing much, certainly no retraction of Nina's death," Jack said, putting the paper down to finish his Arbuckle, the coffee was just as he liked it and he did not want it too cool to much. "The main news is of the number of beatings and attacks on individuals around the city. The area to the northeast of the stockyards, where the Black Hawks are seeking to take control, seem to be an area of particular violence at the moment."

"We have not spoken of the future," Martha pointed out, she had determined to wait until Jack brought up the topic but, against her own better judgement, she wanted the matter resolved between them.

"What is to discuss?" Jack almost shrugged, it wasn't that he did not care but things were as they were.

"Perhaps we should move from the city," she suggested, having given it much thought during the night, "to a small place out in the country, with its own grounds and stable so you can ride again. We could live a quieter life, the children can visit, if we find somewhere not far from the railroad, to the south, we can always come up for the theatre and such."

Jack gave her a long hard look. She sat, as she always did, straight-backed and poised, she had all the bearing of a lady and the morals of an alley cat but he had known this throughout his married life and thought little of it. Jack knew himself no model husband either. Though the war had hurried him along his path even if it had not occurred he would still be the man he was: ill-tempered, morose, a drinker, restless and unable to find peace within himself. Perhaps he would have taken fewer lives but his readiness to kill would have remained within him, dormant and waiting for the opportunity to emerge and take possession of his soul. There was no undoing the past, the war had kindled the fire within him, his years as a bounty hunter then sheriff had simply been excuses for his continuing to kill. His retirement to the city had brought no peace and his black soul continued to reach out and take lives, always with the excuse that they were in someway deserving of their fate. He had long ago become judge, jury and executioner but he knew it was not justice that he metered out.

"Jack?" Martha spoke to him for the third time, almost scared by his unresponsiveness as he was so still, he seemed hardly to breath, if she had not known him so well and seen him thus so often she would have thought he had died where he sat. "I do not suggest we decide this now nor today, but we should give it thought. I know you need to help find the killers of those two poor women you found and help get to the bottom of what has happened to Nina. I have suggested the idea only as something for us to consider for our future."

"To put the past behind us once again, do you think that possible? Are you willing to give up everything you have here and try again?" Jack asked though not doubting it.

"Yes," there was only certainty in her mind, "I know we have tried before, each time with limited success but I am for trying again. There is nothing to hold me here," she assumed Jack understood the reference was to Minsky, even if he ever returned alive, and not her children. "You will always be my husband and I will do all I can to remain at your side. No matter how it may seem, I do not give up on our marriage."

"Nor I," it was the only reassurance he could give her, he could not imagine to what dark and foul ends he would have travelled had not Martha been at his side, his marriage to her a small guiding light that kept him from racing further down the road to hell.

Jack knew he needed to speak with Hank and Brandon to ensure that his story about Martha's involvement was clear but he was in no rush and wondered if he should call on Boat first or whether it best to leave them to their grief. However, as he slowly got ready a message came from Hank, he was now the proud father of a baby boy. His sister and godfather were with him at his mother-in-law's house attending on his wife and newborn son. Martha smiled at the news and talked of presents to be bought and flowers for Beatrice's funeral, she advised Jack to stay at home as he could hardly go to the Partkis family and keep the news of the baby secret and they would not thank him, in their grief, for learning of the happy event.

It was a little after lunch when O'Leary and his sergeant knocked on their door. They were polite and sat in the parlour, drinking coffee and eating cakes like any other guests but with just, "A few questions to clarify matters," as Cage put it.

"You had already spoken to Mr Henry Tipwell before coming to us?" O'Leary asked Martha, smiling as he took another piece of the angel cake.

"Yes, that is correct, Inspector," Martha said a little too formally to sound at her ease. "That is before Jack had completed his enquires and discovered the truth of the matter."

"You knew Minsky for many years, a man whom Mr Tipwell described to us a 'complete scoundrel and a low life of no account'," O'Leary looked at his notebook to get the wording correct.

"I knew him, many years ago as a business associate of Mr Brandon O'Shea's," despite her even tone Martha almost squirmed in her seat, angered by the description but also at the implication of the question that she knew Minsky better than she had claimed; which of course she did. "This was before Jack and I had moved back to the city and I knew Brandon as a friend of Mr Jacob DeWert, who was my daughter's father-in-law to be."

"I am not clear how you became involved with him on this current occasion, how exactly did you meet him again?" the inspector asked as if clearing up a small misunderstanding.

"By accident," Martha smiled, glad Jack had questioned and tested her on their revised version of events. "We spoke of old times, he invited me to tea, he mentioned a woman, a charity case in need of help, it all seemed so casual, so natural. When we parted I offered to look the woman up and help if I could."

"You were not at all suspicious?" the inspector did not accuse but his tone of incredulity hinted at disbelief.

"What exactly is it you want, Cage?" Jack cut into the conversation, making no attempt to sound polite or any less angry than he was. "We have told you all we know, I looked into this Minsky's story and discovered it false, then asked around about him and realised he was in all likelihood your robber. You should be thanking us not here questioning what more we know."

"What I am trying to clarify," Cage raised his voice sufficiently to remind Jack he would not be spoken to in such a manner, "is why Mrs Stevens did not inform us of Mr Minsky's identity and her longstanding acquaintance with him when first questioned."

"And we have already told you, my wife was in shock at the news of Mrs O'Shea's death," Jack was far from calm and not in the least concerned about Cage or his official position as a police inspector, "and, as she thought Minsky had left the building immediately after delivering his message, she did not consider his actions of any consequence."

"It was an error on my part, I accept that it was a silly mistake," Martha tried to be conciliatory. "I honestly thought I saw him descend the stairs, but he must have slipped back up without my seeing."

"About that..." the sergeant began.

"No!" Jack was on his feet. "Enough of your insinuations. If the pair of you had done your jobs correctly in the first place... "

"Calm yourself," the inspector jumped up, shouting almost as loudly as Jack, "I have a perfect right to…"

"If you would take your seat…" the sergeant was also on his feet, arm out towards Jack and motioning him back down.

"Or you'll do what?" Jack boomed, his voice loud enough to travel the length of a parade ground, his right hand instinctively going to his colt, his eyes staring, his entire demeanour that of a man about to draw and shoot.

"Jack!" Martha was on her feet and grasping his arm, pushing between them. Both the inspector and sergeant where to freely admit sometime later that they thought their time was up, that the old time gunslinger was about to put a bullet into their heads and there was not a thing either could do about it. "Please, I will answer any question Inspector O'Leary puts to me. I have made a silly mistake, I was shocked and embarrassed to have been the means by which that man gained entry to the house. I am sure our friends here understand that. No one suggests it was deliberate, they simply want to ensure they now have all the facts and that Minsky is the man they need to find. Isn't that so, Inspector?"

"Exactly so, Mrs Stevens," O'Leary agreed, even he was not so thick skinned as to have poured more oil on the flames by suggesting he had his doubts. "I fully understand your embarrassment. It was simply that, as you had known him previously, it is possible that you might have further ideas on how he might be found, possibly the names of old associates?"

"Mr Stevens, please," the sergeant motioned Jack to resume his seat and allow the interview, now virtually concluded, to continue, "this is simply a matter of formalities, I am sure you understand. We are all friends here."

"I have no idea why you should think that," Jack stated grimly, letting the colt slip back into his shoulder holster, and striding out of the room and house.

9

MORE SORROW

It was a cold, wet night and Martha could not rid herself of the anxiety and dread she felt because, no matter how much she did not want to believe it, she thought Minsky must either be dead or have deserted her; she would prefer the latter to the former whatever it said of the man. To add to her woes, Jack had not returned. The inspector and sergeant had left shortly after Jack had stormed out, both declaring they understood his anger, though both were shaken at the thought he was close to shooting them, and O'Leary apologising if she thought he believed her involved in the theft but they had to, "clear up all the loose ends," he had explained.

The cab driver would not take her to the River Bar, "Not the place for a lady," he had insisted, adding under his breath, "and too dangerous for the likes of an honest cabriolet driver." Unable to think where else Jack might be she gave him the address of Jack's bachelor apartment. She stood outside the door marked 'Stevens' for some while listening to the subdued noises from within, the occupants moving around the small apartment and speaking in low indistinct voices. She could not make out what they said, nor even if they were male or female, but she knew neither was Jack.

In the end she knocked, after all her name was on the door and whoever was in might know where Jack would be.

"Good evening," she began, as the door opened, trying for an imperious tone, "I am looking for Mr Jackson Stevens."

"He's not here," a gruff voice told her. Martha recognised what little of the brown checked suit she could see and tried, from the small portion of the face that glanced round the edge of the door at her, to work out who it was. The face was familiar but for a moment she could not place it.

"Do you know where I might find him?" Martha asked, moving her head to see slightly more of the face.

"No…" the response came but got no further as light dawned on Martha to whom she spoke.

"Katherine McGuire!" Martha was tall and, despite her age and matronly ways, she was strong and now angry. The force with which she shoved the door caused it to hit Kitty in the face and sent her reeling back. "What are you doing wearing such clothing?"

Martha was in the room and standing over Kitty, who had instinctively slunk back and onto a chair, as an odd looking woman burst into the room from one of the rear bedrooms.

"What's going on, what are you doing?" the woman demanded, looking both confused and angry, then without further thought stepped towards Martha. Barty, in an ill fitting dress that did not quite do up, had only intended to push the intruder back out of the room and slam the door on their face but Martha delivered a right-hander to his face that put him on his arse and left him sitting dazed, with a bloody nose.

"It's you!" Kitty exclaimed, though she felt for Barty's predicament it was Martha's dress that arrested her and stopped her flying to his aid. "I recognise you now, in that dress."

"What!" Martha shouted back, a satisfying if unpleasant pain, resulting from the punch, shooting from her knuckles to her shoulder.

"You, and the little Russian man who lives above me, you

are his woman," Kitty stated, now certain, though she had not seen more than a glimpse of Minsky's visitor's face but the dress she would know anywhere as she would have loved a similar one herself: the dark blue patterned cloth, a bird motif, a small bow at the rear, the bodice and puffed sleeves having a lighter blue trim and lace at the wrists and neck, the whole was so elegantly modest.

"What?" Martha suddenly felt like Jack, responding monosyllabically to a series of questions, but the bizarre situation had befuddled her completely.

"You! I see it now," Kitty stated, reaching over to Barty so as to hand him a handkerchief to staunch the blood from his nose. "I would not have connected you to him even if I had clearly seen your face but your dress is a different matter; it is the same one you wore when I last saw you visit him, your hair is the same but the hat and jewels are different."

"You are so observant," Martha said calmly enough, she had renounced shame and made no effort to hide her liaison with Minsky, especially to the trollop sitting before her whose own reputation was now much in question. "However, that is of no matter, it is Jack I look for; do you know where he is?"

"I do not," Kitty answered honestly enough, slipping from the chair to kneel and help Barty.

"I do not care what depravities are practiced in this place but if you want to help Jack then tell me what you know of where I might find him, it is urgent that I speak with him."

"Jesus, Mary and Joseph that's a hell've punch you have there," Barty, nasally intoned, getting unsteadily to his feet with Kitty's help.

"Perhaps, you should leave the fighting to your *gentlemen friend*," Martha mocked, at least Kitty looked the part of a youngish male but Barty was a travesty in the dress, his shoulder length blond hair could not hide the evening shadow on his jaw nor his bulging arms and shoulders that burst from the upper portion of the dress.

"There is no depravity here," Kitty assured her, taking command of the situation, closing the door and offering Martha a chair, hoping her actions were masculine enough for Martha to accept, "nor any need to mock. Bartholomew was trying on my dress for fun, to see how it looked, not from desire. If I wear male attire it is from a need for independence not lust of my own kind."

"You look comely enough to turn a few heads," Martha conceded, hoping that by playing to the other's vanity she might gain her trust and knowledge of where to find Jack, "but I do not come here for the pleasure of it, I must find Jack."

"I really do not know where he is," Kitty again explained. "Please, Barty, go change before you get more blood on my dress. We have been waiting for Jack, so I might tell him of my plans."

"He knows you dress like this? As a man?" Martha tried not to sound judgemental, but found it hard to accept that her husband might find excitement in such things.

"He looks after me and has tried to dissuade me but I have been in the cage of my skirts for too long and wish to escape," Kitty explained, then drawing breath as there was something in Martha's disdain for her that gave her strength. "I will part from him tonight, cut my hair and renounce my dresses and female finery for a better life. I travel to Canada with Barty to start a new life." Martha made no response as Barty, now the figure of a finely built young man dressed in trousers and shirt, joined them; his nose no longer bleeding but he held the bloody kerchief to his face as a precaution.

"It is money we need," Barty explained as he took a seat at the table, Kitty going to stand beside him, "we wait to ask if Mr Stevens will loan us a stake."

"It is a liberty I know," Kitty jumped in, seeing Martha frown, "and we can cover the fare by boat or train but need something to get us started. We will look to travel a while then find a business to open perhaps a clothing shop or dry goods."

"Such plans," Martha could not think of anything to say, how Jack spent his money she cared not one jot.

"Bartholomew's a good man, aren't you Barty lad?" Kitty went on trying to lighten the mood, still yet far from trusting Martha as she was afraid that if Jack's wife left now and sent word to Hank they could be still be stopped. "He is a loving and trusting sort, so our being partners makes sense as we give each other cover and the lie to our true natures."

"How much do you need?" Martha's tone was still far from friendly but neither was it one of disgust as many might have felt, she understood the woman's need to be able to act more freely as it was her own skirts that stopped her from roaming the streets and bars to hunt for Minsky and Jack.

"No great sum, I would not presume on our friendship," Kitty said, determined to run the moment when Martha left, not daring to risk being caught by her brother. "Two or three hundred, or less, whatever Jack thinks."

"I will give you five hundred if you both help me find Jack tonight," Martha told them. "You are right in as much that two men will be able to go where I cannot and where it might be dangerous for only one to go."

"You have that sort of money?" Barty spoke up, disbelieving that anyone he knew could have such a sum to hand.

"I will go to my son at breakfast, such an amount means little to him and he will not ask why I want it, so you can leave first thing," Martha smiled, holding out her hand. "Is it a deal?"

They tried a number of places, starting with the River Bar before Kitty began to realise that Jack may have gone to the one place she had thought the least likely, Ruby's. The driver flatly refused to go that close to Black Hawk territory at that time of night and neither Barty nor Kitty thought it safe to go on foot. Martha told them all plainly they were a disgrace to their sex and she would go on her own if need be; the irony of addressing Kit with these words escaping her in her annoyance and frustration.

Barty was in the process of telling them all that he would go and do so on his own when the sounds of an oddly groaning melody reached their ears.

"Cockles and mussels alive, a lively oh!" Jack lurching, in parody of a man sauntering along at his leisure, along the side street in which the cab had halted, whilst alternately taking swigs from a near empty bottle and singing catches of the song he regularly heard at the River Bar but could only remember one line of and that not with any accuracy. "Why Martha?" Jack stated in surprise as his wife stepped from the cab in front of him. "Kitty! Or Kit as is," Jack waved his bottle, looking confused by what he saw, wondering if he was dreaming. "Barty! Old man, you make up the full set: king, queen and knave," Jack laughed inordinately at his own joke, repeating it and snatches of song as his three companions waited in stony silence.

Day Twelve – Saturday April 26th 1886

Jack awoke the next day with the feeling he had lain, without sleep, on a bed of rocks. He ached from head to toe, was bathed in sweat, exhausted and in desperate need of a drop to bring him too his senses and alleviate his woes. As he struggled out of the bed and into the parlour, he found Kitty, still dressed as Kit, and Bartholomew sat at the table with a sailor's knapsack and a suitcase stood by the door.

"I had the strangest of dreams," he informed them both, slumping into the only other chair in the room.

"It was no dream, Jack." Kitty informed him, doffing her hat to show him her neatly barbered hair.

"Dear God in Heaven," Jack blasphemed, incredulous at the sight, Kitty's masculine haircut making her look like a man in his thirties, now even without make up to darken her chin she could pass down a street in broad daylight.

"Martha went with me and paid the barber a fortune to cut it in the latest of mens' fashion," Kitty explained. "Even then I thought he might stab us with his scissors, cursing us both under his breath for having unnatural desires. Martha, however, was fierce enough to cower him, stating, in no uncertain terms, 'if she wanted her *friend* to pass as a man it was no business of his'. Afterwards we went to my place to collect the few things I'd need," she nodded to the suitcase. "Then I dropped her at your son's house and returned here. Barty has collected and returned with his things whilst I kept watch on you. Martha will be with us in a short while."

"My son's?" Jack pondered, trying to make sense of what he heard.

"For money, your wife has promised us a grub stake," Kitty told him, sighing slightly so that Jack would know she was sad at what she now told him. "Barty and I leave today for Canada, to make new lives for ourselves."

Jack sat for a long time in thought, then perplexed Kitty by asking, "You knew John Wesley Blackstaff tolerably well, isn't that what you told me? And about these tarot card things?" Jack had recollected the conversation but not when it took place, it coming to his mind at that point must, he thought, mean something.

"Yes, tarot cards. An old colored woman read my future with them," Kitty, having expected Jack would raise objections to her leaving, was not happy to be asked such an odd question.

"And these cards are special to coloreds?"

"To many types of people, of many races and stations in life, many that pray for guidance from God still want to divine their future if they are able," Kitty told him, realising Jack was not going to try and stop her from leaving, it not only confirmed she did the right thing but also how little she really meant to him.

"How? What do the pictures mean?"

"The compass means 'good fortune ahead'," Barty put in but could add no more, he never fully understood the working of the cards.

"Two people hung the wrong way up," Jack wanted to know, ignoring the Canadian, "what does that mean?"

"'The Hanging Man'," Kitty corrected Jack. "A man hung by his ankle with his other leg crossing, like an upside down four. It is the symbol for treachery; treasonous actions by or against you, someone will lie to you or deceive you. Why?"

"And, John Wesley knows about this code?"

"He knows how tarot cards work, we spoke about them when I was in his office," Kitty told him. "Jaunty, who was acting as my protector for the day, made fun of it afterwards, 'only a darky could be so superstitious,' he said. But, I know plenty of all types that heed the cards."

"Does it denote anything different if it is a woman that is hung so?" Jack asked, interrupting Kitty's recollections.

"Not that I know," Kitty despaired at Jack's addled thoughts to bring up such a matter at this time. "My old maid once said that female slaves where whipped so if they displeased their masters. Her mother had been a slave, had been brought over on the ships as a child and had told how she remembered her mother being hung upside down and beaten. She learned later that women were beaten if they did not lie willingly with their masters when required; on the ships the sailors would hang them by their ankles, thereby weakening their legs and adding to the agony of being whipped."

Jack remained silent, the other two watching the minutes tick by on Kit's pocket watch, until, not long after, Martha returned. Thinking that Kitty was more likely to be recognised at the docks, the pair instead departed from the train station. Martha, despite being tired, said that she and Jack should return home, freshen up, eat and then visit Mr and Mrs Hugh Partkis; it would be wrong not to do so, now that Beatrice had been publicly declare dead.

Intruding on others grief is never easy, no matter if socially correct to do so. Banjo, another of Jack and Hugh's old war buddy's was leaving as they arrived; a tall, lean man whose normally sunny disposition was clouded over, his only acknowledgement of Jack and his wife being a stern nod.

Hugh paced the rooms of the small house telling Jack there would be a retribution, that there would be payment for Beatrice's death. After a short while Jack stopped trying to engage the distraught father and left him to his anger and grief and joined the women. The younger daughter served coffee and cakes whilst speaking of the funeral arrangements. Mrs Partkis was swathed, as was much of the house, in black crepe she said little and when she did speak between sobs it was only in the lightest of whispers. Jack could not make out what she said but the other two women both spoke as if they did, offering some uplifting quote from the bible or a sympathetic word, whilst Jack held his tongue not knowing what to say.

Jack was equally silent over dinner, which suited Martha as she was tired and it had been a trying day, she had no intention too attempt to further clear the air between them, as to do so now would be a mistake. Martha retired early whilst Jack sat and mused over everything, trying to put the puzzle pieces, that floated in his mind, together in a way that made sense. Eventually, as the sips of whiskey he took became fewer and he started to doze before the guttering fire, he determined with absolute certainty two things.

Firstly, Jack must find a solution to Mrs O'Shea's disappearance before Boat went in all guns blazing. And, secondly, he needed to speak with Inspector O'Leary about his suspicions that John Wesley Blackstaff was the killer of his own sister and Mary Walsh: the flask, the man's knowledge of Ruby's and what the women did there, how the pair were killed all suggested JW was the killer. The brother would consider the pair traitors; they were traitors to the Knights of Labour, on whom they jointly spied, and to their own sex for their actions at Ruby's.

Jack slept soundly in the chair, only the tugging at his right ankle by the cold hand of some unseen dread finally waking him just after dawn as the servants began to stir.

Jack had not used his cane to walk with since storming out of the house the day before last, the swelling had gone and he walked much as normal, but still it gave him a twinge every so often, especially now having spent the night asleep in a chair. He had washed, changed and started to eat breakfast before Martha stirred and he had a tray sent up to her, that she might rest a while longer. A note had been delivered for him and, as he ate breakfast, he was mulling over the message, coldly giving thought to the implications of what it required him to do and how this might fit with his plans, when there was a knock at the door. A tired looking Sergeant Magnuson was shown into him by a concerned Hortense, who had been told by the sergeant he must speak urgently with Mr and Mrs Stevens.

"I apologise for interrupting your breakfast," Magnuson began having removed his hat and, still standing, looking much like an errant schoolboy before the senior master, "but we have found a body." Hortense in the process of closing the door behind her gasped and stopped, her shocked curiosity overcoming her sense of propriety in acting as a servant, "We believe it to be the diamond thief."

"Is there any doubt?" Jack asked between mouthfuls, noticing Hortense's reluctance to move from the doorway and scowling at her.

"The body was taken from the water late yesterday, it had been caught between two barges and had probably been there a few days," the sergeant explained. "There were no papers on him so only his height and general features have led us to believe it is the thief, Minsky."

"Hortense, stop dallying there and go to your mistress, ask her to come down as Sergeant Magnuson is here," Jack instructed, "but say nothing of what you have heard." When, some minutes later Martha entered the room in her night attire covered by a robe and followed by Hortense, the sergeant had been given a seat at the table and was hungrily devouring the ham and eggs Jack had served him from the tray.

"We await fresh coffee," Jack explained, rising to help Martha to sit before she started to ask questions. "The sergeant is here to tell us of yet another death, they believe it is your erstwhile friend, Minsky."

Martha took a deep breath, lowering then raising her head before saying, "I see, I had already feared the worst." There was pause enough for Hortense to rush back from the kitchen with a fresh pot of coffee and to begin serving it, slowly, so she would not miss anything of the dramatic tale.

"From the description Mr Stevens has given us of what Mr Minsky wore when delivering the message to you at the O'Shea's ball," the sergeant went on, pausing in his much needed meal, "it would confirm both that he is the deceased and that he was drowned the same day or the day after the ball."

"He was drowned," Martha was aghast at the thought.

"We believe he was put unconscious into the water, there are marks to his head that suggest this though we can't be certain…"

"The sergeant,' Jack interrupted, noticing his wife turn pale at the detail of the sergeant's answer, "has told me he was found near the bend in the southern branch, late yesterday. Obviously they are trying to work out who might have done this and he is here to ask if we know the names of any of his acquaintances."

"That is correct, Mr Stevens," the sergeant realising he had said too much in the presence of a lady, confirmed.

"There was only one name he mentioned, Black Rube," Martha stated, confused and shocked she could not remember what she had already told the police and, for the moment, she was done with the tangle of lies and deceit.

"A dangerous fellow," the sergeant informed them and not thinking of anything else to say looked at Jack for any further information as Martha had fallen into a reverie.

"I believe," Jack went on, "he had only returned to Chicago a little while ago and was keeping himself away from his old friends, his meeting with Mrs Stevens being the exception. Given what we now know that meeting is suspicious and I doubt if it was accidental on his part." Martha glared at Jack but said nothing. "You might have more luck asking Brandon O'Shea about those Minsky used to consort with, perhaps he was unlucky enough to run into an old enemy."

"The inspector is with O'Shea as we speak," the sergeant informed them, rising to go.

"No," Jack stopped him, "finish your meal, 'Eat when you can' is my motto. But, you will excuse us as we must get ready for church."

Martha did not have to ask what errands Jack had so urgently needed to run after church, on his return after midday, she could smell the drink on his breath. Fortunately, his grandchildren didn't seem to notice as he played soldiers with them, little Harland advancing his lead troops towards his grandfather's cannon whilst Sarah sat beside him trying to intrude one of her dollies upon the game, or as Jack told Abby and Martha, "At last the much needed reserves, the 'little fillies' come to the rescue of the beleaguered cannon which fall under the mighty onslaught of Major General Harland Jackson Jacob DeWert's gallant men."

Despite the gaiety of the family dinner both Martha and Jack were subdued as they were driven home in the carriage Jack had hired for the day, the long package he had placed under the seat before they had left in the morning unheeded. A young, uniformed police officer waited for them on their doorstep.

"What now?" Martha sighed, tired and exasperated. "What more can they want to know about poor Ibrahim?"

"Perhaps they have found the diamonds?" Jack wondered as they pulled to a stop and Gideon, their man-of-all-works, who had obviously been keeping a discreet eye out for their return, hurried to open their carriage door. "The sergeant was reticent to talk about them this morning."

"Tell the inspector I will be there shortly," Jack informed the young copper after a brief conversation, then turning to Gideon, "Have the carriage wait and take the package under the seat up to my study."

"What is it now?" Martha irritably demanded her nerves drawn bow tight. "Haven't they questioned us enough that they must summon you to answer for Minsky?"

"It isn't about Minsky that they wish to consult with me," Jack took her hands and led her to a chair, seeing her seated before continuing. "There has been another murder, this time it is Brandon, he has been shot and killed." Martha could not comprehend his words at first, but stared up at him, her face blank. "Four deaths in almost as many days, it is a terrible thing. They are obviously linked, Brandon, Nina, Beatrice and Minsky, and the motive would seem to be the diamonds but O'Leary wants to discuss with me how Brandon was shot."

"Why? Why you, Jack?" Martha suddenly asked as her brain finally managed to absorb and piece together what she was being told.

"To be honest I don't exactly know," Jack confided, "but the message referred to Brandon being shot with a rifle and the killer has escaped so I fear they suspect Boat."

"It is no great shot," Jack informed the inspector as he peered over the roof ledge down the street to the front of O'Shea's hotel, "but would have taken a steady hand."

"Really? That is an insight we would not have gleaned without your expertise," O'Leary, having missed a meal or two and after only having had a few hours sleep between the finding of Minsky and now Brandon's killing, could be excused the sarcastic response.

"There are marks on the parapet here," Jack ignored the rebuke and was casting around the roof for something, quickly spotting the planks and crate thrown against the disused rabbit hutches in the opposite corner of the roof. "Constable would you mind helping, I have trouble bending as a result of a stiff knee."

"Someone used to breed rabbits for the pot up here not so long ago," the constable pointed out, hoping to be useful though from the inspector's disapproving look he decided silence would be a better option to adopt.

"You can see a small indent has been made here on the edge of the parapet overlooking the street," Jack pointed out, wishing he had his cane as it would have been a useful pointer. "It was made to steady the end of the rifle, suggesting the shot was lined up before Brandon arrived."

"So the killer would have some knowledge of O'Shea's movements," O'Leary muttered.

"To have expected Brandon to mount or dismount from a carriage at the steps into his hotel may not have taken much forethought," Jack pointed out. "Knowing he regularly attended the Sunday morning service at the cathedral, roughly when it ends and he would return, is not that much of a secret either. However, the mark on the ledge, showing where the planks were rested on it, and the mark on the roof where the crate was placed for the other ends to rest on, does show us whoever did this knew what they were about."

"How is that?" The sergeant asked, as O'Leary bent to examine the marks and the constable positioned the planks and create.

"A man without training or experience would probably have knelt to fire over the parapet, it would have been harder to maintain his position and to keep a steady rifle. To have lain on the planks, would have given him a lower profile, so less chance of being detected from below, a steadier aim and a position he could have maintained at ease for sometime."

"Clearly a professional then," O'Leary concluded.

"As you can see," Jack took up a shooting position on the planks, again wishing for his cane that would have made a passing

175

substitute for a rifle, "a taller man would have had his feet overhang the boards positioned as they are, the end of the planks cutting into his shins would not have been pleasant, whilst a broader man would have struggled to keep his elbows in place."

"So, a man of your height and build," the sergeant commented, glancing at the inspector as he considered the obvious.

"Yes, roughly so," Jack agreed. "Boat certainly, being so much wider in his girth than I would have struggled. Whilst Banjo is taller, though you can check his shins for any marks as they would have rubbed."

"You rule out Hugh Partkis and… " O'Leary paused looking expectantly at Jack.

"Mr Graham Chappell," Jack explained, "whom we called Banjo because he could not play the harmonica worth a spit and, with Boat's aid, saved my life on more than one occasion."

"And you theirs, no doubt," the inspector said, stopping both the sergeant and constable from derailing the proceedings by asking how 'Banjo' was derived from an inability to play the harmonica.

"Yes, it was the way of things."

"From what you have said a man of your experience and stature probably made the shot?"

"Yes," Jack agreed.

"We will check on your friends, though with a daughter to bury tomorrow I suspect Mr Partkis would have been with his family and to eliminate all other lines of enquiry, before I disturb him in his grief, perhaps you can tell me where you where?"

"I'm surprised you have not dragged my wife up here to interrogate her," Jack smilingly complained. "She is quite a good shot with a rifle or pistol, I taught her myself you know. Nor have you said exactly when he was killed but if it were after morning service, it is my habit to take a stroll after church then we go to my daughter's for an early dinner. I was reenacting the Siege of Petersburg, with my grandchildren. My grandson, who is but five marshals his troops with considerable strategy, whilst my granddaughter, barely three, makes an impetuous calvary commander and leads her dollies into the fray with gusto; though with little thought for the cannons she charges." The constable did his best not to smile at Jack's description, whilst the inspector pondered why Jack seemingly tried to obfuscate his answer to a simple question.

"Sergeant, can you make a note of all this, the position of everything and so forth," O'Leary said. "We will go down."

"How is Hank?" Jack asked as the pair clattered down the stairs.

"He was splattered by his godfather's blood, as he stood on the hotel steps, so I do not believe him happy," the inspector threw over his shoulder at Jack, who lagged a little behind hampered still by the stiffness of his knee.

"You are in a foul mood, Cage," Jack observed out loud, causing the other to stop and turn to look up at him. "What do you think the motive is here?"

"The diamonds play a part, of that I am certain," Cage told him, the edge of frustration in his voice clear for Jack to hear in the echoes of the stairwell. "The insurance values them at nearly three quarters of a million, to be broken up and sold as stolen property perhaps half or a third of that but still a vast fortune. I believe Minsky was used for the robbery simply on the basis that he could bilk Mrs Stevens into helping him with getting in the house. Why Miss Partkis was killed to cover Mrs O'Shea's disappearance is not clear to me. There is no evidence of Mrs O'Shea being abducted so the only thing the poor maid's death achieved was to briefly throw suspicion onto Mr O'Shea. It is possible that the robbery and shooting are unrelated but I believe that too great a coincidence."

Cage paused, thinking he should be treating Stevens as a suspect not as a confidant. Then looking again at Jack, who waited patiently for him to resume, swept the thought aside and continued, "Either the O'Shea's concocted this whole subterfuge themselves to swindle the insurance or it has been done to discredit them. If either wanted the other dead there are easier ways to go about it. As for Brandon's killing it has been done for revenge or because there has been a falling out within the family."

"Do you think Hank, has a part in this?" was Jack's only comment, he could not fault the inspector's logic.

"You could say he now comes into his inheritance early," O'Leary mused. "With Brandon discredited he had all but taken over the running of the Irish gangs, both their criminal and more legitimate businesses. With or without the diamonds he has much to gain, nor can we find his sister who also seems to have disappeared perhaps she takes the loot to safety."

"It is a plausible theory," Jack decided to keep his knowledge of Kitty's going to Canada to himself currently. "Though I sense you have a hesitancy in this theory compared to your other lines of thinking."

"Mr Tipwell seemed genuinely distressed at his godfather's death," Cage explained his doubts, "visibly shaking as we spoke. He has also returned to his wife and newborn son, leaving his lieutenants wondering what steps to take next. That hardly sounds like the actions of a man taking a firm grasp of the reigns, had he planned the shooting he would have been better prepared to deal with the aftermath."

"Revenge, diamonds, whatever the causes and why-for's of this, I think you will only find your answer if you find Mrs O'Shea alive," Jack told Cage.

"And if she is dead?"

"Then you may never know."

It was only as he returned home to comfort Martha that he remembered he had yet to tell Cage about his suspicions concerning John Wesley Blackstaff, but given all that had occurred that day he realised it could wait a while.

Beatrice's funeral was attended by family, friends and some of the servants she worked alongside at the O'Shea household, including Fellows. The small offering of flowers the servants had brought were gratefully received, though the large wreath from Mr Henry Tipwell went 'missing' and did not make it to the service. The brightness of the warm April day and the spring flowers that filled the cemetery were at odds with and provided a stark contrast to the black clothing, the sorrowful expressions and tears of the mourners.

The wake that followed was a livelier affair, expressing a life honoured rather than the grief at an early death. Jack managed to get five minutes alone with Boat and Banjo, both claimed neither happiness nor grief at the report of Brandon O'Shea's death. Both had been discreetly questioned by Inspector O'Leary, Banjo amused that he had been asked to show the police his shins, which were unmarked. Both men had spent the previous day in each others company along with many of their friends and family. They had been at church together and then in the company of the deceased, who had been in a closed coffin in the parlour to receive less formal goodbyes from her kith and kin.

Jack, slipped away in the early evening, leaving Martha who was happy to be accompanied home by Banjo or Fellows much later. Jack stood awhile outside listening to the song that had struck up as he left, Martha's strong voice matching that of Boat's deep baritone, it had been sometime since he had heard the strains of 'San Antonio Rose'; an oddly apt love song for the occasion:

> "Deep within my heart lies a melody,
> A song of old San Antone.
> Where in dreams I live with a memory,
> Beneath the stars all alone.
> It was there I found beside the Alamo,

Enchantment strange as the blue up above.
A moonlight pass only she would know,
Still heard my broken song of love.

"Broken song, empty words I know,
Still live in my heart all alone,
for that moonlit pass by the Alamo,
And my Rose, my Rose of San Antone."

10

BAMBOOZLED

"Now here comes the worst criminal in the city," Pinky waved at Jack as he entered the Gripmans. "If you yearn to use your Beans, sergeant, then clap them on Stevens' wrists, it will be a certainty that he has been up to no good."

"If it is advice on getting your man you are after," Jack retaliated, addressing the sergeant, as he took a seat squashing the sergeant and inspector on one side of a bench table, "then go elsewhere but if you want to know how *not* to go about it then ask Pinky how he went after the James gang."

"Now, Jack," Pug interrupted before Pinky could respond, the last thing either Pinkerton wanted was Jack telling stories about them and the James Gang.

"The press are not full of headlines about the James brothers," O'Leary pointed out, "but about the deaths of the O'Shea's and how these and the deaths of the two women remain unsolved. I'm being pushed by my superiors to bring an end to all the calls of 'police incompetence' by arresting the men responsible."

"If the Tribune is anything to go by," Pug commiserated, "you're lucky to still have a job as they seem to put responsibility for the lack of action directly at your door." O'Leary made no response other than to finish his beer and order another round.

"Anything new come to light?" Jack asked them collectively.

"Minsky's neck was broken, the wounds to his head seem to have been caused when he was in the water," the sergeant told them, seeing no reason not to share the information as they met at the Gripmans to do just that, even if Stevens was not officially invited none seemed able or willing to keep him away. "And, as far as anyone can tell, he went into the river not far from where we found him, which is in reach of the Hawks."

"Black Rube jumps to mind," Jack said what all were thinking, "Martha has said that Minsky mentioned him."

'The Black Hawks are as mad as hell at the loss of Ruby's to the King's," Pinky put in, "but there has been no word of Black Rube for weeks. To all intents and purpose Ruben, Rube's nephew, was pretty much running things."

"Perhaps Black Rube wasn't happy with that and did for him?" the sergeant ventured, he toyed with his beer whilst the others drank, each taking it in turns to buy another round.

"Broken necks are more his style," Stevens pointed out. "Vitriol is something Joseph Mannheim is noted for."

"There's been no sight of him either for a few days," Pug gave them the news they already knew, whilst trying to relight his pipe. "The Kings seem to be splitting apart since old man Mannheim took to his bed."

"What ails him?" O'Leary wanted to know.

"Heart apparently, been on the books for a while and they say he'll be a goner soon."

"Didn't know he had a heart," Sergeant Magnuson made the obvious joke but raised a laugh all the same.

"Though Joe, the younger son, is in hiding he and his half of the Kings have taken over Ruby's, whilst his elder brother flounders, trying to keep the peace between the irate Black Hawks and his own divided gang," Pug informed them. "Looking for Joe and keeping tabs on the Knights of Labour has led us all over the city and the only talk we hear of is the trouble between the gangs."

"They are heading for war," Pinky told them.

"The Black Hawks are nowhere near big enough to take on even one half of the Kings," Magnusson pointed out. "They would need the help of the Dead Hands, however, with O'Shea dead and Hank in mourning they seem leaderless."

"Isn't it your turn for a round?" the inspector reminded his sergeant.

"Err… yes. Is that four beers then?"

"I'll have a brandy, double," Cage stated unsmiling, the others wanting whiskey's, again doubles. As the despondent sergeant waved a waiter over and made the order, Jack mouthed, "Bastard" at Cage and the inspector smiled back.

"How are the bairns and the misses?" Pug asked Magnuson as the sergeant turned back trying not to look as if he was mentally calculating the value of the coins he had in his pocket.

"They'll be waiting on new clothes, at this rate," Magnuson said, half seriously and half in jest at himself.

"Put these and everything else on my tab," Jack informed the waiter when he brought the drinks.

"Now look, a sergeant's pay may not be much but I can pay my way," Magnuson angrily turned on Jack, insulted by the offer to pay his round.

"Pull your horns in," Jack laughed back, "it applies to all and I only do it because I am thinking of buying the place."

"Really?" Pinky asked, though not doubting that Stevens could afford to do so if he wanted.

"Yes, though mainly so I can have you thrown out," Jack sniggered at the thought. He might even speak with Andrew about doing so as the bar diner always seemed to have plenty of customers and he'd enjoy barring Pinky. "So, the gangs are ready for war but none have sufficient advantage to kick things off ."

"That will change when Hank recovers his wits," Cage said,

thinking a partnership in a small but prosperous diner would make a good investment for a police inspector's retirement, "then the Dead Hands will have the upper hand."

"Yet the Knights of Labour suck them all dry," Pug saw another side to the argument. "Workers of all kinds from across the city are flocking to the ranks of the Knights. As they grow in strength they resist not only the exploitation of their employers but the gangs who also profit from their labour."

"Although the Knights have their divisions as well," Pinky took up the line of thinking. "There are extremists in their ranks who seek political ends beyond an improvement in workers rights, they could unsettle things yet."

"So, to sum up," Jack waved the waiter for another round, "the gangs are at logger-heads, but are currently stalemated, whilst the Knights of Labour, unless they are torn apart by the factions in their ranks, threaten the profits of both the city's employers and the gangs."

"That is pretty much how things are, Jack, a powder keg," Pug agreed, Pinky nodding alongside.

"Minsky is likely to have been killed by Black Rube," Jack continued his summary, "who may or may not have the diamonds and hasn't been seen for weeks. Ruben is likely to have been killed by Joe, probably so he could get his hands on Ruby's, and has since dropped out of site. Brandon O'Shea has been shot, for what reason isn't clear and Mrs O'Shea has disappeared."

"There is no word on any of the three we seek," Cage mournfully confirmed. "Obviously finding them is key, especially Mrs O'Shea as I believe that what she knows will clarify much."

"At least, I think I can help you with the two murdered women: Blackstaff and Walsh," Jack informed the inspector, finishing his glass.

Blackstaff's Chandlery was closing for the day, the majority of its employees had already left and the remainder were going out the door as the inspector, sergeant and Jack drew up in a police carriage. John Wesley Blackstaff was still at his desk, usually being the first to arrive and the last to leave, his equally hardworking office manager showed the three in before going home himself. The day had been warm and sunny and, though the air along the river was now chilly, the room was stuffy as the windows had been kept closed all day.

"Do you have news?" Blackstaff asked without welcome, surprised at the visit but seeming more tired than angry.

"We move ahead," Inspector O'Leary informed him. "Though we have a few more questions in order to clarify some points."

"Questions of me?"

"I believe you will be able to answer them and I did not want to disturb your parents."

"No, they are not well," Blackstaff wearily commented, his energy ebbing away and his tiredness looking to overwhelm him. "It has been a heavy blow to them both. It has even struck at my father's faith and that troubles him deeply."

"Though you are a younger man, with different needs and a different view of your faith," Cage stated rather than asked.

"Your meaning?" Blackstaff started up, momentarily alert like a fox run to ground hearing the bugle horn.

"We are men of the world here," O'Leary said in a mild tone of comradeship, "single or married, younger men have their needs, do they not? You went and sought out what you desired at Ruby's"

Blackstaff hung his head, he could not deny the facts the others already knew but whether this caused him shame or frustration from being found out the others could not tell. "Yes," he finally admitted, "I went there at times, not often. After each visit I told myself it would be the last, but what I saw invaded my dreams, even my waking thoughts, and eventually drove me back to view more."

"To observe, rather than participate, seems less of a sin," the inspector hoped to make the path towards a confession a smooth one, "little more than the shadow of a sin."

"At first I thought so as well," Blackstaff admitted, "but as time went on and I thought more and more of taking part, of the unnatural lusts those sights aroused in me; then I realised how far along the road to damnation I was."

"Then you saw the one thing you could never have imagined seeing," O'Leary took Blackstaff a step closer to the admission he looked for, "your own sister, performing those lewd, unnatural acts herself, giving the lie to her innocence. Perhaps you felt responsible in some way, had opened up the path to hell along which she had travelled so much further than yourself."

"Yes," the word was barely audible, carried on the slightest of breaths, as John Wesley struggled to hold himself in control, to hold what plagued and harried him, inside himself.

"No doubt you thought at first only to punish her, to drive out the lusty devil that had gained entry and taken over the innocent soul. Unfortunately things went further than you expected, she was after all a traitor: to you, your parents, her sex, even to the Knights of Labour. To the very things you both believed in, so you thought to make an example of her?"

"What?" Blackstaff was shaking his head, his expression one of confusion and bafflement at the words. "No, I was horrified by what I saw, I could not believe it was her, not at first. By the time I was convinced of her identity I was already gripped by lust. Her flesh, the smoothness of her skin, her thighs and buttocks, the roundness of her breasts. How she touched the other woman, their caresses and kisses had already inflamed me, engulfed me like the fires of hell." The three watched, stupefied and embarrassed, as Blackstaff writhed before them, fighting to remain in control of himself.

"You took them, dragged them to that out of way place where none could see, hung them with tackle from your own shop, beat them and strangled the life out of them," the inspector, angrily told the 'guilty' man, demanding a confession in the face of overwhelming motive and evidence, but only meeting an incredulous shaking of Blackstaff's head in denial. "You left them naked and obscenely tied as a message, based on your own superstitious beliefs handed down to you by your grandfather, from you to the world of sinners. Isn't that the case?"

"No!"

"Or was the message for you sister only, to carry to hell with her? She also knew of the tarot cards, she had been shown them as a child, seen them on your wall. She would understand the evil you had seen her commit, would know the sign you made of her."

"You speak madness... "

"It must have been hard work, perhaps you needed to fortify yourself or steady your resolve with a drop of rum but you dropped your flask and left it as testimony to your responsibility for those foul actions," Inspector O'Leary had risen and now towered over John Wesley, leaning with both his hands on the desk, his eyes staring the other man into submission.

"No! No, it is not so. It was I who sinned! I who lusted after her! I who should be punished!" Blackstaff intoned, his voice pleading not for mercy nor for understanding but for recognition of his guilt; not murder but lust for his sister's flesh. The two men stared at each other, both breathing hard, Blackstaff cowering in an agony of shame whilst O'Leary looked on in revulsion.

"When did you leave Ruby's?" Sergeant Magnuson asked in a quiet voice, yet causing Blackstaff to jerk his head round almost as if he had been slapped, whilst O'Leary continued to stare watching every facial tick that passed on the black man's face.

"I don't know the exact hour, but not long after midnight?" despite a slight hoarseness in his throat, Blackstaff's voice was oddly clear, his answer concise.

"When did your sister leave?"

"I do not know, she had finished sometime before, I had a drink or so before going."

"You stayed to watch other performances?" Jack asked, remembering the token system the club operated. Blackstaff nodded, almost imperceptibly, not looking at Jack or the others.

"You are lying! This is all pretence!" Inspector O'Leary bellowed, the force of his voice causing Blackstaff to push back in his chair, cringing in fear.

"No, I swear, upon the bible, I swear," Blackstaff suddenly gathered himself and pulled open a draw on his desk, pulling out a bible and placing his right hand on it, stated, "I solemnly swear as God is my witness on this bible, His holy word, that I speak the truth. I, John Wesley Blackstaff, am a sinner. I lusted after my sister's flesh, I undertook foul, lustful acts but I have not murdered, not taken any life." O'Leary's eyes never left the other man's, who in turned held his eyes steady, for a seeming eternity they held each others gaze, the room growing darker around them.

"Did you go straight home?" Magnuson's quite voice eventually broke the silence.

"I did not," Blackstaff broke from the inspector's gaze and looked at the sergeant, his voice calm as his sworn confession had seemingly given him ease. "I returned here, I often work late and sometimes stay over night at a nearby house. I was not alone."

"Who were you with?"

"A woman, I arrived there about 1 o'clock, and was with her for the night. A young colored woman by the name of Matilda Devine. Others in the house will have seen me."

"You saw nothing more of your sister?"

"Nothing until she was in her coffin, I swear… "

"Enough," O'Leary barked, "we will check your story whilst you remain here with Mr Stevens, you need not sully the good book further with you polluted touch."

Jack sat studying the tarot cards framed on the office wall with just half an eye on Blackstaff, who sat unmoving and silent his eyes closed in prayer or self-recrimination. Jack neither knew nor cared as his thoughts were on another who'd been in the room, had seen the tarot cards and, no doubt, had pocketed unseen a hip flask which he would have later filled with rum. The pair of capuchins finally had their silence broken by the return of the two police officers.

"It seems they know you well at that disorderly house," the inspector said, his tone mocking Blackstaff. "They consider you quite the gully, charging you ten times the value of the canes you pay Matilda to break across your back. She, and others, remember you that night and confirmed you stayed until dawn. They also said that you have been there since, wanting punishment for your sins, when it would have been better to seek repentance from God."

"I try… "

"Give me none of that, your weak-willed tries count for nothing with me," O'Leary was in a cold rage and both Jack and Magnuson watched him lest he finally broke and went for Blackstaff with his fists. "I watch you from now on, I will set eyes upon you around the clock. If it were not for your parents I would arrest you now but it would be a death sentence for them both to learn of your disgusting behaviour. Your slate is wiped clean but should you put any mark on it from this hour forward I will know it and will have you before a judge and publicly condemned. Do you understand me, you damned rogue?"

"Yes, yes I understand," Blackstaff almost fell to his knees at this reprieve, but stood instead as if to shake the inspector's hand. The sergeant already had O'Leary by the arm to stop a blow that would have come in response to the outstretched hand.

"Remember the inspector's words well," Jack told Blackstaff, also ignoring the man's outstretched hand and helping Magnus quietly usher O'Leary out the room, "or arrest and public shame will be the least of your worries."

"I thought him on the verge of a confession," O'Leary muttered once again. Jack had insisted they accompany him home for a nightcap, the police constable who drove the carriage was sent to the kitchen for a supper whilst Jack, Cage and Magnuson had whiskey in the parlour.

"I expected the same," Jack sympathised, "but I don't think he lied, though it wasn't his putting his profane hand on the bible that convinced me but the decanter of brandy in his office, no rum at all."

"The inspector raised hell at the brothel house," the sergeant confirmed his superior's thoroughness, "and put the fear of God and the Chicago police force into every man jack of 'em. Though they stuck to their story in support of Blackstaff being there. It wasn't until then that I was convinced."

"It still leaves the question of who is responsible, if not Blackstaff," Jack mused, emptying his glass and topping everyone up.

"We know they went to Ruby's to find out more about Chicago Joe," Cage revived, having downed his glass and waited for a refill. "Their ruse to take the part of participants gave them entry and a degree of safety, but either Joseph Mannheim or Ruben grew suspicious. With Ruben dead that leaves only Joe as our quarry and we seek him in any case."

"It is our most likely path," Jack agreed, "though the flask and the manner of the women's death still troubles me." The sergeant was about to ask why when there was a clattering at the front door, Jack beat Gideon to opening it and found a tipsy Martha, who he had assumed already retired for the night, and an embarrassed Fellows on the step.

"Hello, dear Jack," Martha greeted her husband with a smile and a wave. "I stayed behind to help clear up after the wake. Fellows here was a marvel, he cleared and tided the place in a flash while I washed the glasses and plates, Mr and Mrs Partkis were most taken with our mutual skills in the household way of things…" her words petered out as she spied the inspector and sergeant, though not for long as she took up another line of thought. "Why, if the Pinkertons were here we'd have quite the set of detecting nitwits." Jack smiled indulgently, Fellows bid them all a "Hale goodnight," and the inspector and sergeant beat a hasty retreat. "I grow more like you everyday," Martha stated, pushing past Jack, "coming home drunk and ill-tempered appears to be catching."

Martha was determined to prove her witticism at the detectives expense correct, insisting she and Jack go over every aspect of all the deaths that had occurred since the two hanging women had been found. With little grace and much ill-temper, she criticised the many dead ends the police and Pinkertons had explored. Then wondered why, if they all believed Black Rube responsible for Minsky's death, the killer had not been brought to justice.

Jack weathered the storm at anchor, the gales and icy blasts leaving him unmoved; his only comment was, "These things take time, whilst the others scour the streets for sightings and information I will go to Hank, it is time he took things in hand and brought his influence to bear in resolving this."

"It is odd," Martha wearily said, as they fell asleep, "that there should be so much love at the centre of all these horrific acts."

"What?" Jack asked, suddenly wakeful again at Martha's thought but she already slept.

Day Fifteen – Tuesday April 29th 1886

"Let me guess, Jack, you are here to persuade me to put my grief behind me and take up the mantle that Brandon's death has placed at my feet," Hank smiled across the desk in his study.

"Yes, though not in such prosaic terms," Jack replied. Martha had insisted on coming with him to Hank's smart Rush Street home and was upstairs with the other womenfolk viewing the newborn babe, "I take it I am not the first."

"A relay of senior members of the clan have been in and out already this morning, the last being that jumped-up little turd, Jaunty."

"No doubt he presumed on his close blood relationship to

you," Jack assumed, Hank seemed unexpectedly calm, a man who had already decided on his plan of action.

"He did, and no doubt expects a considerable reward for his troubles," Hank went on, "though he might be disappointed on that score. It surprises me that you are here on the same mission, you not even being a blood relation."

"Nor Irish or Catholic, God save me from the shame of both," Jack said, just earnestly enough for it to sound insulting. "Is that Jaunty's glass? On the tray by the decanters there?"

"Yes it is," Hank laughed, Jack cared for no man in this world but himself and Hank rather admired that in the old-timer, "he helped himself, much as you did, though to the rum rather than the whiskey."

"I was beginning to think him a rum drinker," Jack mused, swirling his whiskey in his glass, to watch the legs drain down the side.

"He is that, for many a year," Hank said, puzzled at Jack's twisting conversation. "The only answer I can give you is the same as I gave him and all the others, is that I will not do anything until Brandon is in his grave, two days from now."

"Only it won't be what any of them expect," Jack concluded. "You are at a crossroads and I think you have chosen your path, but it isn't the one you have been raised to take."

"No, though you'll do me the honour of keeping this to yourself."

"Of course," Jack shrugged as if saying there could be no other way, "you are a straight dealer and I respect that."

"In a very short while I and my immediate family, that is my wife, child and mother-in-law, all leave for the west coast," Hank stated, leaning back in his chair, his tone almost daring Jack to put forward arguments to counter him.

"This does not sound a recent decision," for some reason Jack felt relieved, glad that Hank had chosen a different course for his life.

"A year ago I sent my nephew, Kitty's son, west to buy properties on my behalf. He has done well and I move out there to lead a quieter life as a legitimate business man on my own account. I will keep him on as general manager if he wishes it."

"You have managed to keep this secret? Even from your godparents and sister?" Jack could see there had been much intriguing going on in the O'Shea household.

"Some while ago I realised Brandon had been converting many of his personal assets, including a quantity of the diamonds that were presumed stolen, to buy into legitimate businesses such as DeWert Holdings and to purchase political capital for Chester DeWert. Your son-in-law, as I am certain you know, is the *coming man* and Brandon wanted to be certain he had his ear. His intention was to create a financial empire for me to inherit so that I could shake off the need for the Dead Hands."

"Is that so different from your own plan?" Jack asked, helping himself to another glass and offering Hank one, which was turned down.

"Severing links with the Dead Hands, with the Tipwells and my kin, would be no easy thing for me, despite what Brandon thought. Do you think that any of my clan would give up their old ways simply to give me an easier time of it?" Hank was almost arguing his case to Brandon, taking the opportunity to do now what he did not have the chance to do whilst his godfather lived, "I will not have my son grow up in the shadow of the likes of Jaunty, and there are a good few of my clan as bad as my cousin."

"So you will move away and leave your clan to find a new chieftain?" Jack asked, though seeing Hank's resolve clearly showing in his face.

"Jaunty brought me a package this morning," Hank said in way of an answer, reaching into a draw and putting an open box on his desk, Jack could see the glittering diamonds it contained. "About two thirds of the diamonds that were actually stolen, a third of the originals having already been sold by Brandon and replaced with paste ones."

"That's about about $300,000 or so," Jack calculated, noting that Jaunty had been the delivery boy.

"I have no idea, probably a great deal less as they are without the settings and depending on how and where they are sold. Though it is more than enough to live in luxury," Hank seemed almost scornful of the thought, glancing at the box and its contents as if he looked on some piece of excrement.

"They are from your Godmother, Nina?" Jack felt the ground growing firm beneath his feet as he saw a path that could lead to finding her.

"Who else? She hated Brandon for many years, the humiliation of his many affairs, the parade of fancy girls and floozies. Worse still he had by-blows enough, some say me included," Hank glanced up, realising he had said more than he meant but seeing no judgement, not even surprise, in Jack's eyes. "Well, she could not have children of her own, so I became her son. My sister, being older and more independent fought off the affection offered her and the pair never were at ease. But, I was happy to gain such love again.

"My father and Brandon were close cousins and grew up friends, they both fell in love with the same woman. But Brandon was destined for the leadership of the clan, following on his uncle as chieftain, as such he was expected to marry with the interests of the clan in mind. The choice was Josephine Patricia O'Brione, plain and shy but daughter of the family which led the dock, river and rail workers, men on whose shoulders Chicago's wealth is carried. It was a powerful alliance."

"Until the Knights of Labour came along," Jack realised, putting another piece in place.

"The Knights did not need to take power from Nina's family, they made converts of them and her family gave it all to the cause," Hank, sighed at the fragility of human nature and how good intentions could lead to bad outcomes. "It left my godmother, Nina, with nothing to hold over Brandon."

"Brandon also saw the threat the Knights posed but, rather than fight them decided to take a different path. Leaving Nina fearing he might win you over and she might lose you as well," Jack filled in another piece for himself.

"I did not see it as a battle between one or the other," Hank stated sorrowfully, "but for her it was all or nothing. She wanted her vengeance and my undying gratitude." Hank paused, he knew it was his love above all else she wanted, a son's love and respect for his mother, but she could not win from him more than he already gave. "She has been using Jaunty to manipulate and diminish the Kings and Black Hawks, as well as to plot against the Knights. I do not know the details but I can see the confusion and uncertainty that grows on the streets. She wanted Brandon humiliated, as he humiliated her, before having him killed. All done so she could hand me an empire: the gangs, workers, industry, finance, the political support, everything that is required to run this city."

"You've no idea where she is, I take it?' Jack already knew the answer but had to ask the question, he intended to leave no reason for Cage to question Hank.

"None, or I would send these back," Hank tapped the box causing its contents to rattle. "Jaunty was silent on the matter, he is under the strictest of orders to say nothing of how he is in contact with her and he fears her retribution more than my persuasion."

"What about Joe Mannheim? or Black Rube?"

"Jaunty is in touch with Joe, I know he goes to a place north of the stockyards but I haven't found out the exact address. Black Rube hasn't been seen around for some time, all I know are the old rumours that Rube used to work for my godparents," Hank stated, pausing before adding, "I should thank you for helping Kitty."

"Oh. How is that?" Jack could think of nothing more to say.

"You can take your finger off the trigger of your revolver,"

Hank gave a hearty laugh. "I know it your habit to keep your hand on the revolver in your pocket but you have no cause to shoot me with it. My thanks are sincere. Kitty is safe in Canada, I may not like the look of her travelling companion but she has only ever wanted her independence and I regret I stood in her way of gaining it."

"I see," Jack stated, not at all clear that he did.

"I have had her watched for a few days past and I know you and Martha helped her, even to the disguise and money. Somehow you both seem to have that instinct to help others without question." Hank's gratitude seemed sincere and heartfelt so Jack decided not to disillusion him and instead rose to shake his hand, wishing Hank and his family good fortune.

Jack took Martha to lunch and talked about going to the theatre, they had not been out together for some time and, given recent events, he thought it would help repair any rift between them.

"There can never be any rift between us," she assured him. "Though a play or the opera would be a pleasant change."

"Good," he agreed, "then all is settled and harmonious between us?"

"Of course Jack. We have traversed many difficulties and always come out the other side stronger in our love for each other."

"I am glad of it," he smiled. "Then we should be getting back in order to prepare."

"Prepare?"

"Yes, for dinner, with our friends from the Pinkerton agency and the Chicago police force," Jack explained, finishing his last mouthful of steak, "I have sent word to the four of them to dine with us so we can discuss our plans."

"Of course, our plans," Martha smiled, though her eyes spoke of a less than happy emotion. "I take it these are the plans to bring Minsky's and Beatrice's killers to justice?"

"The very same," Jack saluted her insight by raising his glass. "Along with Miss Blackstaff's and Miss Walsh's was well."

The beef soup was hot, thick and perfectly flavoured, so Jack was taking his time savouring it. The table had a lack of 'balance' as Martha and Fellows expressed it when commenting on the fact there was only one female diner: Martha. However, doing their best to accommodate this, they placed Pug opposite Cage and Pinky opposite Magnus with Jack and Martha at the table ends. Jack had asked Hank if Fellows could be drafted in before he had left the younger man to both mourn his godfather and rejoice in his new son. With the O'Shea residence temporarily shut, and likely to close permanently, Fellows was more than content in doing service for the Stevens'.

"As soon as I had your message about Mr Jaunty Tipwell I had a watch set upon him," Magnus Magnuson told Jack, whilst trying his best not to slurp his soup and making a mental note of everything he saw and heard in order to relate it to his wife later that night.

"I don't know why I don't just turn my entire section over to you," Inspector O'Leary bemoaned Jack's intrusion into police affairs.

"You should be thankful for my husband's assistance," Martha pointed out, giving O'Leary a stern look just in case he was serious in his observations, "given his wide experience in law enforcement."

"Just try keeping his nose out," Pinky ruefully pointed out, then resumed eating his soup as Martha glanced his way with a clear warning in her eyes to 'mind his manners'.

"I simply passed on information and your sergeant acted on it, rather efficiently as it seems," Jack explained, nodding and smiling at Magnus.

"Forgive my surliness," O'Leary, who was much more socially adept and used to dining in elegant company than he let on, "however, I have spent the morning explaining to my superiors my lack of progress and the dead ends I have run down. Whilst the afternoon has brought in no new information or leads."

"Then perhaps we should change the subject," Martha suggested. "If Fellows will bring the fish whilst Hortense clears the table."

"We also have had a busy day," Pug pointed out as Fellows served him. "The rumour that the Knights of Labour plan a big rally have been confirmed. It is to take place in a few days, 3rd May to be precise, at the McCormick Reaper Works in support of the strike there."

"These strikes are a terrible thing," Martha stated, "Chester said they are costing the McCormick's thousands of dollars, I believe he and Andrew are dining with the father and elder son tonight in order to discuss what can be done."

"Along with the Pinkerton brothers," Pug informed them all, "as well as the police commissioner and the deputy mayor."

"Quite the gathering," Jack commented. "Let us hope they eat as well as we do, Fellows please tell Hettie this fish is delicious."

"Yes, sir," Fellows smiled an acknowledgment of thanks on behalf of the staff, he'd been in the house only a few hours but had already established himself as the head servant.

"Do you have any truck with these Knights and strikers?" Pinky asked the Englishman.

"I have no thoughts on the matter, sir," Fellows was quick to respond, noticing Mrs Stevens' look of annoyance at her guest's question he sort to smooth over the contentious debate. "On the whole I have found house servants are generally loyal to their masters, when working in a household, no matter how large, one is in contact with the family. Whilst for the average labourer, working in their hundreds and without site of the owners their loyalty goes to the man at their shoulder."

"Much as it is in the army," Jack pointed out, taken by the thought. "You fight for the men either side of you, not the officers or some great ideal."

"Not unlike the gangs that run the streets," Magnus pointed out, he had enjoyed the fish and wine more than he thought he would, "most have grown up in the same neighbourhood and many are related by blood or marriage, it creates a close bond. Though they are quick to exploit the weak and vulnerable that live and work around them."

"The pork, if you would Fellows. The fish has been so well received it has disappeared from our plates," Martha did her best to lighten the table conversation. "How are your children, Mr Burke? And your wife is well I take it?" Martha turned to Pug.

"All in excellent health, thank you Mrs Stevens," Pug told her, his face lighting up at the thought of his family, then quickly returning to a less happy countenance. "I have not been home much recently, we have been keeping a close eye on the more extremist elements who associate with the Knights as we are fearful they will resort to violence."

"I thought the Knights of Labour only supported peaceful protests and rallies," Martha stated, her curiosity of current events overcoming her desire for a more genteel dinner conversation.

"That is their public view, but the struggle for worker rights is not an easy path to tread and the employers can be as robust in defence of their capital as the workers are in demanding improvements in their rights. And men, like Joseph Mannheim, exploit the situation by providing the means to turn the throwing of fists into the hurling of lead and dynamite," Pug stated without thought, causing Hortense to drop a fish knife as she cleared the table. "I apologise," he quickly added, "I dwell too much on the evils in society."

"I hear that the Reverend Blackstaff might speak at the rally following the protest," Pinky told them, believing himself to be on a safe topic as far as Mrs Stevens was concerned, "though I believe he is still far from recovered from the news of his daughter's death."

"I fear, as things stand, he may never recover," Cage told them without thought, the roast pork being his main focus.

"Our prayers, are with him," Martha stated, looking genuinely sympathetic of the parents loss. "It is a tragic thing to loose one so young, with such potential as I understand the daughter had."

"Amen to that dear wife," Jack agreed, realising that they had a daughter of a similar age and what her loss would mean to them. "You said love was at the heart of these foul deeds, as strange as the thought seems, I agree."

"How so?" Cage asked, the idea intruding on his enjoyment of the pork and wine.

"The love that existed between the two young women, I believe, gave them them the courage to visit Ruby's and it was the *love* of violence that led to their murder."

"That is not what I meant, Jack," Martha was obviously aghast at the thought.

"It is hardly the same thing," Cage also protested.

"Love is never the same for any two people, even those that love each other," Jack explained, raising his glass and nodding to his wife, receiving a 'blushing smile' in acknowledgement of the compliment from Martha. "However, if you define *love* as being an intense relationship with someone, then it can apply to many situations. Even to a killer, who so lusts after pain and humiliation of the one he destroys, that it is a love of sorts and is undoubtedly remembered by the killer with considerable pleasure for the remainder of his days. Which hopefully will not be many."

"Fellows, I must apologise for my husband," Martha had turned to the English butler in despair. "You understand our normal table conversation is not so dark and grim as it is currently. Our guests profession and the absence of their wives turns the talk to such low and unpleasant thoughts."

"It is perfectly understandable, Mrs Stevens," Fellows was unperturbed, it not being his place to listen to what was said as he served at the table, though truth was he found the discussion considerably more interesting than many he had overheard in his years of service. "Such political theories and deep philosophies are rarely heard outside of the most refined households."

"There, Martha," Jack raised his glass again, "I have been called many things but never *refined*, now you have the truth of it. I am not the dog you all think me." The sentiment raised a laugh as well as Martha's despairing eyebrows.

"What is more," Cage determined to continue, as Fellows started to clear the meat course, "if what you told us about Mrs O'Shea and your belief she is at the back of all these acts, then it is the *love* for her godson that is her motivation."

"Though Black Rube is a dark mover in all this," Martha said, surprising them all that she continued in the same vein that she had rebuked her husband for, "and I can see nothing of *love* in his actions in these dire events." The conversation might have continued in this manner through dessert, cheese and port but a knock at the front door and a message, brought in by Fellows, for the sergeant interrupted proceedings.

"We have them!" the sergeant stated triumphantly, having read the message and passed it to the inspector. "Jaunty Tipwell has led my men to an address in a residential area to the northwest of the stockyards. It is outside the Kings main territory but a convenient distance from Ruby's, an area of quite and unassuming apartments of the middling sort. My men are watching the place and have seen many they identify as members of the Kings go in and out and have now also seen Joseph Mannheim at one of the windows. I can take a detail and arrest him within the hour."

"It will need preparation," O'Leary contradicted his sergeant, though gently as he understood the other's desire for action after so many days of frustration. "Have more men sent discreetly to the area to lock it down, though under no circumstances inform the local coppers in case one is in the pay of the Kings. Then have plans ready for a dawn raid, using only our most trusted men. I assume we can also count on the support of the Pinkertons?"

"Ourselves and four others, perhaps half dozen more if we can get hold of them," Pug assured him.

"Then meet us at the precinct station an hour before dawn, if we catch them sleeping it will be a less bloody affair." The meal was over and the four men out of the door too attend to their preparations, apologising and thanking Martha, whilst Jack waved and nodded and finished his desert, then starting on the cheese and port.

Fellows was sufficiently startled by the sudden turn of affairs to look slightly perplexed, but continued calmly to pour the port, quite a good bottle he thought, for his temporary master. Martha, having fulfilled her hostess duties of seeing her guests out of the door, returned and took her seat, sat upright, hands folded in her lap and giving Jack a hard stare.

"Habit, I am afraid dear," he said, motioning that she should join him in a port now they were alone, "formed long ago. I always eat a hearty meal before a dawn raid, in case it intrudes on breakfast and lunch." The jest, however, did not seem to alleviate Martha's anxieties.

11

AN UNRAVELLING

Day Sixteen – Wednesday April 30th 1886

Jack was the last to arrive at the police station. He had jogged along on the horse he had sent Gideon to rent for the day, surprised at how many birds filled the air with their dawn chorus. The air itself seemed sweeter in the half-light of dawn; it was damp from the overnight rain with the mildest of breezes bringing a slight but pleasant chill that woke and heightened the senses. The deserted, birdsong filled streets hardly seemed like the city and he could almost imagine himself out on the prairie again, if it wasn't for the plodding mare on which he sat. He had used to own a good horse for many years, a powerful and clever animal, but it had not taken to city life, the noise and bustle spooked it and the paved roads were not to its liking and, after a short while, Jack had sent the creature back to the small western boomtown he had been sheriff of; a present to a young man of color he had known.

"You look like a gunslinger," O'Leary had told him, much to Jack's annoyance, though given that he wore his range clothes, more suited to riding and the work ahead for the day than the town suits Cage and the sergeant wore, and with his stetson, three pistols, Winchester and pockets that rattled with spare ammunition, it was an understandable observation to make. "But as a civilian I can't let you come with us. I have a dozen officers in street clothes already at the scene and two dozen uniformed men to take with me and five Pinkertons, as much as I'd like you beside me Jack I can't let you attend."

"Six," Pinky stated loudly, standing to the side of them, his comment cutting across whatever response Jack was about to make.

"What's that?" the inspector turned to the smartly dressed diminutive detective, who also carried a Winchester.

"Six Pinkertons," Pinky smiled broadly, knowing Jack would be as put out having to thank him as the ex-sheriff and bounty hunter would be at being called a gunslinger. "Mr Stevens is with us, under my command as a temporary agent. Given his shooting skills we thought he would be an asset to have with us today."

"Very well," O'Leary was not displeased. "Stay with the Pinkertons who will cover the rear of the property we raid whilst I and my men go in at the front. Apart from myself all other men entering the premises will be in uniform so take care who you shoot at."

"I'll try not to put a bullet in my own foot," Jack sarcastically replied to Cage's back as the inspector strode off. Then turning to Pinky, "What are you waiting for? An Invite?" and followed the inspector out of the station.

Jack and the other Pinkertons were on horseback whilst the police rode on their specially made wagons, on which the uniformed men sat back-to-back facing outwards towards the side.

"The house we go to," Pug, who rode on Jack's right on a huge gelding suitable for a man of Pug's great stature, informed him, "is at the end of a row, the gable end is windowless and faces across the street to a high wall of a manufacturing works on the opposite side. We are to cover the rear of the house, there is one large courtyard that serves the rear of the entire block and the one behind, it will have all the usual outbuildings, privies, laundry rooms and washing lines and such; plenty of places for cover."

"The police led by O'Leary will go in the front, a half dozen will burst in the door, the others to remain outside with their wagons as cover to fire on the windows if needed," Pinky, who rode on Jack's left, explained. "Though the inspector hopes they will catch them all asleep at this hour and he will be inside and have them before a shot is fired.'

"A desirable outcome but unlikely, I expect," Stevens commented. "There is always someone on watch or wakeful enough in such places. What happens if they can't breech the front door?"

"They retreat behind the wagons, pushing them over for cover and return fire from there," Pinky told him. "The inspector plans to have men on the roof who will try to gain entry from there as well."

"The buildings have flat roofs," Pug said, pulling his horse, that seemed keen to get to its destination, back in line with the other two that jogged along at a more leisurely pace, "he will have two men on the roof opposite as well to cover the upper story windows. Other men will clear the apartments opposite the house we raid so the occupants are not caught by stray bullets."

"More men follow on behind," Pinky looked back as they crossed West 31st Street and continued heading south, but could see no sign of the additional force, "they will cordon the streets to keep onlookers and passersby away."

"It sounds a well thought out plan," Jack commented. "How many apartments in the house?"

"Five, we are told," Pug commented. "One on the first floor opposite a kitchen, that extends out the back, then upstairs on the second floor are two apartments and same again on the third floor with stairs continuing up to the roof. The sergeant says they have counted sixteen men inside including Jaunty and Joe, with four fancy girls in addition."

"All well armed no doubt,' Jack assumed.

"Given what they found when they raided Ruby's they suspect there may be dynamite as well," Pinky added with a deep scowl, he had experience of blowing up a house and had not liked the results so did not enjoy the possible outlook of a repeat of the situation.

"It'll be hot work then," Jack commented sourly, he had had his fill of such actions many years previous in the war and preferred those situations he could control as a sniper. "Who covers the gable end? I take it they will have men there to co-ordinate what is done out back with what is happening at the front?"

"Magnuson on the front corner, another sergeant on the rear," Pug said, struggling with his horse who still hankered to take the lead. The streets remained near empty as the small convey headed southwest, the delivery wagons and occasional pedestrian taking little heed of them. Jack had expected a destination closer to the stockyards, from what he had previously been told, and was surprised when the wagons pulled over much further to the northwest then he expected. They were on the corner of a street with the wall of the manufacturing works to their left and the gable end of the Kings house opposite, the large communal rear yard could be seen in front of them and the turning into the street that fronted the block of houses was just a few paces beyond the gable end to their left.

"You all know your orders," O'Leary told them standing on the driver's seat of the first carriage and calling back in a stage whisper to the others. "You will follow my lead, I will blow a sharp whistle as we burst in the front door, fire if we are fired on, cease fire once you hear a second whistle." With that the inspector dismounted, five other men following him to stand at his side. Magnuson and a uniformed sergeant took up their positions at each corner of the gable end, two other constables ran, doubled over, one to the apartments opposite and one through the yard to the house next to the Kings, to tell the officers waiting inside that O'Leary was in position.

The remainder of the policemen were preparing the wagons to follow the first wave into the street, the horses would be taken off once the wagons were in position to avoid their injury or panic in any gunfire. Whilst the Pinkertons and Jack drew their mounts up ready to canter forward and take their positions at the rear, Jack already decided to ride over to the kitchen extension and clamber onto its flat roof as the raid started. Inevitably things where not to go as planned.

Inspector O'Leary led his men round the corner and barely before they reached the front door, shouts could be heard from inside followed by the breaking of glass and shots. The inspector's whistle sounded a piercing blast, followed by shouts of, "Police! Open up!" For a moment the advance force were pinned down, either huddled in the porch or crouched against the wall, though they returned fire as best they could to stop those inside leaning out to shoot them. However, their predicament quickly changed as as the police carriages pulled round the corner and those on board opened fire, as did the men positioned on the roof opposite, pinning the defenders down. O'Leary tried shooting the lock but the door was heavily barred on the inside so he and his men retreated to the wagons, now forming up at either side and opposite the house front.

Jack and the Pinkertons set out for the rear yard as the whistle sounded but Jack peeled off and pulled his horse against the wall and, using the saddle as a step, hauled himself up onto the flat roof of the kitchen. Almost immediately he found Pinky climbing up behind him,

"Pug and the others will watch the back," the Pinkerton, almost gleefully, told Jack as they stepped up to the rear window of the second floor, gable end apartment. Not stopping to look in, the pair smashed the glass with their rifle butts and tore down the curtains, waking a women sleeping in the bed who screamed like a pricked demon. A man, half a sleep, was with her in the bed and the naked pair tumbled over each other trying to get free of the bedclothes. Another man lay in a second cot to the left of the window and, as Jack and Pinky smashed their way in, he sat up gun in hand. Neither Jack nor Pinky hesitated, smoothly reversing their rifles, and fired killing the man instantly.

The first man, now shrieking to match the banshee wail of his bed companion, threw up his hands and shouted, "Don't fire, I'm unarmed. Don't fire!"

Pinky reached over the woman and clouted the man with the butt of his rifle, knocking him senseless. Then pulled the naked woman out of the bed, shouting, "Get underneath and stay hid, keep out of the way." Jack jumped past him to the bedroom door that led to the front room, ready to fire as he dropped to his knee in the doorway. There was a man with a rifle already halfway across the room to help repulse the attack on the rear bedroom, another knelt by the window firing out into the street.

Jack put two bullets into the man advancing on him, a shot from the man's rifle splintering the wood above Jack's head. The man by the window turned, firing as he did so, as Jack ducked back. One of the man's bullets hit the open door, another smacked into the wall beyond the door and the third hit the floor just beyond Jack's knee. Jack could hear gunfire from both the front of the house and the rear, shouts and calls from all over but through it all he listened intently for the sound of the man moving position and was rewarded by hearing him crash into a chair as he attempted to flee the room. Jack barely had to poke his rifle round the door frame and the man, retreating through the door into the hall, put himself squarely in Jack's sights. Stevens squeezed the trigger as the man half flew out of the room but wasn't certain if he had hit the fleeing man.

Jack was up, but Pinky was quicker and was through the bedroom door and at the hall door before Jack could take a pace, his left leg still slowing him. Pinky put two shots into the man who sprawled on the hall floor, then launched himself out into the hall aiming to cross it and enter the room opposite. However, shots from inside the other apartment, the door of which was open, caused Pinky to do a neat duck and roll to seek cover at the top of the stairs going down to the floor below. As Jack reached the door of the first apartment Pinky was already returning fire with those in the front room of the second apartment. From the cover of his doorway Stevens was in a much better position to see the occupants of the other room, opening fire himself and sending the three men he could see diving for cover.

Above him on the third floor he could here shouts of, "Police, put down your weapons!" intermingling with gun fire. The men O'Leary had put on the roof had forced their way in and down the stairs onto the floor above and were clearing the two apartments up there of combatants. Jack signalled to Pinky that they should move to either side of the door opposite so they could shoot into the room at different angles and keep the occupants pinned down. Even as they went to move the gun battle that had raged at the front of the house suddenly went quite and shouts of, "Police, put your weapons down! Hands up!" could be heard from the front downstairs rooms, the police having finally entered the house from the street through the windows, the frames of which had been virtually shot out.

The battle for the house, with just a few remaining defenders at the rear, was almost over. Jack nodded to Pinky that they should move now and take the room opposite when a roar shook the house. The floor seemed to jump and both Jack and Pinky instinctively threw themselves down. A pall of dust and smoke billowed up from the first floor rear, where the kitchen was, its door blown out by the blast. Shouts, screams and gun fire could be heard from all directions. Jack, his ears ringing, could see figures moving in the smoke through the blown out kitchen doorway below.

"Hold them here, Pinky!" Jack yelled at the detective huddled on the stair top. "The police will join you from above and below in a few seconds." As Pinky, nodding in understanding, fired a shot through the door opposite to keep the occupant's head down whilst Jack leapt up and back into the room they had just vacated. As he scrambled out of the window, he had only recently smashed in, he took in two images, one was the naked female coiled up in the corner of the bedroom hands over her head and crying pitifully, and a man half-hanging out of the window above. The latter had obviously been shot through and now hung down his hands flapping like the ends of curtains in the breeze. As Jack moved across the flat roof of the kitchen he saw the Pinkertons, led by Pug, climbing into the rear window of the first floor back room and smashing into the kitchen.

As Jack reached the edge of the kitchen roof, he saw smoke and dust still billowing out across the street, debris where the wall had been blown out were strewn across the street to the high wall of the works opposite. Figures were running through the smoke, the uniformed sergeant was sprawled in the road unmoving but Jack could not see anything of Magnuson. Jack was stood directly over the hole blown in the gable end wall, a man emerged with a second close behind.

"Stop! Hands up!" Jack shouted, firing down between them for emphasis that he meant business. The second man jumped back into the building but the first ducked and turned to face upwards pointing both the pistols he held, one in either hand, up at Jack. Jack fired down, two more shots, directly into the upturned face of the man he did not recognise as Joseph Mannheim. Jack quickly let himself down the wall to the ground, he could hear the police and Pinkertons shooting at those now trapped in the kitchen to, "Give up! Drop your weapons!" Jack had no intention of getting himself shot by sticking his head in the hole that gaped in the wall, knowing whoever was to emerge next might come out shooting he backed away a few paces. Then he heard a shot from behind him, from the street they had first paused in, where O'Leary had given his final brief orders, only minutes though feeling a lifetime ago.

The smoke and dust cloud from the explosion was clearing and, turning to where the shot had come from, he could see two men fighting on the ground. Jack rushed over, his injured leg forgotten, and seeing that one man was Sergeant Magnuson and the other not, brought the butt of his rifle down sharply onto the head of the man who wasn't a police sergeant. A second man lay prone on the ground a few paces off, another escapee but this one shot by the sergeant before tackling the man Jack had knocked out.

"Tipwell, Jaunty Tipwell, has made off, down the road," Magnuson shouted as Jack hauled him to his feet, the sergeant leaping away after the fugitive before Jack could take in what he'd heard. Stevens, slow to follow, turned the corner to the front of the manufacturing works, the back of which was opposite the gable end of the house they had raided. Had the police, that had followed on the heels of O'Leary's main detachment, not been occupied in keeping a few early workers and residents of the area back from where the raid was taking place, Jaunty might not have gotten through.

"Which way did they go? Which way?" Jack shouted at no one in particular, "Two men came running this way, which way did they go?"

"Down there!" a number in the crowd shouted back.

Then a constable seeing Jack and guessing he pursued someone who escaped the raid, pointed up the street, "Up there, a man run past heading for the stable further down." Even as the uniformed man spoke, Jack saw a man in a colourful suit burst out of the stable on horseback, it could only be Jaunty making good his escape. A cabman stood in his seat well, leaning on his cab roof so he could get a better view of what occurred over the top of the growing crowd at the works gates.

"Follow that horseman," Jack shouted to the driver, running over to the cab and grabbing the door handle.

"No way copper," came the emphatic reply, the driver looking down as if at a madman, "I ain't paid enough by any fare to get myself shot at."

"Then get out of the way," Jack yelled back, using the wheel spokes like a ladder to launch himself upwards and half-leapt half-scrambled onto the seat. The driver, taken by surprise, fell backwards, arms flaying for a handhold to stop him falling. By the time he had righted himself and started to shout at Jack to, "Stop, get out you thief! Get off!" Jack had the reins and was urging the horse to turn and set off.

"Get off yourself," Jack pointed his colt at the driver, causing him to freeze, as the cab started to bound off, the horse jerking it forward. "Jump down or ride in the back but get in my way and I'll put a bullet in your dammed guts." The driver, ashen faced, took his cue and jumped down from the side of the moving vehicle, landing on his feet then tumbling head over arse in the road, ending up sitting upright in the middle of the road staring in disbelief at the back of his vehicle racing away.

As Jack settled to his task of getting to grips with the reins and setting the horse off to a fast trot, his Winchester on the seat beside him, his colt back in his shoulder holster, he realised the rider not more than a hundred paces in front of him was Sergeant Magnuson; Jaunty Tipwell being nowhere in sight.

Pug and O'Leary were both covered in dust, so much so that they looked like walking statues of themselves.

"Pinky will be bringing the women out, he has found them sheets and blankets enough to cover them," Pug explained, spitting to clear his throat, as he coughed up more smoke and dust. "Where do you want them, sent to your station or somewhere closer."

"We are still getting the injured and dead away, until we have appropriate covered carriages free have them put in one of the houses across the street," O'Leary instructed him. "The good people living opposite have opened their doors for the comfort of the wounded. There is water to be had in there," the inspector went on as Pug continued to cough, "to clear your throat."

"A good idea, I feel like I have eaten a bucket of dirt," Pug nodded his thanks as his throat was starting to feel raw. "What is the tally?"

"Fifteen men from the house are accounted for, five are killed, two others badly wounded from the explosion, the remainder with minor injuries," the inspector recited, the numbers were indelibly engraved on his mind as this had not been the normal raid that had left a few with broken heads and bruises but something far more deadly. "Of our officers, one constable is fatally wounded and there is a priest with him… "

"God give him comfort," Pug muttered, seeing O'Leary's dour expression beneath the layer of dust that covered his face. The Pinkerton realised this one death meant more to the inspector than the the others combined.

"Yes," O'Leary seemed grateful for the few words, "we pray for him but the doctor has said it is beyond hope, he was shot twice in the chest. Sergeant Henley has a broken arm and is still dazed by the explosion but otherwise uninjured, three other men have minor wounds that need tending, the others have nothing worse than cuts and bruises."

"Given the number of bullets fired back and forth we are lucky the count was not higher," Pug opinioned. "Is there any news of Sergeant Magnus or Stevens in their pursuit of Tipwell?"

"None," the inspector said, turning away to help Pinky and another of the Pinkertons to assist them in escorting the fancy girls, all of whom seemed shocked and distressed by the events they had witnessed, "though I take that as a good sign as they have obviously not given up their pursuit to report back."

Jack soon realised their chase was a bizarre one, both Jaunty and Magnus must have taken animals from the stables that were being prepared to be hitched to wagons, just how this occurred Stevens had no idea but it meant both men rode without a saddle, hanging on to what little harness had been placed on the animals. Both animals, being unused to being ridden, barely reached a canter, just fast enough to out distance a running man but little more. Jaunty, a city boy all his life, was the worst of the two riders and more than once nearly fell off his mount, bouncing around on the beast's back like some clown in a wild west show. Magnuson was, therefore, slowly closing the gap between them but so imperceptibly that it would take a couple of hours for him to actually catch-up to the man he chased.

Jack drove the carriage pell-mell, the horse was strong and seemed to savour being given its head, but dragging the cab behind gave it a considerable handicap. On the straights he actually managed to make up ground but each corner or swerve round another road user put them back and slowly they were losing ground on the two riders. As morning broke the roads were getting busier and presented more obstacles to Jack and the cab than the men riding horses. At one busy intersection Jack almost caused a collision which was avoided only by his mounting the pavement with a crash and bump that almost threw him over. Almost having lost sight of those he followed, Jack had stood up, whipping his horse on; the game animal responded with a turn of speed that would have rivalled that of an ancient chariot charging into battle. Cornering was now a game of russian roulette with the cab in considerable danger of turning over, other road users cursed and struggled to avoid the out of control cab that hurtled down the centre of the street.

"Tell Inspector O'Leary we have passed here," Jack tried to shout at one cop, controlling traffic at a busy intersection, but the red faced officer failed to hear him over his own oaths, shouted at Jack to stop and the noise of two delivery wagons crashing as one lurched into the other to avoid the speeding cab. Despite the best efforts of Jack and his horse, eventually they lost sight of the other pair, as the riders turned down a back alleyway the cab could not pass down. In the unlikely hope of catching sight of one or the other rider Jack had decided to turn down a cross street to see if he or any passerby, to whom he called, had any sight of them. Two blocks on he saw the sergeant still on horse back and trailing the second horse, emerge from an alley.

"Do you have him?" Jack shouted, pulling up to the other man but seeing nothing of Jaunty.

"Only the horse he rode, I lost sight of them in the back alleys then came upon his horse standing halfway down this one. He either hid in the shadows until I passed or has run into one of these buildings," the sergeant was breathing heavily and cast about as if expecting to catch sight of their quarry as he gave Stevens the bad news, "but it could be any building in either block backing onto the alleyway."

"We need reinforcements to help with the search," Jack said, still optimistic, getting down to help the sergeant tie the harnesses of the two horses he had to the rear of the cab. "If we can send for help we can watch the buildings from opposite corners to see if Jaunty emerges," even as he spoke Jack realised the impossibly long odds of this working and he could see from the sergeant's expression that the chase was over. "Damn, we were close."

"It's not over yet," the young sergeant reassured him, squaring his shoulders in determination, "we will scour the city for him, I will raise every station and have men out on every street looking for him."

"I know this place," Jack had stopped listening, they had moved to the corner of the main thoroughfare, a section of South Clark Street, and he was looking at the diner opposite. "Coming here by the meandering route we took in the chase I did not recognise it but this building here on the corner is the hotel Martha and I first stayed at when we came to the city six years past."

"That is good to know Jack and if we continue over in that direction we will find a police emergency telephone," the sergeant informed him, not understanding what Stevens was on about.

"I think I know where Tipwell has gone," Jack said heading for the hotel entrance but stopping by a shoeshine boy sitting in the early morning sun on the edge of the steps. "Has anyone been in here during the last few minutes?" Jack asked the ragged boy, dropping a quarter into his box of polishes, brushes and rags.

"None but an elderly couple leaving a little while back," the boy looked up, happy that the first money he earned that day came with such little effort. "They and their bags got a cab up to the station."

"Then I wager Jaunty went in by the back way, not far from where you found the horse he rode with such a lack of grace," Stevens turned to Magnuson. "Write a note for the boy to take to the nearest police station, I'll give him two more quarters and they will tip him a dollar. That's a fair rate of pay isn't it boy?" Jack smiled down at the lad, who smartly jumped up his face beaming his luck at the thought of such wealth.

"How do you know he is here?" the sergeant demanded as he hastily scribbled a note with instructions to alert Inspector O'Leary of where they were, to send reinforcements and to tip the boy a whole dollar.

"Because he has run to the one person he thinks will help him get away, a woman who has her own escape route long planned," Jack told him with a grim smile. "I believe this hotel is where Mrs O'Shea and Black Rube are hiding out."

"How can you know that?" Magnuson incredulously asked, handing over the note and watching the boy sprint off faster than the nag he had ridden in the chase.

"I have sufficient history with Mrs O'Shea for me to be certain and it will be quicker to prove my theory by entering than standing here in explanation," Jack told him, reloading his weapons as he spoke. "Take care as we go in, if I'm right, there will be armed men watching for us."

Six years previous Jack had been laying on his bed in a room on the second floor when Mrs O'Shea had knocked on his door. It was a short and angry visit, with Jack holding a gun on the tall, muscular colored man who stood in the shadow of the corridor, whilst Mrs O'Shea lambasted him. At first she thought he would angrily go after Brandon and Martha at being given news of their affair but, when realising he already knew and cared little about the situation, she resorted to goading.

"What sort of coward are you?" she demanded, every inch of her stout figure aquiver with indignation and anger. "A pander? Or a weak willed, fawning cuckold?"

Jack, torn between amusement at being so accosted and annoyance at having his rest disturbed, answered in a like vein, "And what sort of lady are you to come to a man's room with a colored ape in tow?" Jack had already levelled his pocket revolver at the 'ape' in anticipation of an attack provoked by his words, but had also managed to hook his colt out of his belt and holster hanging on the end of the bedstead with his left hand and aimed it at Mrs O'Shea. "Feel free to step forward and I will put a bullet in you both," Jack assured her, as she rained cuss words down on him and his family heritage.

After a moment or so, Jack sat himself back on the bed, keeping his guns levelled on the pair in front of him, taking his ease to show he had all the time in the world and no worries about his current predicament. Faced by such profound indifference and realising that Stevens would not hesitate to shoot, and being a sheriff thought himself above the law, Mrs O'Shea recognised the stand off and throwing further curses and cuss words over her shoulder she left. For a moment the 'ape', still a hulking shadow at the edge of the doorway, remained motionless perhaps thinking that taking two bullets to the chest a small price to pay to get at Jack's throat, but turned and left as Mrs O'Shea called, "Come Rube, we waste our time on the horned fool."

Two coloreds sat in the hotel foyer, ostensibly reading newspapers, one to the right of the stairs at the far end of the reception desk, the other to the left of the front entrance, between them they could cover each other, the stairs, door and foyer. It was as much the strategic convenience of their seating positions as the thin, pale receptionist throwing himself to the floor, as Jack and the sergeant entered, that gave the game away. Magnus had left his rifle on the stable floor, having been knocked flat as Jaunty bolted out the door on the stolen nag's back, but had his pistol at the ready. Jack had his Winchester against his shoulder as they went through the double doors, the bottle glass of its windows not giving them much hint of what lay beyond.

"Police! No one move!" the sergeant shouted, noticing the receptionist ducking down, he turned his pistol onto the man sitting to his left. "Stay put and keep your hands in view."

"Move and I shoot!" Stevens, dropping to his knee and taking aim, shouted at the man in the chair at the opposite end of the foyer. "You are a dead man if you do."

The pair of guards, despite being warned that Jaunty was followed, were taken by surprise at such quick and determined action and both raised their hands, their own guns in their laps having hoped to trap the pair between them in the foyer. Magnuson used his Beans to handcuff the two men, one wrist each through the banister rail at the bottom of the stairs, ordering them to stay quiet if they valued their skulls remaining in one piece.

"Where did the man who ran in here from the rear entrance go?" Jack demanded, pulling the quaking receptionist to his feet.

"To the second floor," the man blurted out, his voice shrill, "to the owners rooms.'

"Owners?" Jack kept a firm grasp on the young man, lest he fall down again.

"Mrs Hall," came the response, "they have the four rooms at the front, behind a locked door in the corridor for their privacy."

"They? Who are they?"

"Mr Roberts, the manager, his two associates and now the

man who just came in," the receptionist found his legs at last, though supporting himself on the desk, and Jack let go of his grasp to allow the young man to stand free.

"Roberts is a large, muscular man of color?" the youth nodded and nodded again when Jack added. "His two associates like that pair over there?"

"Do you think they know we are here?" the sergeant asked Jack as they crouched at the end of the corridor, looking at the door which kept the four front rooms sealed off from the rest of the corridor.

"We should assume so, using the rooms at the front gives them sight of the streets to the front and sides, though it blocks them from the stairs," Jack replied, thinking hard about the next move to take. "It'd not be an issue for the men who could easily climb down to the pavement but Mrs O'Shea is no climber, not even down a single storey, but then they probably never planned on Jaunty bringing us down on them."

"We should wait on Inspector O'Leary's arrival, we'll have them trapped like rats then."

"You should go and watch outside in case Jaunty tries to escape, I doubt the others would leave Nina but he would run."

"Very well, but if I hear shots I'll be back."

"Keep to your post, I'll be fine," Jack assured him, "I'll use one of the empty rooms for cover and they won't get past.'

"It won't be long before a relief force is here," the sergeant said, and he wasn't wrong. The shoeshine boy had delivered Magnuson's message and the superintendent at the local station understood its importance and was organising men to assist. Inspector O'Leary had also been informed and was racing to the scene with Pinky, Pug and two officers noted for their marksmanship, using the horses the Pinkertons had taken to the raid.

Jack waited until he had counted to one hundred, enough time for Magnus to get outside before he opened fire. His first volley of shots smashed the door lock and sent the door flying open, and the two men behind diving for cover into the first two rooms beyond.

Screams from behind him, alerted Jack to the occupants of the rooms trying to escape, he shouted for them to, "Get back and take cover!" although on the whole he was ignored, apart form one woman who hid in a wardrobe, and they threw themselves in disarray and most only partially clad, down the corridor and stairs. Jack continued to fire methodically at anything that was fool enough to poke itself around any of the doors before him.

The commotion the guests made, coming down from both the second and third floors and into the lobby, which combined with the noise of gunfire sounded as if a massacre was underway in the hotel. And, Sergeant Magnuson was on the verge of rushing back inside when he heard a noise from the street on his left. Changing direction and turning the corner Magnuson found Jaunty and one of the guards helping each other down from the floor above and bade them both to, "Put up your hands," to which instruction they complied, realising he had a pistol levelled at them whilst their own were in their pockets.

Jack, meanwhile, decided to take a calculated risk. He reckoned that Nina was in the end room on the left, probably with Black Rube, as this had been the room Martha had occupied six years ago. Whilst the rooms on his right had fallen silent with shots only being returned from the one on his left and this room was the one that had an adjoining door into Nina's room. So that is where he aimed to go. He put his last two bullets in his Winchester into the door frame of the room, expecting this would cause the defender to keep his head down, then pulled his old colt from his waist band fanning the hammer to rapidly fire four more bullets, one for each of his strides, to keep his man pinned down and to hide his footsteps.

A more experienced defender would have guessed the manoeuvre and quickly beat a retreat behind the bed, taking aim with his gun at the doorway to shoot Jack as he entered.

Fortunately, Jack's gamble that the guard, though a hard man of the streets, lacked experience and remained crouching behind the door waiting to return fire when there was a gap in Jack's fusillade, was correct. The man never got the chance to return fire as Jack put his last two bullets into him the moment he reached the doorway and had him in his sights.

Jaunty though a sadistic and violent bully was no street fighter and in such circumstances was inclined to let others take the lead. He pushed his companion into the sergeant's path then leapt past the grappling pair to hightail it down the street. However, the sergeant was no raw recruit, having as the saying goes 'seen the elephant', and clubbed the the second man to the ground with the butt of his revolver then turning to take aim on Jaunty. But, there was no need for the sergeant to fire as Jaunty had, literally, run into the arms of a burly uniformed constable who had only that second arrived on the scene.

Jack laid his empty colt carefully on the washstand, took his five-shot pocket revolver in his left hand and his newer, single-action colt in his right, paused to calm his breathing and listen. If he had the wrong room it would not matter, but the slightest shifting of a body's weight behind the adjoining door told him he had chosen correctly. Striding forward he shot the lock with a bullet and kicked the door in with the same movement, only his misjudging the way the door opened saved him from the shotgun blast, that blew a hole in the door and sent it crashing back on its hinges into the room where Jack had fallen back from his misplaced kick. Jack, in his turn, put a shot from his revolver through the open doorway, causing Nina and Black Rube, both armed with shotguns, to step back.

"Stevens, is that you?" Nina shouted, though not having any doubt who their assailant was. "We nearly shot you, what is this fools game?"

"No game Nina, put the guns down and come out."

"There is no need for this Jack," Nina reasoned, "you can say we blasted our way out to get past you. Our deal is done and scores are settled. Your killing Brandon in return for my leaving you and Kitty in peace was a fair trade and leaves us square. I've had my little revenge on Martha with the killing of her friend and you will get Jaunty for murdering the two women, a foul and unnecessary murder he deserves to hang for. We are square Jack, nothing more to be served by our shooting it out. A ship waits to take me and Rube to Europe. Hank will restore order here in the city and will soon be calling all the shots. It's an end Jack, best for us all."

"Only Beatrice is unaccounted for," was Jack's only response.

"Are you alone? We only saw you and O'Leary's sergeant arrive, and he is out front, no doubt chasing Jaunty by now."

"I have two capable friends with me each with more bullets than I need," Jack almost laughed, he felt exhilarated. The world had suddenly turned against its axis and he was again in the forests of Virginia, or perhaps the Black Hills, stalking his prey.

"Then step forward and let us see their faces," Nina cooly returned, not a shred of fear in her tone, knowing their two shotguns were more than a match for Jack. The quiet that followed allowed Jack a moment of tranquility and calm he rarely experienced, monetarily he was free of the rage and fear that had haunted him from the earliest days of the war, from his first encounter with death when his best friend died. He did not breathe, his heart did not beat, his head slightly tilted so he could almost feel the cool, wooden stock of his sniper rifle on his cheek as he took deadly aim on his target. He stepped forward and put a bullet from his colt directly into Nina's face, the roar of Black Rube's shotgun deafening him, as the bullet from his pocket revolver hit Rube in the guts.

Jack died before his body hit the floor, whilst Rube lasted long enough to crawl to Nina's side and lay his heavy, black head in her lap.

12

REPORTAGE

Day 18 – Friday May 2nd 1886

The four men, Cage, Magnus, Pinky and Pug, had gathered in the inspector's office at an hour before midnight. Exhausted by two days with little rest or nourishment to keep them going, Cage had broken out a bottle of whiskey and was filling the four mismatched glasses. The police station was finally quite with barely a soul but themselves about.

"The papers did your young constable proud," Pinky tapped a broadsheet, one of half a dozen that sat on O'Leary's desk with various other papers and files. "They made him the hero of the day."

"They did," O'Leary sighed, "I emphasised it enough when I spoke to the newsmen. He may have been young but he had a wife and son, so there must be no doubt about his pension."

"Here is to the death of a good man!" Sergeant Magnuson, raised his glass, clinked it with the others and took a mouthful of the smoky liquid, as they echoed his toast and followed his example.

"You have also had it reported as a raid on another disorderly house, but one met with resistance from the Kings," Pug said as way of a 'thank you', to the inspector for agreeing to the subterfuge. "It has allowed us to look into the papers we found at the house."

"Have they told you anything of use?" The inspector wanted to know, his first reaction was that with Joseph Mannheim dead, the notebook they had found offered little enlightenment on its own.

"More than we could have hoped," Pug told him. "We have cross-referenced the initials he put beside the number and type of guns and *sticks* sold with the reports made by Mary Walsh and have found six names into which we have looked more closely."

"She had been doing a good job," Pinky acknowledged. "She had mapped out the hierarchy of the Knights of Labour, though that was widely known and no secret. However, against each name she listed those with whom they had links, such as significant supporters, other groups, men and women like Reverend Blackstaff who helps indirectly and the O'Brione's who give active and direct support, those who are successful recruiters, and so on. She also had lists of the extremists whom the Knights are in communication with but do not entirely trust. It is from these groups we believe we have identified six men who have bought guns and sticks of dynamite from Mannheim over the past weeks and months."

"They have been stock piling weapons?' O'Leary, despite his exhaustion, felt he should be stirring to action at such worrying news.

"So it seems," Pinky stated, taking another sip of his drink. "And, we have traced four of the men and are having them watched. All six are part of two or three different organisations, though they seem to interlink and their memberships overlap and are fluid."

"Anarchists to a man," Pug told them disdainfully, he had no truck with such men whose ideologies, unlike those of the Knights of Labour, seemed to do nothing for the ordinary man.

"We should have them brought in," O'Leary told them, sitting up as if ready to go that moment, "and sweat them for information. I find such men quickly give up their fellows when faced with the stark reality of prison. We could have all concerned in the cells in no time."

"I would happily break a few heads to get at the knowledge they hold inside," Pug agreed. "But we have have passed on everything we have found to our bosses and they have met with your chief and the deputy mayor. We have been told to keep watch only and not tip our hand whilst they decide on a strategy."

"When will we hear?" the sergeant asked, scowling at the delay, like the others he wanted to continue what they had started, even though they had not originally known how far things would go.

"Early next week," Pinky snorted. "Let us hope these extremists have nothing planned before hand."

"I will drink to that," O'Leary told them, raising his glass.

"And to the work done by a fine female detective," Pinky added.

"We paid our condolences to Mrs Stevens this morning," Magnuson informed the Pinkertons, "she seems quite stoic, almost as if she doubts the reality of it."

"It is the second time I have had to tell her that her husband is dead," Pug explained, his face troubled and sorrowful at the remembrance of knocking at her door, he could barely remember what he had said, but there could have been no doubt this time as to the truth of what he told Martha. The look on her face, as if something in her died, was an expression he would remember until he went to his own grave, "I think there is no doubt of it in her mind on this occasion."

"A stronger-willed woman you could not find," Pinky pointed out, he would dearly have loved to take some of the pain he had seen in the grieving wife's eyes onto himself but he had not been able to do or say anything except breathe, 'I'm sorry'. Pathetically shallow words that covered a deep well of his own grief, an emotion he never thought he would feel for the likes of Jack Stevens. "She is the sort of woman you take to help you conquer some new frontier."

"Here is to the strength and devotion of a good woman!" Pug raised his glass and clinked it with the others as they acknowledged his toast.

"You have obviously not seen the late editions," O'Leary postulated, nodding to the newspaper on top of the pile. "My sergeant here has had himself named the man who has brought the murderer of Miss Blackstaff and Miss Walsh to justice."

"Under your instructions, Inspector," the sergeant stated, somewhat bashfully, "before the legal representatives of Mr Jaunty Tipwell could get his side of things out."

"He has confessed then?" Pug guessed.

"We have had a hard time stopping him from doing so," if it wasn't for the mournful circumstances and his tiredness Magnuson might have been gleeful, even danced a jig, but all he could manage was a shrug and shaking of his head. "He finally admitted the crime but ever since has said his actions were *justified*. Can you believe it, he says he killed as a matter of *morality* and acted as any christian thinking man would have."

"Has he lost his mind and gone insane?" Pinky was dumfounded at hearing Jaunty's defence.

"Not in the least of it," O'Leary informed them with a scowl, "his lawyer has taken up the theme and has all but demanded his client's release and a reward for his actions."

"The world has gone mad," Pug could not refrain from laughing, thinking there must be punch line to this joke as he could not take what he was hearing seriously.

"He says," Cage pointed out, his deepening scowl showing this was far from a joke as any matter could be, "that when he first met the pair he had nothing to doubt that they were whores. Degenerate whores, at that, who shunned men and engaged in the most abnormal acts of depraved lust that would be abhorrent to any christian woman."

"I would have thought him more knowledgeable of the ways of the world to believe his own deluded thinking," Pinky discounted Jaunty's plea as fabrication.

"What he thinks does not matter," Magnuson pointed out, "if he can convince the judge and jury he believed the women debased and prostitutes he is unlikely to hang, he may even get off. He says they went willingly with him and Mannheim, and it was only afterwards that Jaunty became angry with them and what *they* had led him and Joseph to. He is quite full of how they were willing to do any lewd act yet afterwards scoffed that nothing a man could do could bring them to the heights of ecstasy their touching and kissing each other brought."

"And, as they are not here to deny it and staff from Ruby's to attest to their performance, it gives credence to his words," O'Leary heatedly pointed out. "He even has the gall to say that in his anger and shame he determined to punish them for their immoral behaviour and make them an example as a warning to others."

"He was most calm when he told me," the sergeant went on, "how Joseph slept off the effects of the rum he had drunk in the carriage, whilst he took the pair into the derelict warehouse and using the rope and tackle he had picked up on the way, hung them by their ankles and beat their buttocks. And, when they failed to repent," Magnuson's anger boiled over at the word and he banged his fist on the table making the other three jump though they could not fault his anger. "Repent, mark you, *their* wrongs he strangled the *defiled* air from their lungs. You see how he turns the crime, like his victims, upside down," Magnuson shook his head in disbelief, drawing breath to calm himself. "Forgive my anger at this but you can see how, with a God fearing jury they might just forget the nature of his crime and acquit him."

"Which is why, we called in some reporters and gave them the facts and that Mr J Tipwell, gang leader, criminal and member of the Dead Hands had confessed the murder. We made no mention of his plea but much of the heinous way in which he had committed the murder, having first violated the pair with the aid of an accomplice, now dead. We also spoke of the good works Miss Blacksmith had done for her father's, the Reverend Blacksmith's, foundation and how many ordinary men and women of the city would attest to this. I also explained that Miss Mary Walsh had only gone to Rubys to discover more about the criminal activities there. And, that she had already passed on much information to the police which led to our recent raid on the place. In the light of this our chief has instructed that we should now take action to shut Ruby's down for good."

"To the power of the press," the sergeant raised his glass again, the others clinking theirs in approval. "Let us hope that on this occasion it works on behalf of justice rather than perverting it."

"At least Jaunty will not have any friends to call on," Pinky went on, shaking his empty glass before Cage to indicate a refill was in order, thinking that Jack would have been on his fourth or fifth glass by now. "Rumour has it that Mr Henry Tipwell and family leave for an extended vacation on the west coast. This has left his clan and the Dead Hands in disarray and fighting each other to take control."

"The Kings are all but spent," Pug went on. "Our raid on their house and the killing of Joe Mannheim has seen to that. Nor will the Black Hawks ever recover from their losses."

"At least there is some good that has come out of this," Magnuson said, trying to think of another toast but failing, simply taking another drop in consolation. "I had wondered if Black Rube really existed, until I saw him dead."

"Our bosses were less than happy to read," Pinky told the two policemen, "that Mrs O'Shea had been killed by her abductors, members of the Black Rube gang, whilst a lone, unnamed Pinkerton attempted her release."

"The reports did go on to say the Pinkerton had acted heroically, having chanced upon the gang, he took what action he could and gave his life in trying to protect Mrs O'Shea." O'Leary said in way of apology, adding, "Besides all the papers seemed interested in was the recovery of the diamonds and their great value; which was only a fraction of what we had been led to believe, though a grand enough amount, about $100,000. I still think there was an insurance scam behind all this and a falling out amongst thieves which resulted in Ibrahim Minsky and Brandon O'Shea being killed."

"I do not understand why Jack acted as he did," Sergeant Magnuson stared hard at the drink in his hand, his brow furrowed trying to solve the conundrum, "he had but to wait for reinforcements to arrive. Yet all the evidence shows that he went forward and killed both Mrs O'Shea and Black Rube. The shotgun in her hand showed she was partner in the crime and not victim as put out in the papers."

"Better for the public to believe the woman was abducted and died innocent, there would be too many questions if it were known she orchestrated the robbery and her maid's murder," Pug pointed out.

"Even so," the sergeant worried at the question that gnawed at his brain, "why did he go forward on his own, why kill them at the cost of his own life?"

"Once Jack got on the trail he never gave up," Pug explained, "never gave heed to anything else until he had seen his task through. When we worked together in the Black Hills it was often said that the only way to avoid being shot when Jack Stevens had you in his sights was to dig your own grave and pull the earth in over your own head."

"Here's to Jack Stevens," Cage said, filling each glass to the brim, then lifting his own.

"To a true and sure aim," Pinky stated, lifting his glass.

"To a full glass of whiskey," Pug toasted.

"May he rest in peace," Magnus clinked his glass to the other three and they all downed theirs in one.

'A HELLISH DEED

A dynamite bomb thrown inot a crowd of policemen. It explodes and covers the street with dead and mutilated officers – a storm of bullets follows – the police return the fire and wound a number of rioters – harrowing scenes at the desplaines street station – a night of terror.

A dynamite bomb thrown into a squad of policemen sent to disperse a mob at the corner of Desplaines and Randolph streets last night exploded with terrific force, killing and injuring nearly fifty men…'

Obituaries

November 20th 1886: Reverend OM Blackstaff, much loved Husband of Mrs Essey Blackstaff and Father of Mr JW Blackstaff, died at his home after a long illness. Reverend Blackstaff, noted writer on social, moral and theological philosophy was the founder of a charitable organisation aimed at improving the minds and physical wellbeing of less fortunate working men and women. Reverend Blackstaff had been an active man, tirelessly working for the community in which he had grown up. The son of an ex-slave, who went on to found a prosperous business, the good reverend understood the value of education and faith in God as being the basis for prosperity and a contented life.

It is with sadness we must relate that Reverend Blackstaff did not fully recover from the shock brought on by the murder of his talented, young daughter, Philomena, last April. Following the execution two days ago of the man convicted of his daughter's murder Reverend Blackstaff suffered a stroke and died in the early hours. His family, friends, congregation and this city mourn his passing.

May 12th 1905: It is with great sorrow we report the death of Mrs Martha Fellows, who passed away yesterday afternoon, from pneumonia. She leaves behind and is greatly mourned by her second husband, Mr S Fellows, her daughter and son-in-law, Mr and Mrs C DeWert (Mr DeWert is our much admired Governor), and son, Mr A Stevens, wealthy Chicagoan businessman. The grieving family offer their heartfelt thanks for the many condolences they have already received at this tragic news.

Mrs Fellows remarried after the death of her first husband, many years previous, who is reputed to have been the man responsible for the recovery of the O'Shea diamonds. On remarrying and moving to Springfield she soon became an integral part of its upper social echelons, regularly entertaining our most noted citizens whilst also engaging in and supporting many charitable works. She frequently spoke of her own humble origins in Albany, the daughter of a carter, her days as a pioneer in Nebraska and Iowa before the family made its fortune in railroad stock and moved to Chicago. Her strength of character and determination is a lesson to us all, she will be sorely missed by the many that knew and admired her.

August 12th 1909: citizens of Fort Simpson, North West Territories, Canada, were shocked yesterday to hear of the demise of a local trapper and 'man of character'. However, following the local doctor's examination of the deceased, they were even more surprised to learn that Christopher 'Kit' Jackson Stevens was actually a *woman*! The hard living, drinking, cussing individual spent a great deal of time in solitude, hunting and trapping for furs. When in town 'Kit' told stories of *his* past to anyone that would stand *him* a drink; of *his* time as a prospector in the Black Hills, Indian fighter and army scout in Dakota. It is believed, this *unique* character died as a result of injuries sustained whilst hunting.

ACKNOWLEDGMENTS

I do not pretend to be an expert on the midwest states of America of the 1880s. However, research on any topic has never been easier and the internet, with the likes of Google and Wikipedia for example, is a great source of information on almost any topic under the sun, including details related in this story. Research from original newspaper articles and reports from the 1880's helped give flavour to this work. Details of period clothing, food stuffs, guns and the everyday conditions of life abound in a wide variety of articles, autobiographies and biographies of those who lived at the time.

So many and varied are these reports, scattered across the internet in small snippets, that it is impossible to list them all. Though I would recommend to anyone that an interesting afternoon can be spent following a theme and its many side-shoots through a long trail of websites. However, I would like to offer particular acknowledgement to the following online works which proved to be a regular source of information:-

- 'Berdan's Sharpshooters'
- 'Chicago Public Library'
- 'Encyclopaedia of Chicago'
- 'History.com' – 'History in the Headlines'
- 'Legends of America'

- 'Library of Congress – American Memories'
- 'Lone Hand Western – Reliving History'
- 'Military Factory'
- 'Maps Quest.com'
- 'New Perspectives on The West'
- 'Old West Writers Guide'
- 'Pinkerton'

Finally, I would like to thank the many Americans who have enlivened my travels across their country with stories of 'The Old West' when men-were-men and the gun spoke loudly for retribution if not for justice or the law.

Notes:

- Black Hawk was a native American war band leader of the Sacs (Sauks) and Fox Indians who led an unsuccessful 'invasion' of Illinois in 1832, to take back lands the tribe had lost.
- The American Civil war, 1861–65, was the first modern war, with the industrial might of the north giving it an advantage in the production of: iron clad gun boats, high explosive shells, trench warfare, gatling guns, the railroads used to move men and provisions, etc. And, perhaps most characteristic of the two world wars to come, senior officers such as Grant and Sherman believed in the concept of total war and thought that only the annihilation of Confederate forces and shattering the South's economic base would end the war. More than 1,800 African Americans from Illinois fought in the United States Colored regiments, USCT, most notably in the battle of the Crater.
- 1833 Chicago was incorporated as a town and in 1837 it was incorporated as a city.
- 1847 saw the first publication of the Chicago Tribune.
- 1871 witnessed the destruction a nearly 3.5 square miles of

Chicago in the great fire; leaving 300 people dead and more than 100,000 homeless.

- 1876 saw the election of the first African American to the Illinois General Assembly, representing a south side district.
- 1885 the Home Insurance Building on La Salle and Adams was the world's first ever 'skyscraper', ten storeys high with a steel frame.
- Chicago Joe was a woman, Mary Walsh, an Irish prostitute born 1844, who moved from Chicago to Helena, Montana and became the 'Queen of the Red Light District' and owner of the Red Light Saloon. She married Mr JT Hensley, aka Black Hawk Hensley. Then, in 1885, the Montana legislature passed a law closing the Hurdy Gurdy Houses but Chicago Joe managed to retain a number of businesses until her death in 1899. She is the arch-typical 'whore with a heart of gold' and is reputed to have done many good deeds in her life.
- In 1881 the Chicago Police Patrol and Signal System was introduced by installing booths equipped with telegraph and telephone units from which officers could contact the closest police station. Thereby, along with the introduction of the first Patrol Wagon service, Chicago implemented the first modern law enforcement communication system. The Chicago police have, at times in their history, been riddled with corruption. However, many of their number have died in the line of duty and the eight officers killed and fifty nine wounded in the Haymarket riot and bombings of 1886 still mark its darkest hour.
- The Pinkerton Agency, established 1850, had a formidable reputation as a detective agency, eventually becoming almost a de facto federal force, before moving into 'security' and leaving detection to others. In 1856 Kate Warne was hired, she was the first female detective in America and her abilities were highly regarded by Allan Pinkerton. In 1884 the founder, Allan Pinkerton, died and his sons, Robert and William, took over.

- The growth of labour unrest at this time went hand in hand with the rapid growth in industrialisation and the exploitation of workers; with violence occurring on both sides of the picket line. The Knights of Labour movement grew rapidly in the 1880's as it supported better conditions of all workers, male and female, regardless of race. Their rallying song was 'Hold the Fort', a civil war song to inspire their members to persevere despite the violence they often faced. In May 1886 the Haymarket riot and bombings, though known to be caused by unaffiliated anarchists, destroyed the Knights of Labour's reputation and membership collapsed.
- We think of street gangs as being a phenomenon of the modern age but the reality is they have existed for as long as there have been cities. The early gangs of Chicago were formed mainly round ethnic and family ties, usually for the protection of the neighbourhoods in which they lived, over time they turned malevolent and criminal becoming the forerunners of modern gangsters. Several large Irish gangs, such as the Dukies and the Shielders, existed in 1880 Chicago though mainly around the stockyards (the Black Hands was the name of the early mafia, who began to take hold at the turn of the century).
- Politicians of the day were no more corrupt, hypocritical and self-seeking than they are today. Which isn't saying a great deal.